always
you

a novel

STEPHANIE ROSE

To Brooke,
    Never settle,

        ♡
        Stephanie
            Rose

Cover designed by:
Najla Qamber Designs
www.najlaqamberdesigns.com

Formatting by:
Perfectly Publishing
www.perfectlypublishable.com

dedication

*To my Batman and my
Superman~my husband and son.
You save me every day.*

playlist

Alone—Heart

See You Again—Carrie Underwood

Still Into You—Paramore

(You Want To) Make A Memory—Bon Jovi

Come To Me—The Goo Goo Dolls

Run—feat. Sugarland—Matt Nathanson

Beneath Your Beautiful—Labrinth

Lonely Tonight (featuring Ashley Monroe)—Blake Shelton

Colorblind—Counting Crows

Make You Feel My Love—Adele

Stay—Rihanna

Somebody That I Used To Know—Gotye

Start of Something Good—Daughtry

I Touch Myself—Divinyls

Hanging By A Moment—Lifehouse

It Was Always You—Maroon 5

Superman Tonight—Bon Jovi

Endlessly—Green River Ordinance

Love Someone—Jason Mraz

Almost Is Never Enough—Ariana Grande

Say Something—A Great Big World, Christina Agullera

Without You—Max

I Won't Give Up—Jason Mraz

Sorry—Buckcherry

All I Wanted—Paramore

Thinking Out Loud—Ed Sheeran

All In—Lifehouse

By Your Side—Tenth Avenue North

Turning Page—Sleeping At Last

Marry Me—Jason Derulo

You & I (Nobody In The World)—John Legend

A Thousand Years—Christina Perri

Playlist is Available on Spotify

prologue

Samantha

August 2004

DROPS OF SWEAT poured down my face as I waited by the bar for a drink. I was growing more and more irritated as the minutes went by. The extra effort I had put into my hair and makeup had now gone to shit by the heat and humidity of this dive bar. My damp hair clung to my forehead and the back of my neck. I had even broken out my push up bra, which made my double D's look 3D in my black tank top. That backfired too, as I was sporting some serious boob sweat—*not* sexy at all.

A crowded bar wasn't for me. I liked a more subdued type of place, but a few friends of mine had been on my case to come out tonight. But that wasn't the real reason I was here with extra makeup running down my face and my boobs hanging out.

Lucas Hunter, the beautiful object of my unrequited affection for the past three years, had mentioned he would be there for a few farewell drinks and he'd 'love it if I stopped by.' He had found a job with one of the accounting big four firms in San Diego, and was leaving his job as college advisor. I couldn't bring myself to think of Lucas not being around anymore. I had very little time left to shamelessly follow him around.

My only saving grace for tonight was the music. Eighties and early nineties rock songs played on a continuous loop. One of my favorites, Heart's *Alone,* blasted from the jukebox. Listening to it now seemed poignant as Ann Wilson belted out the words that described my life for the past three years.

The wait for my Malibu and pineapple seemed to take forever. The female bartender was too busy feeling the biceps of the underage college boys ordering their drinks. I huffed as I tapped my foot.

"C'mon, O'Rourke. Can't you lighten up?" My friend Jason put his arm around me and I smiled in spite of myself. It was true. I was having a tantrum like a child, but my emotions were all over the place.

"It's just frustrating. All I want is a frigging drink." I nodded at the full bottle of beer in Jason's hand. "Of course you bat your eyelashes and get one instantly. She's looking back at you, too." I shook my head and laughed. Jason was a great looking guy, built with sexy hazel eyes—but she wasn't his type. He preferred someone with less makeup and more penis. Jason shrugged with a smirk. "I guess the joke is on her, then. We're seniors in a month, we've been dying for you to come out with us. Alexis isn't even that weepy tonight. You look hot, so get your drink and have fun with us. You deserve to let loose a little bit. And the other thing that's got you all worked up, I just saw him walk in." Jason smirked as he swaggered away to where our friends were sitting. I took a deep breath and tried to get a better attitude.

"Let me guess. Malibu and pineapple, right?" I was gutted by the deep voice that now broke my heart as much as it thrilled me. I spun around and found Lucas Hunter standing next to me in the smoky haze. Why did he always have to look so damn good? Even in the dimly lit bar, I could make out his piercing blue eyes. His sandy brown hair was tousled like he just got out of bed, and his black V-neck shirt stuck to every ridge and hard muscle of his torso. Lucas made sweaty look hot—*really* hot.

"How did you know that?"

"Daina told me that was your favorite drink when I made fun of her for ordering it at our cousin's wedding. Wait here, Baby Girl. I'll get it for you." Lucas always had a way of swooping in and fixing things. I had the damsel in distress act down pat, always needing help with something. Lucas always came to my rescue and looked out for me. Now he would be saving the day for some chick in California. Maybe I should've changed my order to a shot.

Of course, Lucas had our drinks in under five minutes.

"I'm glad you came out tonight. The company found me an apartment so I have to leave earlier than I'd planned to get settled." Lucas took a long swig of his beer.

"How much earlier?" I tried to keep the panic out of my voice as I slurped my drink. Lucas was *not* my boyfriend. He had become a good friend over the years, but he was never attainable to me in any way, shape or form. But knowing I wouldn't see or talk to him anymore made a lump form in my throat so large it was choking me. This reaction couldn't be rational—or normal.

"Sunday." Lucas gave me a sad smile. *Two days? That's all I had?* What if I finally told him how I felt and attacked his perfect lips the way I've wanted to for the past three years?

I took a deep breath and grabbed Lucas's arm.

"Lucas, would you want to—"

"There he is! Lucas! We've been looking all over the place for you!"

Lucas's friend Derek came over to pull him back with the group. He was good looking too, with his wavy black hair and over six feet in height. Too bad whenever Lucas was in the room, I didn't see anyone but him.

"Excuse me for a bit, Sam. Time to collect some free drinks from these slackers."

"Sure." My voice was a low whisper, my body feeling the aftereffects of the adrenaline pumping in my veins. Trying to be brave made me weak in the knees and a little nauseated.

No, no, no! I was doing this. For once I was going after what I wanted. No regrets!

I headed to the back of the crowded room, just in time to see someone throw her arms around Lucas and kiss him—right on the lips. It was hard to tell who she was since I didn't see her face, but she had a phenomenal body—at least from the back. So much for this being a night of no regrets. The blood in my veins ran cold as I backed away, shaking my head at myself for even trying.

I moped back over to the bar and took a seat, putting my face in my hands. I needed to stop this—*now*. I was always a kid in his eyes—someone he called "Baby Girl" as a joke, or "Sam" like I was one of the guys. I needed to face the hard fact that I'd been denying for the past three years—that the way Lucas saw me was *never* going to change.

Any time I spent with another guy never went past kissing. I didn't give anyone a chance because I'd had Lucas blinders on for the past three years—and where did it get me? *Absolutely fucking nowhere.*

"Hey, is this seat taken?" Marc, one of the guys I recognized from the few frat parties I attended took a seat on the stool next to me. He was about my height, five and a half feet-ish, with black hair and brown eyes. He wore a blue checkered shirt and khaki shorts, looking like he just came back from the beach. The last party I went to that was hosted by Marc's frat, I remembered feeling like I was in the modern day version of the movie *Animal House*—and Marc was the reincarnated John Belushi.

"No. Marc, right?"

He nodded and smiled. Maybe he was a little cute at second glance.

"And you're Samantha. Nice to meet you. I've seen you around."

I narrowed my eyes at him. "You have?"

"Well, sure. You're hard to miss. I've seen you once or twice with Lucas Hunter. Please don't tell me you're a part of his en-tourage! Makes me sick how girls follow pretty boy everywhere around school. I hear he's finally leaving."

"We're just friends. He's headed to California in a couple of days." I tried to say it without sounding as devastated as I was.

"Interesting. Anyway, enough about him. Tell me about you; where do you live?"

"I live in the Bronx." Marc squinted at me.

"All the way up there? I'm guessing you're a Yankees fan. I

live in Queens. I usually don't travel that far, or tolerate arrogant Yankees fans, but I'd make an exception for you."

"Should I feel lucky?" I rolled my eyes and went back to my drink.

"You're a spunky little thing. I think I need to take you out and see how feisty you really are." Marc gave me a wink. It wasn't as sexy as when Lucas did it, but I had to admit Marc was growing on me.

"Could I have your number? There's a good restaurant I know in Queens if you like Greek food. I'll even drive across the bridge and pick you up. What do you say, Sam?"

"Samantha. I don't let anyone call me Sam." That is, anyone except a gorgeous soon to be ex-college advisor who was taking that privilege with him across the country.

It was time to stop fishing in the deep waters when it came to guys, and give someone who seemed to have an actual interest in me a chance. I glanced to where Lucas was standing with his arm playfully around the girl's tiny waist. I looked away before I saw them kiss again.

"Do you have a pen?"

Marc's eyes lit up as he reached in his pocket and handed me one. I grabbed a napkin and wrote down my number. He put the napkin in the front pocket of his shirt and patted it like he had something valuable.

"Sorry, Sam. I got a little preoccupied back there." Lucas came up behind me and put his hand on my shoulder, making me jump.

"No worries. It's your last night out; you shouldn't have to waste it with me." I shrugged and turned back to Marc. I knew that seemed cold, and I felt awful. It wasn't his fault he didn't feel the same way, and he was never mean to me or acted like he didn't have time for me.

"Don't be like that, Sam. You looked like you were about to say something—"

"Jesus, pretty boy, do you have to lay claim on every girl?" Marc shook his head and got up from the stool, turning to me.

"I'll call you tomorrow and tell you what time I'll pick you up." Marc smirked at me and touched the bottom of my chin to make me look up at him. "Good night, beautiful." I chuckled at his boldness and nodded.

Lucas scowled at Marc as he strutted away to join the rest of his frat brothers.

"You're going out with Marc Christensen?!" Lucas had never raised his voice or looked agitated in front of me before. "Look, Sam, I would never tell you who to date, but I really don't like—"

"It's only dinner. A girl's gotta eat. It's not like I'm marrying him or anything." I shrugged and gave him a smile, still feeling bad because of the way I spoke to him. I stood up from my stool and moved closer to where he stood.

Lucas shrugged and was about to say something else when I felt a tap on my shoulder.

"Samantha, we need to leave. Tony is here with that bitch and I can't stare at them all night." My friend Alexis glared at the couple openly making out in the corner. I assumed that was her ex and his flavor of the month. Jason stood behind her, shaking his head.

"Give me a minute; I'll meet you outside." Alexis let out a long sigh and nodded as she sulked her way out of the bar.

This was it. This was goodbye. There was so much I wanted to say. I wanted to tell him how amazing he was and that I would never forget him, but the words wouldn't come out.

"So, I guess this is goodbye." I looked up at Lucas and he shook his head.

"I'm moving to San Diego, not another planet. I still have family here so I'll always be back and forth. I'll email everyone when I get settled."

I took a deep breath. "Thank you for everything. You're an incredible guy, and I know you'll kick ass in California. I was lucky to get to know you and be your friend." I swallowed hard. Lucas was *not* going to see me cry, I wanted to walk away with a little bit of self-respect.

Lucas smiled and held his arms out for a hug. I was more

than willing to comply and held him tight to my body. If he was going to be a memory from now on, I wanted to make sure I remembered exactly what it felt like to touch him. He turned his head and gave me a sweet kiss on the cheek that made my knees buckle.

"You're pretty incredible, yourself. I have no doubt you'll kick ass here too." He whispered in my ear and kissed my cheek again. I responded by kissing his cheek—and lingering. I had a feeling I would compare every kiss I had in the future to this moment, so I wanted to make it a good one.

We let each other go and pulled back. I gave Lucas a sad little wave.

"Have a safe trip, Lucas." *And a fabulous life.* He gave me one more butterfly storm-inducing smile and backed away. The 'pining for Lucas' chapter of my life was, finally, officially closed.

I turned to leave, and locked eyes with Marc by the door. He patted his pocket and smiled at me, making me laugh. Who was I if I wasn't carrying a torch for Lucas Hunter? I guessed I was about to find out.

chapter 1

Samantha

Present day

DOES ANYONE EVER plan to settle? I know I sure as hell didn't. I wanted love, passion, and a man who needed me more than he needed his next breath.

What I got was a husband who couldn't stand the sight of me. Marc wasn't always this way. When I first met him he was cute, even a little charming. We dated for a few years, got married, and while my life was never a romance novel, Marc was a decent husband. I gave birth to our beautiful daughter, and suddenly Marc couldn't stand being home. He had to be out; the walls of our home became a cage holding him back from the man he wanted to be.

I glared at my husband, sleeping on the couch in his clothes from the night before at one o'clock on a Saturday afternoon. I wasn't sure where he spent all his time these days. Asking where he was or where he was going usually lead to hour-long fights, and an Oscar worthy performance of "how hard it was to be un-employed and watch me leave the house every day." Since losing his IT job a year ago, he'd been working freelance jobs here and there, but never anything permanent. I had suspicions that his attitude was the reason he was never asked to stay, not his performance. Thankfully, my marketing director job paid well enough to cover the bills. But instead of gratitude, all I got was resentment when I strolled through the door every night.

He was constantly texting someone, saying he was "making

contacts," but I doubted new IT positions were the reason his phone vibrated into the wee hours of the morning. I heard a rumor or two about who Marc was really with when he was out all night, but when I confronted him, he grunted at me and shrugged it off. He claimed my friends were busy bodies with nothing else better to do than track him, but I never got a solid denial.

I crinkled my nose at the sad sight that was Marc. Shaking my head, I went into the kitchen to finish cleaning up from lunch.

"Mommy!" Bella shouted to me as she ran down the stairs. "There's a new Lego Friends princess castle! I just saw it on TV! Can I get it, Mommy? Please . . ." Bella bounced and folded her hands under her chin as if she was praying she'd get a yes from me. It was like pulling teeth to get her to speak at an audible level at times, so I loved seeing her more boisterous moments when she got excited.

"*Goddamn it, Bella!* Can't you see I'm trying to sleep? Don't run around the house yelling like an animal. *Jesus Christ.*" Marc sat up from the couch, massaging his temples. Poor sleeping beauty was hung over.

Bella put her head down and ran to me, clutching my hip as she quietly cried into my leg.

"Most people don't sleep until almost two in the afternoon unless they have a night job. I don't think getting drunk with the guys counts as working. Bella shouldn't have to tip toe around the house when everyone should be up." I kept my voice even as to not upset Bella even more. Marc huffed and shook his head.

"Can I be up for ten minutes before you start bitching?" Marc raked his hands over his face. I hoped he wasn't about to puke, although rubbing his face in it would feel awesome right about now.

I knelt down to Bella and pulled her hands from her face. I put my hands on her cheeks and rubbed the tears from her eyes with my thumbs.

"I think I may have seen that castle in Target. After mommy's Zumba class, maybe we can go check it out, and we can build it tonight . . . what do you think?"

Buying my daughter big presents just because wasn't the best way to parent, but when Marc had an outburst like that, I needed to make her forget it. It probably never worked completely, but I always had to try.

She nodded furiously and a small smile appeared on her face. My gym had a day care so I always took Bella with me. She got to play with other kids, and I got to channel my frustrations into exercise. I tried to go every day, probably the reason why I wasn't the Queens Lorena Bobbitt yet. My husband probably deserved most of the credit for getting me into the best shape of my life, even though I always heard comments from him about needing to stay there longer, or how I should stop "stuffing my fat face."

Up until this point, he was just a mopey crank. He'd never yelled at Bella like that before and I was going to make damn sure he wouldn't again.

"Why don't you get dressed and I'll call you when we have to leave?"

Bella nodded and ran back upstairs, not once looking at her father.

I marched over to Marc, still on the couch with his eyes closed and head laid back.

"Get up!" I yelled right in his face. Marc jumped and rubbed his forehead.

"Jesus, Samantha! Can't you see I'm trying to—?"

"Trying to what? Nurse a hangover? We're supposed to feel sorry for you? You're in your thirties and think you're still a frat boy. You can say whatever you want to me, but don't you *ever* talk to our daughter like that. Next time, you'll be sleeping it off on the concrete outside, not on the couch. Grow the fuck up and try your best to hide what a jerk you are from Bella. You only actually see her for a couple of hours a day, so it shouldn't be too hard."

Marc let out a deep sigh and got up. His face was almost contrite, but I didn't buy it.

"Look, Samantha—" I held my hand up. I grew up without a father, and I didn't want that for Bella. But was having a father like Marc much better than having no father at all? I was in no mood to hear his latest excuse, and it was getting harder and harder to ignore the miserable way he was. I had tolerated it at first because I felt sorry for him after getting laid off from a job he'd had since college and liked. After being called a nag day in and day out, I started to believe that maybe I was; maybe I made him like this. For the past couple of months, though, it was more evident that the only person to blame for Marc's behavior was Marc.

Being married to him wasn't how I wanted my life to be, but the thought of starting over was terrifying. Men didn't line up to date a woman in her thirties with a small child. I didn't have much with Marc, but I knew what I was getting. I fought the daily growing twinge in my stomach that soon I wouldn't be able to pretend it was enough.

ONCE I BOUGHT that castle, I could barely make it out of the Target parking lot before Bella begged me to start building. Marc had gone back out again by the time we got home, to where I didn't know and really didn't care. I ordered pizza, and we giggled as we connected all the little pieces to make the castle and the princesses who lived in it. My phone chimed with a notification. It had been awhile since I got a Facebook friend request, so I was a little curious. I swiped the screen and gasped when I read the name requesting to connect with me.

Lucas Hunter. *Holy shit.*

"Mommy, what's wrong?" Bella frowned at me. I probably looked like I just saw a ghost.

I guessed I did. A ghost from my past, the man I had wanted more than life for three straight years before he moved away. Since I was still best friends with his cousin, Daina, I asked about him every once in a while. Always still in San Diego, doing well at his executive accounting job, always dating but never serious—typical Lucas.

Lucas and I were good friends back then, nothing more. He was always so nice to me and took me under his wing in college, making him that much more attractive to me. He helped me with my homework and cheered me on whenever I had a presentation or big test. He was a true friend in every sense, except for the fact I would spend half of our time together fantasizing how it would feel to explore his mouth with my tongue.

My index finger shook as I pressed *confirm*. I intended to check out his profile as soon as I got Bella into bed. Admittedly, I'd searched for his name a time or two.

My hand was still shaking as I tried to connect a part of the roof of the castle. I heard my phone chime again and jumped, making the Lego collapse like a house of cards. He wouldn't have contacted me back so quickly, would he?

"I'm sorry, baby. Mommy had too much sugar and is a little jumpy today."

I picked up my phone, and sure enough there he was.

> *Lucas: Hey, Baby Girl! Glad I found you! Guess who's back in New York? Daina told me you work on the East Side in the thirties, and that's where my new office is. So how about a drink after work this Friday? I'd love to catch up. Let me know.*

I hated being called "Baby Girl" like I was a little kid, but secretly loved that Lucas had a nickname especially for me.

Bella was supposed to have her first Daisies sleepover on Friday night. Her friend Julianna's mom was picking her up from school and taking her home with them. Marc couldn't care less where I went, and for the first time that felt like a good thing.

> *Me: Sure. I get out of work around 6, so maybe 6:30? Let me know where you'd like to meet.*

> *Lucas: Awesome! How's 31st and 5th? There's a bar right next to the Starbucks on the corner.*

Me: Sure, see you then. Looking forward to it.

Lucas: Me too!

I was already trying on outfits in my head. I took a deep breath to ease the butterflies in my stomach. I hadn't seen this guy in ten years, and a few messages from him had me all aflutter. This was just a drink, a couple of hours with an old friend— that's all. So why was my pulse racing so fast I was out of breath?

I was so screwed.

chapter 2
Lucas

I COULDN'T BELIEVE it. Samantha O'Rourke had grown up to be a breathtaking, beautiful woman. The pictures she posted on Facebook showed how well she'd aged, but to see her in person was a completely different story.

I noticed her sitting by the bar but didn't walk over right away. I watched as she ordered a drink and crossed her long legs. Our eyes finally met and she gave me a big smile, but then looked down at the floor. I could tell she still had the adorable shy streak that made me give her the nickname she hated.

When I called her "Baby Girl" she shook her head and gave me a hug. I tried to ignore how good her body felt when she pressed it against mine. She was married so I should've been appreciating her beauty from a distance. She was Samantha Christensen now, married to Marc Christensen, the biggest asshat student I knew back when I was a college advisor. I was more than curious to find out how the hell that happened.

"You look incredible, Sam. Time has been great to you." She gave me a little smile that didn't make it to her eyes, like she didn't believe me.

"Thanks, Lucas. You look good, too." I looked over her shoulder and noticed some guy sitting at the other end of the bar staring at her. I didn't blame him, but I didn't like it and asked her if she wanted to move to a table. She stood up from her seat at the bar, her perfectly toned legs and ass now visible under her tight black dress. My eyes traveled upwards and landed on the most perfect tits I'd ever seen. Unlike some of the women I knew in California who were that thin with breasts that big, Sam's rack was natural. I'd never ogled her this much when she was in college. *Get a grip, Hunter.*

"No Malibu and pineapple?" I pointed to the bottle of beer she was drinking as we sat down. Every time she put her lips to the bottle I felt a twitch in my pants.

"This is kind of a sports bar, by the looks of it." Sam crinkled her nose at me." I was afraid I'd get laughed at. So, how was it being a Bronx boy in California?"

I shrugged. "Not so bad."

She threw her head back and laughed. "Of course it wasn't. I'm sure you fit right in with your sandy brown hair and year-round tan. How many girls did you have to fight off at the beach on a daily basis? I totally picture your life out there as a never-ending episode of *Baywatch*. I bet you even surfed."

"I tried surfing but I kept falling on my ass and figured it wasn't for me, and I didn't have to fight off too many." I gave her a wink.

"I'm guessing you didn't try very hard, right?" She winked back.

Look at this sassy little thing. I shook my head and laughed. Shy Sam had a little bite to her now. She was sexy, funny—and off-limits. This was beginning to suck a little.

Three hours later, I couldn't believe how fast the time had flown. We were both on our fourth round of drinks and I couldn't remember laughing so much in one night.

"Marketing director, that's great! I'm not surprised; you were always smart, but never gave yourself any credit. I could tell you were going places back then." Sam gave me a small smile and nodded.

"Thank you. Took me a long time, but I'm happy I finally found a job I like with decent hours. Marc misses the days he only saw me for an hour at night because I was working late. I'm a real drag now that I'm home." She ran her hand through her long chestnut hair and looked away.

Sam was gorgeous and successful but had an underlying sadness and indifference when she spoke. I realized that was the first time she'd brought Marc up all night.

What the hell? I'm going to ask.

"I've watched men check you out all night. Marc must go ape shit when you go out."

"Marc likes to joke that guys may come up to me because of the big boobs, but would run away as soon as I started to talk so he has nothing to worry about."

How was it possible he'd become an even bigger fucking asshole than he was back then?

"If a man got the attention of a woman like you he wouldn't walk away so easily, I can definitely tell you that." I put down my beer and silently cut myself off before I got too forward and made Sam uncomfortable.

"Actually, women seem to flock to Marc when he goes out. At least that's what I hear." She shrugged and took a long drink.

What the hell kind of alternate universe did Sam live in that Marc acted like *he* was the catch in their marriage? I got the feeling there was more to it than that to make Sam look so unhappy.

"Sam, Marc should thank his lucky fucking stars a woman like you gave him the time of day, much less married him. If he doesn't, he's a douchebag who didn't deserve you in the first place." *Shit. I went too far.*

Sam didn't look mad at all. She leaned over and put her hand on top of mine.

"Thank you for saying that." There was a spark of electricity when she touched my hand and looked up at me with those big, light brown eyes full of unhappiness. I was feeling all sorts of things, most of all anger that Sam was treated so badly and didn't seem to think she was worthy of anything better.

Sam looked at her watch. "Crap, its ten thirty already?! The night seemed to go by fast, didn't it?"

It had. We'd been there for over four hours, and I wasn't ready for it to be over.

"I didn't realize that, either. Let me walk you to the subway."

"That's sweet, Lucas, but you don't have to do that." Yes, I did. I wanted that extra ten minutes with her, however I could get it.

"I was raised a gentleman. A pretty girl shouldn't be walking around by herself at night in the big city." I reached out my hand to pull her up and she took it. It felt natural, and it felt right. But it wasn't.

I handed her my business card when we got outside. "Since we work so close, and I live in this neighborhood, too, no excuse to not hang out, right?"

Sam nodded and reached into her purse. "Absolutely! Here's mine. My cell is on it." She pointed to Madison Square Park across the street. "I can't believe they opened a Shake Shack in the park. I've always wanted to eat there. I hear the burgers are really good."

"You've never had Shake Shack? We have to rectify that immediately. Like next week." We arrived at the top of the steps at the train station and she turned around to look at me.

"Yeah, we'll see. Anyway, thanks for a great night, Lucas. I had so much fun, and it was great to see you again." We looked at each other and it was a little awkward. Like this was the moment for the date ending kiss. But we weren't on a date—not really. Didn't mean I didn't want to kiss those full, red lips—because I did. And for a minute, she looked like she wanted me to.

"Good night, Sam." I leaned in to kiss her cheek—and lingered a moment. I thought I heard her gasp. She smelled so good.

Sam gave me a warm smile. I couldn't get over how damn beautiful she was.

"Good night, Lucas."

I watched her as she headed down the steps to the subway. I wanted to see her again in the worst way. I hated seeing her look so sad, but she was married. Marc was a jerk, but there was a child involved and I was sure things were complicated, or else Sam would have left him. Starting anything with her, even a friendship, would be opening up Pandora's Box.

When I got back to my apartment, I took Sam's business card out to get her cell.

Me: It's Lucas. Checking to make sure you got home OK.

Her train was probably underground, but I was worried about her on the subway alone so late at night. Twenty minutes later, I heard my phone buzz.

Sam: Thanks for checking. I'm home now. Hope to see you soon.

Me: Shake Shack, Friday, 1 PM

Sam: OK. Sure. See you then J

Alright, Pandora. Game on.

chapter 3

Samantha

I DIDN'T EXPECT my reconnection with Lucas to go further than that one night. By the time I arrived home, we already had plans to see each other again. It had been almost two months since then, and we saw each other a couple of times a week and texted daily. Working in such close proximity, it was easy to run to Starbucks for a quick coffee break, or lunch when we weren't too busy.

After all this time, Lucas was still sex on legs. His sandy brown hair was shorter than I remembered, but still hung below his ears. He always had the perfect two-day beard growth that made him look downright delicious. I had to remind myself over and over again that we could never be more than friends.

Falling back into our old friendship was easy. Lucas gave me advice about work and listened to me complain about Marc. I shouldn't have brought him up, but he was getting progressively worse and I needed to vent to someone. Sometimes Marc didn't come home at all. When he traipsed through the door the next morning he claimed he'd been staying at a friend's house so he wouldn't have to hear me nag. I could tell Lucas was holding in all he really wanted to say by the way his jaw clenched or he shook his head. But like the good guy he always was, he just listened, and tried to convince me that I wasn't the problem. It was probably on the tip of his tongue to ask me how stupid I possibly was to stick around, but he was nice enough to keep it to himself.

"How could you not watch *Sons of Anarchy?*" Lucas looked at me like I had three heads as he sipped his coffee. I got momentarily distracted as he brought the cup to his perfect lips.

"I usually just read when I put Bella in bed. Other than re-ality stuff, I don't keep up with much TV." I shrugged as Lucas narrowed his eyes at me.

"What kind of stuff do you read? *Please* don't tell me you like the same smut my cousin does."

"It's not all just smut. It's romance. It's a nice escape from real life—and don't judge." I stuck my tongue out at him and he laughed.

"Sticking your tongue out? Guess you told me." Lucas's mouth turned up in a smirk. I crinkled my napkin into a ball and threw it at him.

"You should watch, Sam. It's a perfect mix of sex and vio-lence to keep the interest of both men and women. Hell, even I think Jax is a little dreamy." He wiggled his eyebrows and I chuckled at him.

"Fine, I'll watch next week and give it a try. Speaking of read-ing, I need to see if that guy is selling Kindle covers in the street today. Bella broke mine while she was pretending it was a but-terfly and dropped it."

"Hopefully it was off and she didn't get to read anything. Not sure you want to explain that to the teacher. Didn't you say she was the best reader in her class?"

I cringed, as that was the first thing that crossed my mind when I caught her playing with it. Not that she would know what she was repeating, but that was a meeting I never wanted to have.

"It was off, I think. I hope. Oh, God." I put my face in my hands and Lucas thought my discomfort was hysterical.

"I'm sure she didn't see anything. Sorry to cut this short, but I have to get back. With Thanksgiving this week I have to cram a week's worth of work into three days." Lucas got up, and as usual held out his hand to help me up. It was a cute little gesture, and I couldn't deny the jolt I felt when I put my hand in his.

"I'm sorry. You should have told me you were busy, we could have rescheduled." We headed outside, and I realized we were still holding hands. When I looked down, Lucas let go of my hand.

"But then we wouldn't have seen each other until Monday. I didn't want to go that long. I'm too used to your face now." Lucas gave me a wink and a smile.

I smiled and nodded back. I didn't want to go that long, either. Lucas was always the best part of my day, even if I could never tell him.

"Well, Happy Thanksgiving!" I gave Lucas a kiss on his cheek, and he surprised me by wrapping his arm around my waist to pull me closer.

"Happy Thanksgiving to you, too." He kissed my forehead. "But we'll probably talk before, after, and during, right?"

Whether it was right or not, I was grateful this Thanksgiving that fate had brought this man back to me, even though I still couldn't have him the way I wanted.

He gave me a sad smile as he leaned his forehead against mine. I shut my eyes to control the fluttering in my stomach that didn't feel merely friendly. I was starting to need him, and it scared me. This was getting dangerous.

chapter 4

Samantha

"WELL, THIS IS an interesting place." I looked around at Manhattan's attempt at doing country. Bella stayed with her grandparents that Friday night, so Lucas suggested a barbecue pre-Christmas dinner at a new theme restaurant on Twenty-Sixth Street. The music was getting louder as a group of drunken businessmen tried to line dance. The food was delicious, home-style country goodness with the overpricing that New York City was famous for.

"Open your mind a little. This is a cool place. Maybe we can go next." Lucas stood up and tried to pull me by the hand to dance.

"Easy, cowboy. I'm not tipsy enough yet to feel comfortable making an ass of myself. Have a seat." I pulled him back to sit, but instead of going back to his seat across from me, he landed in the chair next to me.

"Aw, come on." Lucas put his arm around me and whispered. "Pretend I'm a cowboy from one of your books. I've had a long day on the tractor and need a pretty girl to take care of me. Won't you take care of me, Sam?" Every single hair on the back of my neck stood up and my breath caught in my throat as he crooned in my ear.

Sweet baby Jesus. I pictured Lucas in tight wranglers and a Stetson hat, shirt off with beads of sweat dripping off every hard muscle on his chest. The thought created a throbbing ache between my legs. I needed to distract myself before I lost all control.

"What the hell did California do to you?" I backed my face away from his lips, and he gave me an exaggerated pout.

The music got slower, and Lucas stood up again to offer me his hand.

"I know you can keep up with this one, city girl. Dance with me." My mind knew this wasn't the right thing to do, but my legs didn't give a shit and followed Lucas to the dance floor.

Lonely Tonight by Blake Shelton and Ashley Monroe was one of the few country songs I recognized. I tried to ignore the ironically poetic meaning of the lyrics as Lucas took my hand and held it close to his chest as we swayed to the music, inching closer to each other as the song progressed. I let myself bury my head in his neck, and Lucas still smelled the same—like a sweet cologne I could never pinpoint. I'd memorized the scent after he lent me a T-shirt one day in school. I "forgot" to give it back, and then didn't wash it for weeks. I chose to think of that as a sweet— not stalker—type of memory.

I looked up and realized we were the only couple on the dance floor. The music had stopped and we hadn't noticed. Lucas cleared his throat and led me by the hand back to our table. I asked the waiter for another beer to calm my frayed nerves.

We finished our pork ribs and corn bread and got back to ourselves again, laughing and teasing each other as we ordered one last round of drinks.

"Wait, I almost forgot. Merry Christmas." He handed me a wrapped square box with a ribbon on the top.

"Lucas, I wish you hadn't done that. I don't have anything for you."

"It's not that big a deal; don't panic. Open it."

I'd learned to live without presents for Christmas and birthdays the past few years. I was Santa and the Easter Bunny at home, but I couldn't remember the last time I found a gift of my own under the tree. As I undid the ribbon and ripped open the paper, I couldn't help getting excited.

"An owl Kindle cover?"

Lucas gave me a shy smile. "We never saw the guy on the

street, and I know you like owls since you wear that pendant all the time. Now all your trashy novels are safe." He cocked an eyebrow at me as I tried to hold back the tears. It was a small gift, but it meant so much to me. It was evidence that he paid attention to what I said, and what I liked. He *cared.* That kind of a gift was priceless.

Swallowing hard so I could speak, I put my hand on top of Lucas's.

"Thank you . . . so much. It was so nice—" Lucas turned his hand over and interlocked our fingers.

"My pleasure, Sam. I'm glad you like it."

We put our coats on in silence after we paid the check. Lucas accompanied me to the subway station, taking my hand in his when we got to the steps.

"I guess I'll see you next week." As he ran his thumb back and forth across the top of my wrist, sadness took over Lucas's face. He tried to smile, but it seemed forced. *What were we doing? This couldn't end well.* He finally looked at me the way I'd wanted him to for all those years, but I couldn't do anything about it.

"Sure." I put my arms around Lucas's neck. My body had a mind of its own tonight. I kissed his cheek, and he shut his eyes tight. He leaned in to kiss me back, heading straight for my lips. My stomach bottomed out as the moment I'd waited to happen for over a decade was finally here. I was frozen in place and couldn't stop him if I wanted to—which I absolutely didn't. He stopped just short, kissing me on the corner of my mouth.

I took Lucas's face in my mitten-covered hands. Our eyes locked for minutes, hours, I couldn't really tell. He broke the silence with a snicker.

"Mittens, huh? Borrow those from Bella?"

"Don't knock them. They're nice and toasty. My fingers work together to keep each other warm." He laughed and kissed my forehead.

"Text me when you get home, please. It's late."

I nodded. "Yes, sir." I gave him a pretend salute.

We finally let each other go and backed away. I instantly felt empty and wrapped my arms around myself so I could still feel his embrace.

"Thank you again, Lucas. I still feel terrible that I didn't get you anything."

Lucas glanced down at the sidewalk and let out a long sigh. When he picked his head up to meet my gaze, his piercing blue eyes were pained.

"You're my favorite part of every day. *That's* my gift. Merry Christmas, Sam."

"Merry Christmas, Lucas." I smiled big enough to hide the tear rolling down my cheek.

Amazing how the most joy I'd ever felt came hand in hand with painful despair. I finally had the one thing I always wanted, but I wasn't free to take it. God certainly had a hell of a sense of humor.

chapter 5

Samantha

AFTER CHRISTMAS, THINGS shifted between Lucas and me. There had always been some kind of attraction, but now I couldn't deny the fact it wasn't one-sided.

I raced around the house, getting ready for work in record time after sleeping through my alarm. I'd never done that before, but I'd been texting back and forth with Lucas until about two o'clock. We spoke all day long now, and into the night. When I wasn't thinking about him, I was speaking to him. There was no way I could keep kidding myself that we were "just friends." Sure, nothing physical had happened yet, but only because we were always in public. The accidental brushes against each other that sent shivers right up my spine and the hello and goodbye kisses that lingered longer than they should were slowly chipping away at my resolve. It was becoming a question of *when* something would happen between us, not *if*.

Making sure Bella was packed for another Daisies sleepover tonight, I quickly slipped on my pencil skirt and pale blue silk blouse for this morning's client meeting. I was enjoying a quick cup of coffee when Marc sauntered out of our bedroom with a large duffle bag and headed right for the door.

"Going somewhere?"

Marc stopped in his tracks without looking at me.

Maybe he was leaving for good? He was hardly ever home. He picked Bella up from school, dropped her off at his parents' house and then hung out with his buddies. Our house had become somewhere to shower and eat before heading back out.

"Tonight is Rob's bachelor party in Atlantic City. Carmine is picking me up. I probably won't be home until sometime Sunday afternoon."

I shrugged. "Have fun." I put the empty coffee mug in the sink and was about to call Bella downstairs.

"Wow, that's all you have to say? No twenty questions or bitching about me being out. You feeling okay?" Marc laughed.

"What difference would that make? You come and go as you please without giving your wife and daughter a second thought. Why waste energy?" I didn't care what Marc did anymore—at all. So after all these years of being treated like a nag and an inconvenience, why did I feel guilty? Things had been heading this way between us for a long time, but over the past few months seemed to be getting worse at a much faster rate. Was it because my heart wasn't in it? My interests were elsewhere, and the ding of an incoming text from my phone at seven forty-five in the morning confirmed it.

"Whatever." Marc rolled his eyes and hustled out the door. I blamed him for our marriage failing, but it wasn't all him. I gave up on us a long time ago. Our marriage had been two people going through the motions for a long time, and now we didn't even do that.

Lucas: How about dinner tonight?

Me: Sure. I can meet you at six. I'm up for whatever you want to eat.

Lucas: Great, meet me at my apartment after you get out of work. Ring the top bell and I'll buzz you in.

His apartment? What the hell was I doing? The emotional affair we were obviously having was the elephant in the room we never discussed. In my silly little brain, denying it was the only way I could keep it from progressing. Saying "no, being in your apartment is not a good idea" made it truer than I was ready to deal with.

Me: OK. See you then.

I wasn't fooling anyone, least of all myself.

WE'LL ONLY BE *here for a little while. I'll stay as far away as physically possible until we go out. I can handle myself for a half hour.*

I ran up the stairs to Lucas's apartment after he buzzed me in. He was waiting with the door open when I got to the top of the stairs.

"Glad you're finally here." Lucas gave me big smile and a kiss on the cheek as he led me inside. The tight black T-shirt and ripped jeans he wore didn't help my cause.

This was the first time I'd ever been to Lucas's apartment. Taking a quick look around, it was a typical bachelor pad with his oversized TV and plain walls—not that I'd been to any other single man's apartment to know for sure. I was about to ask where we were going when the smell of garlic and roasted tomatoes invaded my senses.

"You're cooking dinner?"

Lucas laughed. "Don't look so surprised. I have an Italian mother; of course I can cook. I figured you had a stressful week and have nowhere to be tonight; we could have a nice dinner here. Everything is almost done. Take your jacket off and have a seat. Want some wine?"

Shit, this is not good. I can't leave now after he went to all this trouble. I'll just eat and then go home—piece of cake.

"Wine would be great, thank you." My nerves were completely shot. I had to make sure to drink just enough to be relaxed, not uninhibited.

I sat in his small dining room as Lucas finished cooking, chatting about nothing like we usually did. We continued small talk during dinner, but the wine had no effect on me. I was just as jumpy as when I walked through the door.

Our fingers touched as we cleared the dishes together. His kitchen was so small, our bodies brushed up against each other with every move we made. My body involuntarily gravitated towards him and it was only a matter of time before I wasn't able to resist the pull we had.

"I should go, Lucas. Thank you for a great dinner." I grabbed my jacket from the coat rack by the door. As I tried to put it on, Lucas caught my arm to stop me.

"What's the rush? We only just ate. You don't have to be home by a certain time, right?" *Of course, he wouldn't make it easy to leave.*

"You're going to make me say it, aren't you?" The more time we spent alone in this apartment, the more dangerous it became.

"Lucas, I'm married. I shouldn't be here. We're getting way too close." I shook my head and put on my jacket again. I needed to get out of there.

Lucas turned away from me. He let out a long sigh and ran his fingers through his hair. I was taken aback by the scowl on his gorgeous face.

"Yes. I know that." He sounded disgusted, like acknowledging the fact left a bad taste in his mouth. "Believe me, I know you're married. To *him*. He doesn't deserve you." Lucas usually did a good job hiding his feelings about Marc, but I supposed he'd reached his breaking point.

I let out a long sigh and glanced up at the ceiling as I tried to find the right words to say. *Yes, he was going to make this as difficult as possible to walk out the door.*

"Lucas, it's not that simple—"

"I know I'm not supposed to think about you all day long. I know I'm not supposed to want to talk to you every minute of the day, or touch you, or kiss you. But, fuck—" Lucas closed the space between us and grabbed me by the nape of my neck, pulling me towards him. "That's all I ever want to do, Sam." Our faces were close enough that our lips were almost touching.

From the hungry look in his eyes, I thought he was going to kiss me hard, but he was gentle. A light kiss at first, gentle pecks on my lips, very soft but lingering longer each time his lips touched mine. His hand slid from my neck to the small of my back as he pulled me closer. My heartbeat thundered in my ears as I realized I was about to completely give in. As soon as it seemed the kiss was about to get deeper, he pulled back. His eyes were shut tight as if he was fighting with himself to pull away. He rested his forehead against mine.

"Tell me to stop. Tell me to stop kissing you and I will."

C'mon Samantha, push him away and leave. Do the right thing.

How many times had I dreamed about this moment? The Lucas in front of me was real, warm, and hard—and willing to step away. Instead, I pulled him closer, taking his bottom lip between my lips and sucking on it—letting it go with a little pop. It was like I always imagined his lips would taste—soft and sweet. I let my tongue dart out and licked the seam of his lips. There was no way I could will myself to leave. He tasted delicious, and I wanted more.

That was all the encouragement he needed. He crashed his lips onto mine, finally kissing me hard with a passion and hunger I'd never experienced before. Lucas grabbed me by the hips and pulled me towards him. I loved feeling how much he wanted me.

In my past experience, the longer you wanted something, the more disappointing it was when you finally got it. It's never as good as what you'd built it up to be in your head. Lucas was the exception to the rule. After all those years I'd spent crushing on him, and full out lusting in recent months, kissing him was mind-blowing. It was better than I ever could have imagined.

Lucas let out a groan and pulled back. He took my face in his hands, looking at me like he didn't believe I wasn't saying no.

"You're sure?" I didn't know if it was a statement or a

question.

"The only thing I'm sure of is I don't want you to stop. *Please,* Lucas." I begged against his lips. Lucas kissed his way down my neck and across my collarbone. His lips—hot, wet and oh so damn skilled—made my entire body tremble.

"Do you know how much I want you?" Lucas whispered in my ear. "How long I've waited to touch you like this?" Lucas's hand traveled up my thigh and dipped inside my panties. I tried to push my legs together to relieve the throbbing, but his hand pulled them apart.

"Tell me what you want, baby—my fingers, my mouth, or both? I bet you taste so fucking good."

His thumb found its way to my clit, as he made light little circles. I lifted my arms around his neck and held on tight for fear of my knees giving out. As he pushed two fingers inside me, I went limp in his arms. Just being close to Lucas made my body temperature rise, Lucas touching me was almost too much to handle. His hands were as good as his lips, and I wanted both on me—*everywhere.*

As he picked up the pace, my insides clenched and my legs went rigid. I whimpered at the unexpected loss when he took away his fingers and stopped kissing me.

"Well Sam, what's your choice?" Lucas asked. He looked unsure again, and I thought maybe he was giving me a final out, but I was way beyond the point of retreat.

"Both. Please give me both, Lucas." There was a hint of begging in my voice again, but I couldn't have cared less.

Lucas pushed me up against the wall, grabbed my panties and dragged them down my legs. He knelt in front of me, biting his lip as he lifted my skirt above my thighs. He hooked my right leg over his shoulder and dove right in like a starving man—moaning like I was the best thing he'd ever tasted. Vibrations traveled all the way down to my toes as his fingers went back to where they were before, making my legs shake. I felt an orgasm building that I was afraid would tear me in half. When he sucked my clit into his mouth, I came so hard I lost my balance and slid down the wall. Lucas caught me and pulled me close.

"You still with me?" he asked with hooded eyes.

I shut my eyes and nodded. I needed him inside me, and I didn't care about anything else.

I had just passed "wrong" and, somehow, boarded the express train straight to hell.

chapter 6

Samantha

LOOKED OVER at the alarm clock on Lucas's nightstand, four o'clock. I didn't want to travel home so late, and Lucas was asleep with his arm around my waist and his head nestled in the crook of my shoulder. As I rolled over slowly as to not wake him, I winced at the soreness between my legs. Laughable since my V-Card had been gone for a long time. One night of incredible sex must've given my lady parts quite the workout. 'Incredible' meant more than just Lucas being amazing in bed. I felt desired and wanted, like he couldn't get enough of me.

"Whatcha thinking about, Sam?" I jumped since I thought he was asleep. He ran his knuckles along my chin as he lifted his head to look at me. I fought the urge to lean into his touch.

"Nothing. I'm going to stay here until seven if that's okay with you. I don't want fight the drunks to get a cab back home."

I had never spent the night at any other guy's house, and I wasn't sure what it meant if I decided to stay—if I looked too needy or clingy. I also didn't know what this was between us or even if I should encourage it at all.

"You really think I'm going to throw you out at four o'clock to go home? Jesus, Samantha. Give me a little credit." Uh oh, I only got "Samantha" from Lucas when he was annoyed.

"Well, sorry. I don't do this very often. Forgive me for not having proper etiquette when someone fucks your brains out and then you have to go home." At 'someone fucks your brains out,' Lucas jerked back like I'd smacked him.

"Is that what this was to you? *Fucking?* I care about you—a lot. I thought you knew that. And yes, this situation is far from ideal and I can't be with you out in the open the way I want, but make no mistake, last night wasn't 'fucking someone's brains out' to me!" Lucas went from annoyed to straight up pissed off in a matter of seconds.

He turned around and sat up, starting to get out of bed; I scrambled up and wrapped my arms around him from behind.

"I'm sorry, please don't be mad. I'm just—I don't know how to deal with this. Please forgive me. It wasn't just fucking to me either, I swear." I found myself kissing his cheek, then behind his ear and down his neck. My hand slipped down his chiseled chest, over the glorious ripples of his abs and wrapped around the long, hard source of why I would be walking funny to the subway in a couple of hours. The tension left his shoulders as he groaned. I'd won him back, and Lucas turned and put his hand on my cheek, lifting my face to meet his.

"I know, and I don't want to push you. Christ, it's going to drive me insane thinking of you in his bed now." Lucas ran his fingers through his hair and hung his head. There was a look on his face that melted my insides. I couldn't tell what it was. Pain? Longing? Was I really getting him this twisted? *Me?* The past 12 hours were a little hard to process.

I couldn't help but laugh. "I have news for you. I haven't done anything other than sleep in his bed in a very, very long time, so you can rest ea—"

Lucas put his finger on my lips and shook his head. "I don't want to think about that now. When the sun comes up, we'll figure out whatever this means and where to go from here. But right now," He moved until he was on top of me, staring right into my eyes. It was a good thing I was laying down because my knees had melted into jelly.

"Right now, you're mine. And nothing else matters to me except how beautiful you look every time I make you come."

Sweet Jesus. This man was going to be the death of me. He kissed me, slow but hard, running his hands up and down my body. He moved his mouth lower and lower—from my neck down to my breasts, tracing circles around one of my nipples with his tongue. I moaned and pulled at his hair as my eyes rolled in back of my head. Lucas knew exactly how to touch me, and as he got to know my body, every kiss and caress was better than the one before. He stopped, looked deep into my eyes again, and ran his thumb over my lips. I felt worshipped by a man for maybe the first time in my life. Lucas reached over to his nightstand drawer to pull out a condom, quickly tearing the wrapper open and rolling it on. He climbed back on top of me and ran his fingers through my hair.

"You're so fucking gorgeous, and you really have no idea, do you?" Before I could answer, he covered my mouth with his. With one thrust he was back inside me, in and out, deeper and deeper. I lifted my hips in rhythm with his movements. Sex with Lucas was like an addictive drug—after only one night. If it were up to me, I would never leave his bed.

I prayed seven o'clock would never come.

chapter 7
Lucas

IT WAS SEVEN o'clock already. Sam had wanted to get up and leave by now but I didn't want to wake her. Her slender arms were draped around my waist and her head lay on my stomach. She nuzzled into me, placing a soft kiss on my chest before letting out a sweet little moan. I wasn't sure if she was waking up so I didn't speak. My chest constricted as I studied her face and gently stroked her long silky hair. She looked so peaceful and beautiful. *So damn beautiful.* How could I let her go home?

I realized a while ago that we didn't have long before we gave in to this insane attraction that had built up all these months, but this was the part I always dreaded—Sam leaving my bed and going back to her husband. For the next five minutes, I decided to pretend Marc didn't exist. It was only me and Sam. Morning sun leaked through my window, telling me my time was running out and pissing me off even more.

"Lucas? What time is it?" Sam's voice was raspy as she stirred awake. I hoped she wouldn't be mad that I let her sleep.

"Seven." I whispered into her hair as I kissed the top of her head. While she was here, I kidded myself that she was mine. And I could touch her and kiss her all I wanted.

She slowly pushed off my chest, rubbing her eyes. She was still half asleep, didn't seem to realize she was naked, and didn't lift the sheet to cover herself as she sat up. All I could think about at that moment was tracing a circle around a light pink nipple with my tongue and feeling her body squirm under me, the way it had over and over again last night. I became very familiar with every inch of her amazing body in the hours before we finally fell asleep, and my cock hardened immediately at the memory.

Sam looked down at herself, and with an adorable blush on her cheeks glanced up at me and giggled. Even though last night was all kinds of wrong, everything felt so very right. She had to feel that way too. I never had such an intense connection with anyone before Sam.

"I need to get going." Sam let out a long sigh, and stood from the bed. She picked up her clothes that were scattered all over the floor, all while still completely naked. She was killing me little by little. I nodded, but didn't pretend to look away.

I grabbed my jeans from last night that had somehow gotten draped over the headboard and slipped them on. Before I got out of bed, Sam was fully dressed and pulling on her jacket.

"I better get home." Sam gave me a sad smile and lowered her gaze to study the floor. I'd expected her to run out of here, and was surprised to see her stalling.

"I'll walk you downstairs." I took her hand—she was still in my apartment and still mine—and walked her down the inside steps to the door.

We gazed at each other for a long minute. I could barely keep how I felt about Sam to myself before, how the hell was I supposed to do it now? I didn't have to wonder anymore how amazing we would be together. Now I knew. *God, how I knew.* I wanted her so much—*all* of her. I wanted her to leave Marc and to finally realize she deserved much better than that asshole. I'd treat her like a princess. She wouldn't want for anything. *Be with me, Sam.* The desperate thoughts in my head were deafening.

Sam leaned against the back of the door as she looked at me, her eyes filling with tears. I took her face in my hands, my thumbs wiping away what she couldn't hold in.

"Text me when you get home. The subways run weird this early on the weekend." She nodded and I kissed her forehead, lingering and inching my lips down to her eyelids and then her cheeks. I meant to give her just a peck, but once our mouths connected we lost all control. My hand tangled in her hair as she moaned into my mouth. I pressed my body against hers as she pulled at the hair on the back of my neck. I realized that pretending to be friends was now a ship that long sailed as my tongue darted in and out of that perfect mouth.

"Oh, excuse me—" Cute little elderly Mrs. Taylor had stepped out of her first floor apartment and was about take her daily stroll to buy the morning paper. She looked at us and chuckled. She'd gotten quite an eyeful of my shirtless self as I groped Sam.

"Sorry to interrupt. I'll be out of your way in a jiffy. She's cute, Lucas!"

Sam laughed into my chest as I pulled us away from the door and nodded. "Yes, she sure is," I replied as Mrs. Taylor scooted her way out the door.

I shook my head, and Sam put her hand on my cheek. "I better go," she whispered as she gave me one last, soft kiss on the lips before creeping out the door. "We wouldn't want to wake anyone else, would we?" She waved as she shut the door behind her.

I leaned my head against the wall. Last night was a complete game changer for us. I only prayed that when she walked out of my door, she didn't walk out of my life.

chapter 8

Samantha

I SPENT MOST of the train ride home in a daze. Nothing felt real, as if I'd stepped into some kind of alternate reality. I could still taste Lucas's lips and feel him moving inside me. I had sex with Lucas effing Hunter—this had to be a dream.

I still remembered the first time I met Lucas at a Fourth of July barbecue at Daina's house, what now seemed like a lifetime ago.

"Hey Lucas. This is my friend, Samantha. The one I told you about. She'll be going to Barnard this September. Maybe you could get her assigned to you, Mr. Hot-Shot Advisor. Samantha, this is my cousin, Lucas."

Lucas swaggered over to where I was lounging on a beach chair. He leaned over, looking at me like he could see right through me.

"Daina told me all about you, Sam. Pleasure to meet you. I'll make it my business to have all the pretty girls assigned to me; nice to have a heads up on one. The man was smooth, I'd give him that. I hated people calling me "Sam" but that mouth could call me whatever it wanted.

I squawked out, "Nice to meet you, Lucas." He gave me a wink.

"Advisors teach the freshman orientation class, they call it Freshman Seminar in the class bulletin. I think I'm doing the Tuesday 10:30 class. Did you get your program yet?" Lucas sat on the edge of the beach chair next to me, resting his elbows on his knees. Was it possible for a guy to have sexy knees?

"Um, no. I, uh, haven't gotten anything." Lucas was so damn good looking he made me forget how to speak English.

"I can check when I go in the office in a couple of weeks. What's your last name?" Lucas licked his lips and my breath caught in my throat. Good lord, those were perfect lips. He probably really knew how to kiss, too.

"Sam? Want me to give you time to think about it?" The side of his mouth lifted in a smirk.

"O'Rourke, sorry." If Lucas was my freshman seminar teacher, I probably wouldn't hear a damn thing he said all semester.

"Hey, Lucas!" Nicole, Daina's next-door neighbor, called Lucas over to where she was leaning against the wall of Daina's above-ground pool, her perfect body showcased in a white string bikini. He excused himself and made his way over to where Nicole was standing. Lucas gave her a hello kiss and hug, making me queasy.

Lucas strolled back toward me, *"I better go inside and say hi to my aunt before she comes out to smack me, but make sure we exchange numbers before you go. Even if you're not in my class, I can still help you out and show you around."*

"Wow that would be great! Thanks, Lucas."

"No problem! I'll take care of you, Baby Girl." Baby Girl? I got another wink as he sauntered away. Apparently, I was counting them now.

"Do you need a napkin to wipe up the drool?" Daina chuckled and shook her head as she sat in the beach chair next to me. I rolled my eyes in response.

"I was not drooling. Does Lucas have a girlfriend? Wait, don't answer me, he's probably got a few." I leaned back in the chair and covered my face with my hands. I shouldn't have been this affected by a guy after meeting him for all of five minutes.

"My cousin is a really nice guy, but he's good looking and unfortunately he knows it. He'll help you in school, but try to keep a safe distance—I wouldn't want you to fall in love and get hurt."

My phone buzzed in my purse, bringing me back to the present.

> *Lucas: Wanted to make sure you got home OK. Is it bad to tell you how much I miss you already?*

I pinched myself. Yep, still awake. I didn't dream spending the night with Lucas. I texted back.

> *Me: I'm almost at my stop now. No. I miss you too.*

> *Lucas: Call me later?*

> *Me: OK*

My neighborhood seemed so quiet. It was the same street, same walk from the train station—but it all seemed different. It was as if I had been living in black and white before, and someone flipped a switch, washing everything in Technicolor brilliance. It was going to be that much harder to pretend I wasn't miserable now. I put my key in the door and took a deep breath. It was time to face reality.

I opened my front door, and I heard Marc in our bedroom. *Crap, he was supposed to be in Atlantic City until Sunday. Why the hell was he home already?* I didn't expect to have to come up with an excuse for being out all night and crept to my bedroom.

"You're home already? I thought you were staying until tomorrow? Since Bella had a sleepover at Julianna's, I stayed at Stacia's last night after we went out after work. You remember her? She moved here from Oregon and she lives by Madison Square Park, and I took the train home this morning."

Lying was not my strong suit. I always felt I had to add all these additional details to make my story sound believable. Anyone paying attention could see through me in five seconds. Since the truth was I rode Lucas's face for half the night, I felt compelled to come up with a believable story that didn't look like it had any holes. I felt my first pang of shame and guilt, followed by a rush of more shame that I was only *now* starting to feel this way.

Marc paid so little attention to me he didn't find it suspicious at all that his wife came home in a skirt and heels before nine o'clock on a Saturday morning. If I knew him, he didn't care one way or the other, but we were still married. Whatever I suspected he did or didn't do in our marriage, adultery was still breaking a commandment—one of the big ones, too, if I remembered correctly from my eight years at St. Anne's.

"I had to get back early since I'm leaving tomorrow morning." Marc didn't even look up, so he hadn't witnessed my walk of shame through the door.

"Rick told me last night he got me that freelance job I've been waiting to hear about. I can finally go back to work."

"Where?" He was packing a very large suitcase. It didn't look like he intended to come back anytime soon.

"Chicago. For six months. Maybe longer, depending on how it goes."

"You applied for a job in Chicago and took it, just like that? Where are you staying?" I realized how ridiculous I sounded, being so indignant after what I just did. Besides, I should expect this from Marc by now. He didn't consider me a partner, or even someone who factored in any kind of decision he made.

Marc rolled his eyes, like he did every time I asked him a question about anything—what to have for dinner, could he pick up Bella from somewhere, or why he took a long term out of state job without considering he had a family.

"Here we go, nagging as usual. You've been bitching about me not working. I finally do get a job, and you still have something to say. I start on Monday morning. Rick has an apartment there already and I'll stay with him. Thank God! I've been going fucking crazy here. I'm on my way out after I pack. I'll be home tonight."

"You're leaving your daughter for six months and aren't even giving it a second thought?" Now *this* was behavior I should've come to expect—he thought of himself and no one else.

I was getting pissed off.

Marc shrugged. "She's a mommy's girl anyway. She won't even notice I'm gone. I'll promise her a present when I get back and she'll be fine. And I don't have to explain shit to you. I can go *where* I want, *when* I want and it's none of your concern. Shut your mouth for once." He pushed past me to keep packing.

Something inside snapped. I was finally done pretending I had an actual marriage. There was no way I could keep getting treated like this just because I didn't have the guts to move on. Being alone was a hell of a lot better than this.

"Maybe she wouldn't be a 'mommy's girl' if you actually spent time with her instead of dropping her off at your parents' every day like she's a burden you don't feel like dealing with. But you know what, Marc, you're totally right. You're not my concern, and I am sure as hell not yours. It's about time we did something about this joke of a marriage. You go your way, and I'll go mine. I'm *done* dealing with your bullshit."

"Oh Jesus, not this again. You're so fucking sensitive, another reason I can't stand being home. Look—"

"No *you* look! Finish packing and do whatever you need to do, then I want you out of here—for good. When you get back from Chicago, you live somewhere else—with your parents, friends, on the curb, I don't care. I deserve better, and so does my daughter. She's unclear on what a real man actually is after seeing such a poor excuse for one the first five years of her life. Let me know when I can expect money for Bella's tuition since you're finally working again." The 'finally working again' was a low blow, but I didn't care.

I stormed into Bella's bedroom and slammed the door. I was a little shaky over what just happened, and pissed at myself for not standing up for myself a long time ago. I lay down on her bed and covered my eyes with my hands.

After our blowout, Marc didn't say anything else or even try to talk to me. We had been over for a long time, but neither of us had the guts to admit it.

There was a lot to figure out now. I needed to find after-school care for Bella—and figure out how to explain everything to her. I closed my eyes to focus on straightening out my clusterfuck of a life. And getting the image of sexy blue eyes out of my head.

I PICKED UP Bella after I managed to pull myself somewhat together. As I pulled up to Julianna's house, Bella saw me from the front window and waved. The door opened and she ran out to hug me, almost knocking me over. She was my little twin—same dark brown hair, pale skin, and light brown eyes.

"Mrs. Christensen, when can Bella stay here again?"

"Soon, Julianna. I promise. Did you guys have fun?"

"Yup! It was great!" Julianna was so boisterous, and my Bella just smiled and nodded.

I strapped her into the car and drove off. I took a deep breath, thinking how I would spin this to be not a big deal.

"Daddy got a new job and won't be back for a while. Looks like we'll be having fun sleepovers, only us!" Even a five-year-old could see through that crap a mile away, and Bella was smart.

She answered me with a quiet okay. Marc was right. Bella was a mommy's girl, but only because her father didn't spend any time trying to be close to her. There were days when he barely spoke to her. I hoped the years before her mother grew a pair of balls and kicked her father out didn't affect her for the long term.

I stayed in Bella's room all night so I wouldn't have to deal with Marc when he got back. Once she fell asleep, I decided to call Daina. If I didn't tell someone about the twilight zone I had entered, I would go insane.

When I told her I threw Marc out, there was nothing but silence.

"You're serious?" Daina gasped.

"As a heart attack, Day."

"Good! Babe, I've been telling you for years. You deserve so much better than Marc—and so does Bella. Maybe I should call my cousin. Since you two formed this cute little friendship he talks about you—a lot. It would make his day knowing you threw that piece of shit out of the house."

I was about to say this out loud. And then it would be true.

"Well . . . about that. Last night when Bella was at Julianna's and Marc was in Atlantic City, I went over to Lucas's apartment. One thing kind of lead to another and—"

"Holy hell!" Daina screamed in my ear. "Are you saying what I think you're saying? What time did you get home?"

I took a deep breath before answering. "After eight this morning."

"*What?*" This time, she screamed so loud I almost dropped the phone. "Wow, you actually spent the night with Lucas? That has been your dream for what, more than ten years? Sort of crappy timing though. Are you okay?"

"Yeah, I think." I paused. No, I didn't think that at all right now. "Ugh, I don't know. When did my life become such a mess?"

"I'm glad you finally stood up for yourself. And, although I'm not condoning doing what you did while you're still married, I think getting close to Lucas made you see how badly you were being treated and made you realize you'd had enough."

At least Daina didn't judge me. I felt a little better.

"So, tell me. How was it?"

"Ew, Daina! He's your cousin! You don't find discussing this a tad bit gross?"

"A little, but you should have your moment after waiting so long. So . . ."

I took a deep breath. How could I describe sex with Lucas?

"It was *un*believable, I think I'm ruined for anyone else. Better than any fantasy I've ever had about Lucas, and trust me over the years there have been a lot—"

"Moment over. Have you talked to him since then?"

"Not yet. He texted me after I left to say he missed me. But I don't know. Daina, I'm damaged goods. I have a daughter. I separated from my husband three seconds ago. What could I possibly offer a man like Lucas?"

"Samantha, you have plenty to offer Lucas. Don't let the way Marc treated you make you think differently. He hasn't come out and said it, but I think Lucas has it bad for you. You may have officially separated from Marc now, but you both haven't really been together in a long time. Have the guts to take a chance on something that could make you happy. Think about it."

"I will think about it. I promise."

"Call me tomorrow and we can burn whatever Marc left behind!"

chapter 9

Samantha

THROWING MARC OUT and avoiding Lucas somehow gave me a crap load of energy. My curtains were now washed and ironed for the first time since I gave birth, the floors were spotless, and there wasn't a patch of dust anywhere. Starting a new life for my daughter and myself was scary, even though I was sure I was making the right decision; mindless housework was a fantastic escape.

As Bella watched *Super Why,* I plopped on the couch, looking around for something else to scrub. My cell phone rang, and I recognized my friend Robyn's number.

"Hey Robyn, thanks for getting back to me so fast!"

"Not a problem! Is everything all right?

Robyn had to be the nicest person I knew, and the most soft spoken—it was why we were all shocked when she told us she wanted to become a lawyer. The only time I ever saw Robyn angry was when her academic ranking in our high school class went from number one to number three. Even though she over-achieved her way all through law school, Robyn never lost her sweetness unless you were a deadbeat dad or an abusive husband. Then, may God have mercy on your soul.

Robyn's father left when she was very young, and her mom worked two jobs because he didn't give her a dime of child support for her or her brothers. I'm sure that had a lot to do with why she was so passionate about family law. I was very thankful I didn't have to explain everything that had happened over the last forty-eight hours to a complete stranger.

"Marc took a job in Chicago and left a couple of days ago. I threw him out, for good." I took a deep breath. "I want a divorce."

"Oh, honey. I'm sorry. Are you okay? What happened?"

"We had an argument before he left and I finally had enough of being abused all these years."

"Has he hurt you or threatened you in any way? Do you need to file a restraining order?" I smiled to myself at how she morphed from Robyn the friend to Robyn the kick-ass attorney.

"No, nothing like that. I'm ready to move on. It's not good for me or Bella to live in this type of situation, and I don't want her to grow up thinking this is how a man is supposed to treat his family. I want full custody, but I doubt he'll fight me. I'm really clueless, so tell me what I need to do."

"First thing I want you to do is change the locks. I've seen this happen before, the husband and wife separate and then he feels like coming back home, so he walks in like he still lives there. Get his name off everything you can. Do you share a checking account? I would either close it, or open a new one and transfer all the money you need for expenses. The faster you take care of all of that, the faster the divorce can go through when the time comes. In the state of New York, we have to prove you've been separated for at least a year before you can file for divorce. So before we do this, are you sure?"

Whatever happened with Lucas and me from this point on, I was done being married to Marc. I felt good about this decision, even if it meant I was alone.

"I'm sure. What else do I need to do?"

"Get me his address so we can serve him separation papers. I'll have them drawn up ASAP when I get to the office. And Samantha, I'm proud of you."

"Thanks, Rob—I needed that."

The restless energy still continued, and I decided to tackle the boxes at the bottom of my closet. I found old yearbooks, photo albums, and my accounting text book from college. I had fond memories of this book since I used all my accounting and finance classes back then as an excuse to get tutored by the hottest advisor in school.

"Hey, Baby Girl. C'mon in."

Lucas promised me he'd help me with some accounting homework. I hated math but accounting and finance were core classes I had to pass to get a business degree. He said to come by the advisor's office after my last class since he'd be filing the new freshman paperwork.

"Baby Girl? I feel like I'm four when you call me that. It's getting a little old."

"Oh, loosen up. Let's see what we have here . . ." *He looked over my shoulder at my notebook, brushing his body against mine, causing the hairs on my neck to stand on end, as usual.* "You do know which side is credit and which side is debit, right?"

"Um, yes, I'm not that far gone." *Truthfully, I could never remember. Plus, Lucas was looking extra hot today with a tight, long sleeve gray Henley shirt and faded jeans. He still kept his sandy brown hair a little long—just enough to grab during a hot, passionate . . . ah, enough, Samantha. Focus! You're here for a reason. I didn't want to look dumb; I figured he'd show me without having to ask.*

He went through the whole assignment with me. It was adorable how he got excited explaining it. Leave it to Lucas to make the most boring subject in the entire world interesting. I had a good handle on it once we were done.

"Thanks! You're a lifesaver! The professor is too old and scary for me to ask for any help." *The professor was, in fact, very nice and reminded us at the end of each class that his door was always open if we needed extra help. Did I look as pathetic as I really was? I almost enjoyed accounting and finance because it gave me an excuse to spend more time with Lucas. He was always happy to help and so patient, and articulate, and sexy, and . . . ugh. Maybe this incurable crush would help my GPA somehow.*

"Anytime. You're like family, you know that." *Family. Ick. Family was worse than being called "kid" or . . ."Baby Girl."*

I noticed a flyer for a Halloween party on the bulletin board in front of Lucas's desk. Advisors were in charge of all the school events. Lucas was, of course, the most popular, especially with the girls. He wasn't supposed to date any of them, but I always overheard stories from girls claiming to have hooked up with him after one of the on-campus parties.

Noticing where I'd focused my attention, Lucas joked, "You should go. It should be fun, and I'm even wearing a costume." He cocked an eyebrow at me.

"Stop it! What is Mr. Hot-Shot Advisor going to dress up as?"

"You'll have to go to find out. If you come in costume I'll even give you candy. The sexier the costume, the more candy I'll give you."

"Right. Sexy costumes aren't my thing. I'm sure you'll have lots of girls lining up for your candy." It was out of my mouth before I knew it, and Lucas cracked up.

"You make me sound cheap, Sam. I don't give my candy out to just anyone." I nudged his shoulder, making him laugh even harder. "I don't know why you think like that. You're beautiful and could rock the hell out of a sexy costume." Um, what? Lucas thinks I'm beautiful?

I could do this; go to the party, flirt a little, and see where it takes us. Yeah, I could do this—

"Hey, Lucas. You said you'd help me put up the rest of these flyers for the party. You wouldn't stand me up would you?" One of the student aides I knew from my Statistics class strutted into his office, interrupting us. She told me the other day how difficult it was to balance school and modeling. There was a picture of her in only a bra and jeans giving a hot guy a back rub in my Seventeen Magazine this month. Needless to say, my heart bled for the girl.

"I'm coming, Karen. Don't worry."

"Oh hey, Samantha. I didn't know you knew Lucas." She gave me a look like 'how could you possibly know a guy like him?'

Lucas looked over at me and gave me a smile, "Sam and I go way back. She's my cousin's best friend."

"Oh, that's cute." She looked over at Lucas, and—once again, it's like I wasn't there. Mousy Samantha, dismissed as usual. "So are you done here? If you're lucky I'll let you guess what my costume will be. I can't get thrown out of the party for showing too much skin, can I?"

Oh for goodness sake, really?

"For once, it would be nice to have a party where I didn't have to speak with security afterwards. Be right back, Sam. Let me go pick up the rest of the flyers out of the printer."

"So you and Lucas are friends?" Karen twirled her luxurious shampoo commercial worthy hair around her finger as she looked me over.

"Yes. Like he said, I'm a family friend." I shrugged as I packed my books into my backpack.

"He's a really nice guy—and an ah-mazing kisser." She closed her eyes and pretended to shiver.

My heart dropped into my stomach as I tasted vomit in the back of my throat. She got to feel Lucas's lips, and God only knew what else. Did I really think I had a chance against girls like her? I was such an idiot for even considering it.

"Okay, got'em. Sam. We can study for a little while longer— Hey are you all right? You look a little pale." Lucas rushed toward me with a concerned expression and put his hand on my shoulder.

"Nope, I'm fine! I'm just going to go. Thanks again for the help." I bolted out of his office, not wanting to look back at Karen's shit-eating grin.

I spent the night of the Halloween party with my favorite creepy movie, Carrie. There was something about watching an outcast slay all the mean girls who made her life hell that made me feel all warm and fuzzy.

I put the book down when I heard my phone chime with a text.

Lucas: Hi, Sam. I just wanted to let you know I was thinking about you.

I typed a dozen different replies, like I'm thinking about you too, I miss you, I'm sorry I haven't called—but I didn't send any of them. All those years ago, I dreamed about a real chance with Lucas. Now I had one, and it scared me to death.

chapter 10

Lucas

"DAINA, YOU HOME?"
I arrived at my cousin's house and rang the bell. She didn't answer so I pulled open the unlocked screen door and went in.

'Oh hey, Lucas. Come on in. Let me put the baby to sleep and we can talk." It had been almost radio silence from Sam for two weeks. I was about to lose my mind, and went to the only person who I prayed may be able to give me some kind of clue as to why.

From the outside of this fucked up situation, the answer why Sam was avoiding me was obvious. I had sex—amazing and fantastic sex—with a married woman who now regretted it and wanted to stay away from me. But there was more to Sam and me than that, or at least I hoped there was.

I plopped onto Daina's couch as she watched me with pity in her eyes. I'd taken the subway all the way to the Bronx after work on a Wednesday night. It was obvious I wasn't handling my sudden separation from Sam well.

"I suspected something was brewing between the two of you. I'm actually surprised it took three months for anything to happen. And since you came all the way here tonight instead of just calling me, I'm thinking this thing you guys have goes deeper than I thought. Did you plan for that night to happen?"

I should've been insulted, but she had a point. Looking back I could see how it seemed that way.

"No. Not consciously, anyway. She didn't have to be home by a certain time, and I wanted her all to myself. I liked the idea of no time constraint and I wanted her with me, and only me. And it was . . ." I trailed off and shook my head. I didn't think my

53

cousin wanted the details of what has been playing over and over in my head for the past couple of weeks. How Sam's lips felt on mine, how her body moved under me, how fucking responsive she was to everything I did to her.

"Stop! I don't need any more details than I already have, thank you!" Daina held up her hand, shaking her head.

"What did Sam say?" I was lying back on the couch in a slumped and defeated position but wanting to know what Sam told her about our night together made me sit straight up.

"She used the word 'unbelievable' but wouldn't really elaborate. She's had a huge crush on you for, um, *forever*. A smart guy like you should have picked up on that. She was always so scared to admit to you how she felt, but you spent enough time with her back then to know without her saying anything."

"Yes, I knew. I liked her, too, but I didn't want to hurt her. She wasn't the type of girl you kept things casual with." I put my face in my hands and pinched the bridge of my nose. I wished I could go back in time—sweep Sam off her feet and take her deadbeat husband out of the equation. "How the hell did she ever wind up with Marc?" I remember dealing with him when he was a college student, and even then it was obvious he'd never change.

There were worse jobs than a college advisor. And paying off my master's degree by showing freshmen around school and planning on-campus parties was a sweet deal. But I hated parties like this one. The members of the hosting frat were complete assholes. I spent most of the night watching the girls to make sure none of them looked drugged, since that's how their parties usually went.

I had just stepped into the empty hallway outside the common room where the party was drawing to a close to get some air, when the sound of soft whimpers got my attention. A girl was sitting on the floor outside the bathroom with her face in her hands. I rushed over to where she curled herself into a ball to make sure she wasn't hurt. When she picked up her head, I recognized her as one of the undergraduate student aides in our office.

"Paige, what's wrong?" I knelt in front of her and she shook her head when she noticed me.

"I'm just really stupid, Lucas. I thought in my stupid little head that Marc and I were exclusive and I came in to find him making out with someone else. When I confronted him, he told me he doesn't do girlfriends and I should learn not to be so clingy. He's absolutely right." She wiped away the tears still streaming down her face. "I'm in college, not high school. I should know better."

As if on cue, Marc Christensen—the ringleader of this douchebag frat—walked out of the party with a girl on each arm. He looked over at Paige and rolled his eyes. I wanted an excuse to knock his teeth down his throat in the worst fucking way, but no matter what he did, I couldn't. He wasn't worth losing my job and source of tuition.

"Paige, why don't you get a cab home? Here." I pulled a twenty-dollar bill out of my wallet. "You shouldn't have to stay here. And you aren't stupid. Be thankful you didn't waste too much time on Marc before you found out what kind of guy he really was."

Paige nodded. "Thanks, Lucas. You're a good guy."

I put my hand on her shoulder. "Not all guys are jerks." I managed to get a little smirk from her. "Get home safe and I'll see you in the office on Monday."

Paige moped her way out of the building. I felt sorry for her, but was also happy she got away from Marc. She was a nice kid, too innocent for that prick.

When Marc pulled the two girls into the open storage closet at the end of the hallway, I marched up to the door and caught it before it closed.

"Take this off campus. This isn't your personal hotel, Christensen."

"What's the matter, pretty boy? Want them both for yourself? I hear you like the ladies too . . ." One night of bad judgment and kissing a student with a big mouth had followed me *for over a year.*

"I mean it. Not here. Leave and do whatever the hell you want." I held the door open and glowered at Marc, who was laughing like the disrespectful asshole he was. The girls looked uncomfortable and scurried away. Marc let out a long sigh and turned to me.

"You're so fucking pathetic, Hunter. I'm surprised you didn't leave with Paige. She would've eaten your knight in shining armor bullshit right up and her panties would've fallen right the fuck off. She could have joined the little entourage of girls that follow your sorry ass around. Don't you get enough pussy around here without having to cock block me and my friends—?"

I backed Marc against the wall and pressed my forearm against his throat. He was a lot smaller than me, and fear replaced the lousy attitude across his face.

"I would love to teach you some manners, but they would be wasted on you. I'm not supposed to touch you, but that doesn't mean I won't if you push me. Got it?"

I shoved him one more time before I let him go. He bent over at the waist, coughing and sputtering to catch his breath.

"Fuck you, pretty boy." Marc straightened and then sauntered back into the party. I couldn't protect every girl in the school from him, but maybe if he saw me hanging around he would think twice.

Marc got the girl he never deserved, and as much as I tried to hide it from Sam, it made my blood boil thinking of them together.

Daina looked down and shrugged.

"He's not my favorite person either, but I don't think you're here to talk about him. What brings you here tonight, Lucas?"

"For the past three months, we talked all day long, every day. Since she left my apartment two weeks ago, I've only gotten a couple of one-word texts. I think I pushed too hard and scared her off, and I don't know what the hell to do."

Daina shook her head and laughed at me. This wasn't fucking

funny to me—at all. It was starting to feel like a waste of train fare to come here and it was pissing me the hell off.

"Well, glad I came over to give you a laugh. Thanks for the help." I stood and Daina pulled me back by the hand.

"I'm not laughing at you—well maybe a little. I admit find this a little funny. You never let a woman get under your skin like this before. In fact, you have the same sad, puppy dog look on your face Samantha had when she was mooning over you in college. Kind of ironic how the tables have turned. Women always fell at your feet, but Samantha is an unattainable chase. You actually have to fight for her. Is that what has you so hooked?"

I tried to rub the tension away from my neck. I was heading into my late thirties, and up until this point never got this emotionally involved with someone. I wasn't a jerk, but I wasn't a saint either. It was the big family joke how women would always slip me their number or approach me. Since Sam came back into my life, all I saw was her. No one else could compare.

Not wanting Sam would make my life a hell of a lot easier.

"No, it's not about the chase. Sam is just, different from other women. She's sexy and smart, and she has the best laugh. I could talk to her for hours and never get bored. She looks at me like I'm some kind of superhero. It's easy to get high on that."

I missed Sam so fucking much. Talking about her made it even worse.

"I know I turned into a big pussy when it comes to her. I realized that when she left my apartment and I had to fight the urge to hold on to her ankles to make her stay. The way I feel about her scares the shit out of me. I know she's married, and it's all kinds of wrong to want her like this. All I think about is going out to Queens like a fucking caveman telling that jerk-off that his wife should be mine, that he would never be worthy of someone as amazing as she is. I could give her everything, Daina. I could make her happy. I need to convince her to let me."

Daina eyes popped open wide. She was speechless. If I didn't feel like such a loser right now, I would've reached for my phone to take a picture since it was truly a miraculous moment.

"Wow. I'm sorry I laughed at you. Listen, Luc," Daina said as she put her hand over mine. It was funny how I used to help my little cousin nurse her broken hearts and now she was comforting my sorry ass. "Give her some time. I don't think Marc is the issue. She's just scared. All you can do for her right now is have a little patience. I have total faith she'll come around sooner than you think."

I stood from the couch, not sure if I felt better or worse, or how much longer I could do this waiting thing without showing up at her office. I resolved to take Daina's advice and wait it out, hoping she was right.

As I arrived back at my apartment, my phone buzzed in my pocket.

> *Sam: Hey, do you have time for coffee tomorrow afternoon? I'm sorry I've been a little MIA, I had a lot going on here.*

Good thing no one was around to see me leap to reply, or they would have confiscated my man card.

> *Me: Yes, is everything OK? Does 3 work?*

> *Sam: Perfect! I'll explain when I see you.*

Did she leave Marc? Was that what was 'going on'? Did she regret what we did? My mind was going crazy with possibilities. I let her slip through my fingers once. She may not have been mine to take, but I didn't want to let her go.

chapter 11

Samantha

I T WAS WRONG, but I ignored Lucas since I left his apartment two weeks ago. I was still trying to figure out what happened. Did Lucas really want me? Or did we give in to the attraction that's developed over the past months and our night together was as far as it would go?

Lucas was on my mind every second of the day; the hunger in his eyes as he touched me, the hot trail of his lips as he ran them all over my body, how it seemed as if he could read my mind. Being with him was amazing, but I didn't feel free to contact him as freely like I used to. Before that night, we would talk all day long, but these past couple of weeks we'd only texted a few times. I didn't want to seem needy or desperate, but when I thought about all the things we did, I felt a gnawing ache at my core, my insides begging for a repeat. It was so much more than just sex. Lucas made me feel special in a way no one else ever had. I felt like the woman I'd always wanted to be—beautiful, smart and worthy of a man's undivided attention. I could fool myself and try to hide it, but needy was exactly what I was. I wanted more, and I *needed* more. If he didn't, I wasn't sure how to handle that. So like the coward I often was, I put off finding out.

I sat at our usual table at Starbucks. When Lucas came in he looked . . . nervous? He was a little fidgety, cracking his knuckles and running his fingers through his hair, frustrated about something. Since when was Lucas ever nervous? He had to be the coolest and calmest person I knew.

I stood up when he started to walk toward me. He stopped

in front of the table like he wasn't sure what to say or do. I tried to give him a hello kiss and hug, but his body was stiff as a board as he glared at me.

"What's wrong, Samantha? Where've you been?" I was 'Samantha.' Not good.

"Nothing, I didn't mean to make you worry. There was a lot to rearrange at home."

"But you told me you'd call me that Saturday and you didn't. In fact, I've hardly heard from you at all in two weeks. Admit it. You regret it, don't you?" The look on his face was panicked and scared. It was surreal to see him this upset. I pulled him to sit down.

"Marc left on Sunday morning. His friend got him on an IT contract job in Chicago for the next six months. I had to figure out what to do with Bella after school."

"Left for good, or left for now?"

"Supposed to be six months but there's a good chance it will get extended longer."

"No, that's not what I mean. I mean—"

"You mean did he leave me? Right?" Lucas took a deep breath and sighed. He narrowed his eyes at me and leaned forward.

"I know figuring out who was going to pick up Bella from school wasn't the reason we haven't really spoken in two weeks." I thought backing off a bit was better for both of us. Maybe it was just better for *me*.

"Lucas, I never meant to hurt you. I guess I didn't know what to say or how to handle it. I didn't have a real marriage. I always knew that, but being with you made me realize how empty it really was. I saw how much I was settling these past few years. You make me feel things and want things I didn't think were possible anymore. And I guess I was afraid of wanting it too much, and having to deal with losing it."

Lucas exhaled like he'd been holding his breath and sat back in his chair.

"I was afraid I'd lost you. You've become so important to me. I thought I pushed you and scared you off." A man caring this much about having me in his life was new territory. I moved closer to him, taking his hand and interlocking my fingers with his.

"Did I sound scared that night? Or the next morning?" I gave him a little smile. He smirked at me, and I could tell *my* Lucas was back.

"I do remember you screaming, but you didn't sound scared, no." *Smartass.* Yes, I started this but my face got hot and I knew it was turning red.

"Really Sam, after everything we've done you're still blushing?" Lucas shook his head.

I shrugged. "I guess you could blame my half-Irish skin." I tried to hide how nervous I was. "I'm divorcing Marc, finally. I really shouldn't start anything with anyone now."

Lucas's face fell. He nodded and tried to take his hand away from mine. I stopped him and held his hand tighter.

"But you've become important to me, too—and I don't regret a single second of that night. Whether or not it's the right time, I want to take a chance. Can we take things really slow?" I squinted my eyes at him, nervous and tempted to shut out his reaction.

A slow smile spread across Lucas's face as he nodded. "I would like that. I missed texting you good morning and good night, and hearing you laugh. I . . . missed you so much."

"I missed you too." It always felt so right when Lucas and I were together—effortless and wonderful. I thought we could have something special, and we deserved the chance to try. I hoped it wouldn't end up hurting both of us.

"I think I should head back to the office. I have a call with a client in a little bit." Lucas was still holding my hand, and helped me up.

"Yeah I should get back too." I followed as he led me outside. "I'll call you tonight after Bella goes to sleep." I wrapped my arms around his neck like it was the most natural thing in the world. He put his hands on my waist and pulled me closer.

"You're *sure?*" He cocked an eyebrow at me.

"Yes, I promise." I gave him a soft, lingering kiss on his lips.

Lucas's eyes got wide and he gave me a surprised look. "I thought we were going to take it slow?"

I shrugged and gave him a big smile. "We don't have to go that slow."

"Well, in that case . . ."

Lucas pulled my arm back and gave me a *real* kiss. A kiss like the one that started everything back at his apartment—hard and wet and wonderful. We were all tongues and lips, and he always tasted so frigging good. I pulled back, feeling a little dizzy.

"Talk to you later."

At the end of the long city block, I looked back and Lucas hadn't moved. He had his hands in his pockets and was smiling, watching me.

"Don't you have a client call?" I yelled across Park Avenue.

He shrugged. "Yeah, but I have time to enjoy the view," he shouted back.

I shook my head and kept walking, not able to hide the goofy Kool-Aid smile on my face. I prayed if this was all still a dream, I wouldn't wake up anytime soon.

chapter 12

Samantha

ONE MONTH PASSED, and I hadn't heard a peep from Marc. Robyn confirmed he was served with the papers, but he wouldn't answer my texts asking if he got them. I did everything she advised—locks were changed and our joint checking account was closed. I called Marc to let him know and he sent me straight to voicemail. He was as done with our marriage as I was, and I hoped he would just sign the papers so we could both move on.

Lucas and I were back to all day texting and long conversations at night after Bella went to bed. One night I fell asleep since it was so late, and I woke up to the phone in my ear and a text from Lucas saying my breathing sounded adorable. I didn't feel right leaving my daughter with a baby sitter to so we could go on a date, at least not right now. When Julianna asked Bella for another sleepover that Saturday night, I asked Lucas if he'd like to go out. I didn't think I was ready to sleep with him again quite yet, even though I was very 'ready' whenever I thought about being with Lucas again. But if we were going to have a real chance, I had to make sure my head was clear. Being drunk off great sex wouldn't put me in a decent place to have good judgment.

Lucas said he had the perfect place to go, and to meet him at the corner of Thirty-fourth and Fifth at six o'clock. When I got there he looked breathtaking as usual and was leaning against the building. Even standing there, the man had serious swagger. He wore a gray T-shirt under a black jacket and black jeans. He made anything he wore look mouthwatering, and at least for tonight, this perfection was all mine. I didn't know where we were going, so I wore a green wrap dress with my favorite black leather knee-high boots and matching black leather jacket.

Lucas met me halfway and pulled me into his arms, giving me a soft kiss on the lips. I shuddered a little at his smoldering look.

"Ready?"

"Ready for what? You never told me where we were going." I was relieved I didn't under or over dress judging by what he had on, but I would have felt a lot better if I knew what I was in for.

"Look up." We were right in front of the Empire State Building. "Ever been to the top?"

"Once, on an eighth grade school trip." It was awful how I never went to any of the famous spots New York City was known for, like most New Yorkers.

"Well after tonight, you can say you've been there twice. C'mon." He took my hand and led me into the lobby. We stepped onto the elevator and traveled up to the Observation Deck on the eighty-sixth floor. Even all those years ago, I could still remember being a little nervous going so high. Lucas must've realized I was tense and squeezed my hand.

I stepped out onto the deck and understood why movies like *Sleepless in Seattle* and *An Affair to Remember* used the Empire State Building as the ultimate romantic meeting place. I got a kick out of looking through the binoculars and looking down on the city I'd spent my entire life living and working in. It was beautiful from this high up, and the twilight made the views more spectacular.

It was so windy, my hair kept wrapping around my face as I was trying to look out of the bars. I glanced over at Lucas and he was staring at me with a weird expression. Like he was in some kind of trance.

"Hey, what's wrong?"

"Nothing, it's . . . you're beautiful."

I strode over to where he stood and ran my fingers along the trimmed stubble on his jaw. He caught my hand and smiled.

"You aren't so bad, either." Lucas smiled and tried to smooth my hair off my face but the wind was too strong.

Lucas whispered in my ear, "Ever been kissed on top of the Empire State Building?"

"I came here with my eighth grade class—with nuns and class mothers chaperoning us. So that's a no."

Lucas pulled me towards him and kissed me, wrapping his arms around my waist. He even dipped me a little like they did in the movies. He pulled me back up and gave me a sexy smile.

"Good date so far?"

"I'd say so."

I couldn't wait to see what else Lucas would show me that would be like I was seeing it for the first time.

WE STROLLED TO a small tavern for dinner. I was surprised when Lucas slid in next to me instead of across from me in our booth. He put his arm around my shoulder and pulled me close as he looked at the menu. I glanced up at him and giggled.

"What's so funny?"

"I expected you to sit across from me. You're cute when you're clingy." I kissed his cheek and snuggled into his side as our waitress brought us our drinks.

"I'm making up for lost time. Do you know how many lunches and coffee dates I wanted to do this?" Lucas kissed my cheek, and inched his lips down my neck. "Or this." I jumped when he licked then bit my earlobe. A moan escaped me and he chuckled.

"Sorry. I know you want to take this slow. Now that I can kiss you, it's hard to stop. I'll try to keep myself in check. Promise." He took his arm off my shoulder and held the menu with both hands.

I took Lucas's face in my hands and gave him a soft kiss, nibbling his bottom lip as I pulled away.

"I know what you mean. I don't want to stop kissing you

either."

Lucas handed me a menu and looked away. He got serious and moved a little further away from me. I made him uncomfortable but wasn't sure how. I put my hand on top of his and he looked back at me.

"Did I say something wrong?"

Lucas smirked and shook his head. "I need to not touch you or kiss you for a little while. I'm afraid I'll shove you into the bathroom in the back or the alley outside, which would be the complete opposite of slow."

I noticed the single-person bathroom and alley outside too—and had the same fleeting thought. Taking it slow was proving to be much harder than I thought it would be.

"We went out of order didn't we? Friendship, incredible sex, and now taking it slow. We probably gave each other whiplash." I laughed, but Lucas shut his eyes and huffed at me.

"Now what? I'm screwing up our first real date aren't I?"

"No, Samantha." Lucas whispered in my ear. "Hearing you bring up the incredible sex just makes me want a lot more of it. We need a change in subject—*now*."

"You thought it was incredible, too?" I gave him a devious smile. Seeing Lucas uncomfortable was rare, and I couldn't resist busting his chops.

Lucas scowled at me and I couldn't help laughing. He leaned in to whisper again. "It was beyond fucking incredible, so unless you want me to drag you under the table for a repeat . . . Change. In.Subject."

Heat pooled between my legs. Joke was on me now—me and my stupid rational thinking and wanting to take it slow.

I scooted away from Lucas in the booth and nodded. "Okay, point taken. We never really talked about your life in California. I usually monopolize all our conversations with my sad little problems. What was it like?"

Lucas shrugged. "There really wasn't that much more than what I told you. San Diego was a nice city, but I worked a lot of long hours so I didn't get to enjoy it that much. I like my job and life here a lot better. It really wasn't the never-ending *Baywatch* episode that you like to think it was."

"Oh, come on. There wasn't an endless string of blonde bombshells trying to get your attention?"

"I dated, if that's what you're asking, but never anything serious. Until recently, no one ever held my interest for long." Lucas gave me a sweet smile.

"When was *recently?*" I moved closer to him and lifted his hand, interlocking our fingers. Lucas picked up our joined hands and kissed my wrist.

"Recently was about five months ago. I met a beautiful woman for a drink and have been ruined ever since." Lucas cocked an eyebrow at me.

"Ruined?" I crinkled my nose at Lucas, and he gave me a soft kiss on the lips.

"Ruined in the best possible way." He put his arm back around me and called the waitress over to our table to take our order.

I was ruined too. And ruined never felt so good.

chapter 13

Samantha

A S I PULLED into Marc's parents' driveway, I felt liberated. The last of my soon to be ex-douchebag husband's things were in a box in the trunk. My house was officially rid of anything that was his, and it was a heady and fan*freaking*tastic feeling. When he got back from Chicago, he would have no reason to come to the house, other than to see his daughter. He hadn't called her once in the four months he was gone, so I doubted he would make an effort to actually see her once he got back.

Marc's mother Jeannie answered the door with a frown on her face.

"More boxes? His old room is almost full. Is this the last of it?"

"Sure is. When he gets back from Chicago he can come straight here." I tried to keep the smile out of my voice as I handed over the rest of her son's belongings.

Her brow furrowed as she glared at me. "I'll keep them here, but it's going to be silly when you just have to take them back home when you make up."

I put my hand on her arm. "Jeannie, we won't be making up. Papers have been drawn up. Locks have been changed. We're done." She let out a long sigh, but didn't look like she paid attention to a word I said.

"Since Marc's job has been extended, we'd like to take Bella a couple of weekends each month. It's nice picking her up from school once a week, but since her father left we don't see her as much."

Bella was close to her grandparents, and since she had no contact with her father, I didn't want to ruin that. Plus, being able to see Lucas on the weekends sometimes would be wonderful.

"I would be fine with that. Wait—did you just say that his job was extended?" Marc hadn't called once in all the time he was gone. I received rare one-word text answers when I attempted to contact him.

"Oh yes—for another three months at least. We miss him but I'm so glad he's doing well." Marc's mother idolized her son. I never knew whether to feel sorry for her or blame her for the awful way he turned out.

"Well, maybe he can speak to his daughter when she's here, since he never calls the house. You can let him know he forgot her birthday."

"Oh, I'm sure he didn't mean to forget. He's very busy, and you should really cut him some slack—" I held up my hands to stop her from talking. Another great thing about getting divorced was I didn't have to tolerate any more guilt trips from my mother-in-law.

"He's not my problem anymore; he's yours. We have no plans for this coming weekend. I can drop her off after her dance class Saturday morning and come to get her Sunday evening. Does that work for you?"

"Sure. Thank you, Samantha." Jeannie had a hint of a smile on her face as she called Bella to the door. She picked Bella up and gave her a big hug and kiss before she handed her back to me. She did love her granddaughter and both of Marc's parents spoiled Bella any chance they got. I welcomed any normalcy I could keep in Bella's life.

"SO, ISN'T THIS great? I don't have to worry about Bella and can focus on the hot older guy who wants to buy me dinner?"

Lucas and I were enjoying an outdoor lunch in Madison Square Park. I loved New York City in the spring. April was always my favorite month, and everything was in full bloom. My good mood made everything seem even brighter. I snuggled into Lucas's side and grabbed his hand, intertwining our fingers.

"Older guy, huh?" He leaned his head on top of mine and pulled me closer.

"Well, yeah, you're still five years older than me. And I *did* say hot, did you miss that?

"Oh, I heard you. Where do you want to go?"

"Hmm, I don't know, I was thinking of Blue Water Grill, but I really don't care where we go. What do you think?"

Lucas glanced away. He was a little hard to read. I thought he'd be happier about this, and I was more than a little disappointed it seemed that he wasn't.

"We don't have to go out. I thought since I didn't have to worry about who was taking care of Bella we could do something. But if you have other plans, it's totally fine." I pulled my hand away and gathered up the trash from lunch.

Lucas grabbed my arm and pulled me back. "Slow down a second, Sam. I can see the wheels turning in your head. Of course, I want to spend time with you. That's all I think about. I have an idea where we can go. How about Thirtieth and Third?"

"Where your apartment is? Is there a new place to eat there?" I didn't remember hearing about any new restaurants.

"I meant my apartment. We could order in. And you could stay the night with me, if you want." Lucas kissed the back of my hand. "Bella is with her grandparents all weekend?" He gave me an unsure smile, like he wasn't sure how I'd react to that.

Did I want to spend the night with him again? *God, yes.* I still wanted to take it slow, but I thought about Lucas all the time—and in most of that time he was naked. If I went back to his apartment, there would be no self-control for either of us. Being alone with no time constraint would have the exact same effect on us it did before. Were we ready for that?

70

I took a deep breath. "Yes, she is. I'll come to your apartment Saturday and we'll order in. Can I get back to you on spending the night?" I gave him a sideways glance. I didn't want to hurt him again or offend him. I wasn't avoiding things like during those two weeks I didn't see or speak to him, but I wanted to be cautious.

Lucas gave me a big smile and nodded. "Sure, Sam."

I was more than a little rattled, and needed time to think.

When I got back to my office, I realized I should have gone home instead since I was useless. I really did want to spend the night with Lucas again, but I still felt uneasy about it. We had a great thing going. A great undefined thing, but I didn't want to ruin it. I kept running pros and cons over and over in my head.

Lucas called after I got Bella in bed. We had packed her bag for grandma and grandpa's house, and I had a strong pang of mom guilt weighing heavily in my stomach. She *should* spend time with her grandparents. And regardless of what—or who—I was doing, I deserved time to myself too. But as much as I tried to rationalize things, the pangs still didn't go away.

"Hey Sam, were you under the covers waiting for me?"

"Now I am. I got Bella packed and in bed and took a shower since I was a sweaty mess from kickboxing tonight."

Lucas groaned. "I like thinking about you being a sweaty mess. Did you decide about tomorrow?"

"Not yet. It's not because I don't want to stay the night—believe me. I just don't want to move too fast."

"I get that, and it's okay. I don't want to pressure you. I'll be happy being able to hold you on my couch while we watch the crap TV you seem to like."

"Crap TV? What are you talking about?"

"Last time you were here, I had to suffer through the *Real Housewives of New Jersey*."

"We only saw maybe the beginning of it before you made me shut it off before dinner, remember?"

Lucas laughed. "No, actually I don't remember. I was preoccupied with something else. I blame it on the skimpy outfit you had on."

"Skimpy outfit? I had a client meeting that day and thought we were going out later. It was a blouse and a skirt, you animal."

"When you took that little jacket off, it was all I could do not to strip you right there and run my tongue along every sexy curve of your body."

My mouth got so dry I couldn't swallow. I'd never had phone sex before—unless you count the time an ex-boyfriend and I tried it as teenagers and his brother picked up the other line.

"At least you were nice enough to let me eat first." Not the sexiest reply, but I needed time to warm up. "What else do you remember?"

Lucas took a deep breath.

"I remember trying to ignore how incredible you looked. The shirt you had on was low cut enough that if you leaned over, I could look right down. I saw you spilling out of a black lace bra and I wanted to rip it off and see how long it took your nipples to get hard in my mouth. You looked so fucking good in that skirt. When I ran my hand up your thighs, you were so wet, and I'd barely even touched you. God, Sam . . . do you have *any* idea what you do to me?"

Holy shit. He was good at this.

"I don't think you know the effect you have on me either." Hearing Lucas breathing heavy made me a little brave.

"Oh yeah? What do I do to you, baby?" His voice went low and raspy and sent a shiver up my spine. "Tell me."

"I still remember the day I met you. You took off your shirt to get in the pool, and I memorized every muscle and hard ridge. I spent the next three years ignoring the need to worship every inch with my tongue. I wanted to lick an outline around your abs, and head lower to see what you would taste like. All these years later, you somehow got even sexier than you were back then. When you kissed me and pulled me close, I felt how hard you were—all over. All I want to do is taste you again."

My hand moved between my legs, my fingers making the light circles around my clit that Lucas drove me crazy with that night. I closed my eyes and pretended it was him. Being with him, as much as I wanted to take it slow, created an aching need inside me more powerful than any college girl crush.

After a few long moments of silence, I stopped touching myself and draped my hand over my eyes.

Way to ruin a moment, Samantha.

"Lucas? Are you still there?" Finally, he breathed an audible sigh.

"Are you trying to fucking kill me, Sam? I'm a minute away from jumping into a cab and heading straight to your house. I would be on my way now if I wasn't so hard I can barely walk."

Lucas groaned, and I smiled at how flustered he was getting over me.

"*Nothing* tastes sweeter than you, baby. I could eat you for breakfast, lunch, and dinner. It was torture not to be able to touch you for all those months. Every time we said goodbye, all I could think about was that perfect mouth, those full red lips. How they would feel on mine or wrapped around my cock. Now that I know, I'm hooked. Addicted to every fucking part of you."

I was lost in the sexy timbre of his voice. A moan escaped me as my eyes rolled back in my head.

"Fuck, Sam—are you touching yourself? Are you wet for me?"

"Very wet, Lucas. I wish it were you touching me. How hard are you right now?"

This was the most worked up I'd gotten since I left Lucas's apartment. I was squirming and writhing against my hand, thinking about his words as flashbacks of our night together that played over and over in my head. Even over the phone, he knew exactly what to do to send me over the edge.

"So hard it's fucking painful. I wish I were doing more than just touching you. I wish my face was between your legs so I could lick it all up. You ready to come for me?"

"Almost, Lucas . . . I want you so much." My words were strained as tremors traveled down the lower half of my body.

"I want you, too. You wouldn't believe how much. I want you

to come in my mouth and slide down the wall like you did that night. I've never seen anything so fucking hot in all my life."

Before I knew it, I was screaming out Lucas's name as he responded with mine, followed by a myriad of jumbled curses. We were both panting as I fell back on my pillow, dizzy and blissfully spent.

"Lucas?" I ran my hands through my sweaty hair.

"Yeah, Sam?" I chuckled at how Lucas's deep voice sounded so small.

"Can I still spend the night tomorrow?"

"Abso*fucking*lutely! How soon could you get here?"

Slow and steady wins the race, but keeping it slow and steady hadn't done much for me in my life so far. And the hell with slow and steady when you were talking about Lucas Hunter.

chapter 14

Samantha

WAS REALLY going to do this. I was going to spend the night with my . . . my—Lucas. What was a label anyway? Useless, right?

I dropped Bella off at her grandparents, and then went home to pack. I was never one for sexy lingerie; the hottest eveningwear I owned was a Victoria's Secret cotton baby doll nightgown so I threw it in. Makeup, contacts, toothbrush, birth control pills (I especially didn't want to forget those suckers), skinny jeans and a fancy black top in case we went somewhere. *Ok, this was dumb.* I'd slept at his apartment before, and only needed one outfit since I was naked most of the time and did fine without all the provisions. I finished over-packing and headed to the train.

My phone buzzed with a text as I reached the subway station.

> *Lucas: I hope you're on the train right now. I can't wait until you're all mine tonight.*

All the bravery I felt after the awesome phone sex we had last night seemed to have vanished. Plus, Bella wouldn't let me go when I dropped her off. I had a mixture of guilt—again—nerves, and, I was ashamed to say, near *dread* floating around in my stomach instead of the eager butterflies I should have been in anticipation of having Lucas all to myself for a night.

I rang the bell outside and he buzzed me in. I ran up the stairs as fast as I could with the stupid heavy bag I needed to bring, and Lucas was waiting at the top of the stairs with a big smile.

"Took you long enough to get here." Lucas joked with a sexy grin and a wink. He looked so good in just a tight white T-shirt and jeans. I gave him a smirk and shook my head.

He took my bag from me and laughed. "Did you run away? This is pretty heavy."

"I . . . I don't know . . . packing all that stuff made sense an hour ago." I groaned and put my face in my hands as I followed him inside. *Way to play things cool.* I was supposed to spend the night and packed like I was moving in.

Lucas put my bag down and pulled me into his arms once he shut the door. "Come here." I put my head against his chest since I was too embarrassed to meet his eyes. He pulled away a little and put his finger under my chin to lift my face.

"We can go as fast or as slow as you want. You're here, and you're with me. That's all I care about. Okay?" He gave me a soft kiss on my lips and cocked an eyebrow. "Okay?'

"Okay." I kissed him back and buried my head in Lucas's neck. He rubbed my back and I relaxed a little.

"So what do you want to eat?" I tried to make small talk but I was still a little too worked up for dinner.

"We can wait, come sit with me for a while." Lucas took my hand and led me over to the couch. He sometimes knew how to read me so well it was a little scary.

I sat next to him and curled into his side, laying my head on his chest. I was still upset about Bella and how maybe I shouldn't have agreed to her staying overnight.

"Something bothering you?" He looked down at me with a little bit of a frown, like he was concerned. Good thing I wasn't a poker player. My tells were obvious.

"Bella didn't want to let me go when I dropped her off. I hope she's stopped crying by now."

"She's with her grandparents, right? And although they raised a jerk-off . . ."

I giggled at him and he shrugged. No arguments from me there.

"You said they were nice people. You're allowed to have time to yourself, Sam—it doesn't make you a bad mother." Lucas ran his fingers through my hair and my eyelids fluttered a little at how good it felt. He chuckled as I melted into his chest.

"Feeling better?" he whispered, still playing with my hair.

"Mmm hmm. That feels good." I snuggled closer to him and he kissed the top of my head. I lifted my head up to kiss him on the cheek, but he turned his head and I got his lips instead. It started out a soft and sweet kiss and got deeper and urgent. I was sixteen again and making out with a guy I liked on his couch. Except for the fact none of the guys I knew then, or ever, had moves like this.

Feeling a little bold, I climbed on top of Lucas and straddled his lap, our lips still moving. I rubbed myself against him and he moaned.

"I'd say someone is feeling *much* better," Lucas murmured against my lips. I smiled as he found the hem of my tank top and lifted it up and over my head. He dragged his hands over my breasts and gazed up at me.

"So beautiful . . ." Lucas grabbed the nape of my neck and brought me back to his lips. He unsnapped my bra, but didn't take it off right away. He pulled me closer as he inched the straps off my shoulders. When it was finally off, he looked up at me with a smirk. "I may be here for a while . . ." He cupped both my breasts with his hands, and when he brought one to his mouth to suck on my nipple, I squirmed in his lap. He brought his hands to my hips to hold them in place. "Stay still, you aren't going anywhere." He sucked on the other nipple and let it go with a pop.

Lucas put his hand on my cheek, rubbing his thumb across my lips. I thought back to when he did that in his bed the last time I was here, how he made me feel worshipped, desired, loved— even though I wouldn't dare say that word out loud . . . yet.

Lucas unzipped my jeans and slipped his hand inside my panties. The second his hand felt my wet and swollen flesh, he dropped his head back and groaned.

"Shit, the condoms are in my nightstand drawer." He lifted me up to get off the couch, but I didn't move.

"I've been on the pill for a long time, for health reasons. When I found out about—anyway I got tested and I'm clean. I haven't been with Marc since, or anyone—until you.

Lucas cupped my cheek and rested his forehead against mine.

"Are you sure? I don't mind using—" I put my finger on his lips.

"Yes. I want to feel you, all of you." I grabbed the back of his head and devoured his lips. This went against "going slow," but I felt the need to give myself to Lucas completely—without anything between us. I may've been opening myself up for a world of hurt, but I felt safe with Lucas.

Lucas flipped me over on the couch so he was on top of me. I lifted my hips as he pulled my jeans off and tossed them behind him. He took his clothes off in record time. I was a little disappointed since I wanted to strip him. He hovered over me for a moment, and I allowed my fingers to drift over every ripple and muscle in his chest.

"You feel so good . . ." Lucas's eyes rolled to the back of his head as he moved inside me. That familiar buildup grew as he went in and out, deeper and deeper. Slowly at first and then he picked up speed. Suddenly he stopped, lifted my left leg, and slid back in quick, hard, and *really* deep. When the shock of his movements and the new angle felt like they were too much, he drove into me even harder. My insides tightened until I couldn't take the throbbing anymore. I came harder than I probably ever did in my life.

Lucas soon followed and we both collapsed on the couch.

"I guess I didn't need all those clothes." I laughed as he grabbed me and pulled me on top of him.

"I was afraid you'd never be here like this again." He rubbed my back and looked at me with a sad smile.

"Believe me, there was never a time I didn't want to be here with you. I needed time to make sure I was ready for it."

"I know, and I didn't mean to make you feel bad." He ran his fingers through my hair, grabbing the back of my head and inched his lips towards mine. "I'm just glad you're here." He gave me a soft kiss that became deeper and urgent, and I felt him getting hard again under me.

I pulled back from the kiss, my eyes wide.

"Really? You could do that again so fast?" Lucas smirked at me and cocked an eyebrow.

"Not bad for an older guy, right?" He slapped me on the ass, making me giggle.

As much as I was trying to take it slow with Lucas, there was no going back now. Every second I spent with him, I wanted him more. I was all in, and there was no way I could hide it.

chapter 15

Samantha

LOOKED AT my reflection in the restaurant window and cringed. *What the hell was I thinking when I bought this dress?* It was black satin and tight enough for anyone to see what I had for breakfast—yesterday. It wasn't too short or low cut, but since I was packing double Ds, my boobs took over *anything* I wore. The dress was sleeveless, so I threw on a black shrug-length sweater over it. I'd gone shopping on my lunch hour with my friend Tabitha yesterday, and when I told her Lucas was taking me to the new trendy restaurant in the meatpacking district, she insisted I buy this dress. She even convinced me to buy a new pair of silver stilettos. I had a short window of time before the shoes gave me a pronounced limp, and prayed we were hopping right into a cab back to Lucas's apartment after dinner. Since it was a night special enough for painful heels, I took extra time with my hair and makeup—even breaking out the hot rollers. I took a second glance at my smoky eye makeup and soft waves in my long dark brown hair. Although I didn't quite feel brave enough to pull this dress off, I thought I looked kind of hot. Hopefully, my date agreed.

Over the past month, my label-less relationship with Lucas had progressed to the stage of keeping clothes at his apartment for my overnight stays, thus eliminating the need for an overnight bag. Thank goodness, as I could barely carry myself in these heels as I made my way to meet him at the restaurant.

I asked Lucas to meet me by the bar. I wanted to surprise him tonight with my more primped than usual self. I noticed him right away, and thought how unfair it was that one person could be that damn good looking. His blue button-down shirt clung to every muscle in his torso, and his black pants fit him to perfection. He looked like he had stepped off a runway, and I hoped my ridiculous shoes didn't make me fall as I strolled over to where he sat.

Lucas didn't see me approach. I came up behind him and wrapped my hands around his waist.

"Hey, handsome." His cheeks turned up in a smile as he reached for me.

"Hey, yourself, baby—" Lucas stopped speaking mid-sentence and his face fell.

Crap, I knew I couldn't pull this dress off.

"You hate it. *Ugh,* I knew it." I looked down at myself, shaking my head.

"Hate it? Um, no. You look—" Lucas's eyes traveled up and down my body, giving me a smoldering gaze that made my heart beat faster. "I can't even put into words how amazing you look tonight. I'm trying to figure out how I'm going to get through an entire dinner without ripping that dress off of you." He stood from his seat at the bar and wrapped his arms around me.

"I should be prepared to get in a fight tonight. You're going to turn the head of every man in this place looking like that. So, let's make sure everyone knows you're with me." He pulled me into a deep kiss and slid his hands to the small of my back, pulling me closer. Forgetting where I was, I moaned into his mouth as his tongue caressed mine.

"Ahem, sir. Your table is ready." A voice belonging to a six foot tall Amazon interrupted us. I guessed you had to be a supermodel to work here. She led us to our table and Lucas took my hand, paying no mind to the gorgeous woman who handed us our menus.

Since we said our passionate hello, Lucas hadn't stopped touching me—his hands and lips taking turns staking his claim as he moved his chair closer to mine. To say he was acting possessive was an understatement, but I loved every second of it.

After the waiter took our order, Lucas leaned in like he was about to tell me a secret.

"So tell me, Sam. I'm a little curious—how long did you have that huge crush on me?" He smirked at me and raised his eyebrows.

I rolled my eyes at him. "*Really?* You have to ask? You didn't know?"

Lucas shrugged and tried to hold back a smile. "I may've had an idea." I kicked his leg under the table and he laughed. "I felt your eyes glued to my ass when I taught freshman seminar."

"My eyes, those of every straight girl in the class, and even a couple of not so straight guys. What brought this on?" I took a sip of my wine. We were 'together' now, but I hated that it was common knowledge how I'd pitifully carried a torch for Lucas throughout almost all four years of college.

"Why didn't you ever tell me how you felt?"

My eyes grew wide. He had to be joking.

"Why didn't I tell you? Lucas, I was nothing more than a kid to you. You practically patted me on the head when you saw me. I heard the stories about all the hook ups. I could never compete with any of those girls. Yet, I followed you like a sad little puppy dog, hoping you'd notice me. That day never came, so I accepted we would only be friends and moved on."

"Moved on to Marc." He looked away, shaking his head as he bit into a piece of bread.

Yikes. This conversation was taking on a more serious tone than I expected.

"He wasn't always so bad." I shrugged and put my hand on top of Lucas's. "And I never blamed you. You were a great friend and always so nice to me. But you were *Lucas Hunter.* Lucas Hunter's don't notice Samantha O'Rourke's. It's just the way life is. You were gorgeous, smart, and had your pick of any woman you wanted. I *was* just a kid in a lot of ways."

"Lucas, is that you?"

Standing next to our table in a tight white dress—still a fan of transparent clothing—was Nicole. With long blonde hair and a perfect tan, she was still stunning and seemed like she hadn't aged a day since I last saw her over a decade ago.

"Hi Nicole. You remember Samantha?" Lucas was polite, but not what I would call friendly. He hardly made eye contact with her, but she didn't seem to notice or didn't care.

"Oh yeah, your cousin's little friend." She didn't deem me worthy of a hello. "When did you get back from California? I haven't seen you since that night in San Diego. When was it—two years ago?" She put her hand on Lucas's arm, and I wanted to twist it right off her perfect body.

Nicole saw Lucas when he lived in California? I knew they sometimes hooked up while he lived in New York, but knowing she was a part of Lucas's life while he lived on the West Coast bothered me.

"Yes, I think so. It was nice seeing you, but I'd like to get back to my date now."

Lucas put his arm back around me and kissed the top of my head. I enjoyed the look of confusion on Nicole's face. He turned toward me and gave me a wink. Nicole had to have gotten the hint by now.

"Oh, well it was good seeing you too. I still have the same cell number if you ever want to catch up, for old times' sake." She was a brazen little bitch, another thing that hadn't changed about her after all these years.

Lucas nodded at her. "Have a good night." Nicole strutted away, and Lucas took my hand.

"Sorry about that. Back then—"

I shook my head and held up my other hand. "No need for explaining. None of my business. I could use another drink. Have you seen our waiter?" I craned my head to see if I could find the waiter to ask for something a little stronger.

Lucas wrapped his arm around my waist, pulling me closer. He kissed my cheek and whispered in my ear.

"Every year, you got the same Jansport backpack in a different color. You always carried an old Discman around with you, and the CD inside was either *Journey's Greatest Hits* or *Bon*

Jovi Crossroads. I saw you at an internship open house in the career center one afternoon. You wore a tight blue jacket and skirt. You may've thought I only saw you as a kid, but I couldn't take my eyes off your amazing body. You were beautiful then, just like you are now."

My eyes filled with tears. All those years I thought Lucas hadn't given me a second look—I was wrong.

"You . . . remember all of that?" A tear ran down my cheek and Lucas wiped it away with his thumb and nodded.

"I remember a lot. Lucas Hunter's notice Samantha O'Rourke's, but sometimes they mess up and let them go." Lucas lifted my hand to his lips and kissed my wrist.

"If they get a second chance, they don't make the same mistake twice."

chapter 16

Samantha

LUCAS AND I had been together for five months, and he still hadn't met Bella. I realized I was compartmentalizing my life and living as two different people. There was Sam, the carefree girl dating the man of her dreams, and Samantha, a single working mother trying to be both parents and not completely screw everything up.

I admit, a big reason why I didn't have them meet was because I was afraid. Lucas really didn't know me as someone's mother. I wasn't sure if actually seeing me with the little person I was completely responsible for would make him think differently of me, and make him question what he was getting into. Lucas was a good guy, and the *idea* of Bella didn't scare him off, but having them meet definitely took what we had to another level I hoped we were ready for.

Bella and I were sitting at the breakfast table, and I was trying to decide how to spend the day. I tried to make our weekends as fun as possible. Marc not being around was a good thing, but she was still without a father.

"Can we go to the zoo, Mommy? They have a new baby giraffe."

"Sure!" I wondered if this would be a good way to introduce Bella and Lucas. Maybe meeting us there would take the pressure off, and he could see what it was like to entertain a five year old.

"Would you mind if an old friend of Mommy's meets us there? I know he'd love to meet you." At least I hoped he would love to meet her. It was time to find out.

"It's a boyfriend?" My daughter had an innocent but excellent question—one that I didn't have an answer for at the moment.

"Yes, he's a boy who's my friend. Is that alright with you?" She nodded yes and went back to her Cinnamon Toast Crunch.

Why it had taken fifteen minutes to work up the courage to call him and ask him, I couldn't say. I was going to be a chicken and send him an aloof text, but you couldn't hear someone's emotional reaction to something over a text message—even with shouty caps or cute little emoticons. If he had an issue with spending time with Bella, it was best for all of us if I knew now.

Of course he picked up on first ring—I wasn't even half-way through rehearsing how I was going to ask him in my head.

"Hey Baby Girl, what's up?"

"Hey Lucas. Would you want to come to the zoo with Bella and me? It's okay if you don't want to but I thought I would ask." I must've said it all in one breath, and I winced as I waited for him to answer. I should've sent the chicken text message.

He laughed. "Were you afraid to ask me for some reason?"

"No, not afraid. But I wasn't sure if you were a kid person since we never really talked about it and—"

"Yes, I would love to meet Bella and come to the zoo with you." Thank God he put me out of my misery—and it looked like he was the kind of guy I hoped he was.

"Probably easier to meet us in the Bronx than to come here and then go together. Can you meet us in front of the World of Birds at like twelve?"

"Sure, thank you for asking me. What's Bella's favorite place at the zoo?"

"Definitely the butterfly garden. She loves butterflies, they're all over her room."

"I'll keep that in mind. Silly question, but who should I tell her I am?"

"I told her you were an old friend of mine who wanted to meet her. Let's not confuse her with labels right now." Or us, since we never used any.

I relaxed a little bit. If he wanted to meet her, it meant that me being someone's mom wasn't a problem for him, and he wasn't afraid of what meeting Bella meant. Introducing Bella to Lucas was a big deal to me. Of course, legally I was still married to Marc's loser ass, but I could deal with only one milestone at a time.

When we got to the World of Birds and I pointed Lucas out to Bella, she grabbed my leg and hid behind me. She always took a long time to warm up to new people. I gave him a look that said sorry and a shrug as I tried to pry her off me to introduce them.

Lucas gave me a warm smile and squatted so they were eye level. "Hi, Bella. My name is Lucas. I'm very glad to meet you." She peeked out from behind me.

"Your mom told me you liked butterflies, so I got here a little early to see if I could find one for you." He showed her a plastic bag and handed it to her. She could never resist a surprise. She looked inside and there was a pink and purple butterfly stuffed animal. We usually got one when we come to the zoo and she put them on her bed, but we'd never found a purple one before. Her eyes lit up and she smiled at him.

"Bella, what do you say?" I prompted her. She replied with a quiet thank you.

"You know, I haven't been here in a really long time." He leaned in and whispered, "Do you think you could show me around?" He offered her his hand, and she let go of my leg to take it. I was in shock. I expected to be walking around with her pulling on me for a good half hour. Lucas sure knew his way around a pretty girl.

"Come on, Mommy. Let's go!" she grabbed my hand and pulled me along with them.

After a couple of hours of dragging Lucas by the hand everywhere, we stopped to have lunch.

"So Bella, where should we go next?" Bella giggled at Lucas. I was still amazed that she took to him so well. I'd been afraid she'd associate all men with her miserable father—like I had been doing until Lucas.

"Definitely the Butterfly Garden! But don't touch the butter-flies, you'll get in trouble." Bella gave Lucas a stern look, and he nodded.

"I definitely won't. Promise." Lucas gave me a little smirk.

"Are you done? Because we could go now." Bella popped out of her seat and tried to pull Lucas by the hand to stand up.

"Hey, Miss Bossy, let Lucas finish his lunch." Bella's face fell and she sat back down.

"Sorry, I didn't want to make him mad." My insides twisted. She was expecting Lucas to push her off and yell at her, like her father used to. Marc had been gone for almost six months, but was still in her head.

"Nope, I'm all done—we can go wherever you want. I'd love to go on the monorail, can we go on that?"

Bella's face lit up. "I love the monorail. There are new an-imals there! We never get to go because Daddy hates to walk."

Marc hated the zoo, and anything else that involved spend-ing time with his wife and daughter.

"Then we'll go on the monorail right after the Butterfly Garden! Come on, Bella!"

Lucas and Bella walked away hand in hand, and neither looked back at me. I'd never been so happy to be ignored.

"Remember, you can't touch them, only look," Bella warned Lucas as they walked into the garden.

Lucas turned around and gave me a wink. I was overwhelmed with joy and relief that they were getting along so well.

The three of us climbed into a car on the monorail. Bella sat between us and pointed out all the animals she saw.

I put my arm around Lucas's shoulder and he turned to face me.

"Thank you." Lucas rubbed my arm and shook his head.

"No need to thank me. It means a lot to me that you invit-ed me today. I know why it took you this long to introduce me to Bella. You wanted to protect her. I didn't need to see you in action to know you're an amazing mother. But the fact that you wanted me to meet her, it shows that you want me all the way in your life—that maybe you like me or something." He gave me a playful shrug, making me laugh. He was turning out to be the guy I'd hoped he was—and so much more.

"Yeah." I leaned over to kiss his cheek, and whispered in his ear, "Definitely *or something.*" He laughed and turned his head to kiss my lips. I let him since Bella wasn't watching and it was only a chaste peck. I wanted today to be fun, not confusing for her.

After we saw everything there was to see, we exited the zoo and made our way to the parking lot.

"I had so much fun with you guys today!" Lucas knelt down next to Bella. "Can I come to the zoo with you again?" She nodded with a big smile and gave him an unexpected hug.

Lucas stood and gave me a lingering kiss on the cheek. He whispered in my ear, "Thank you again for inviting me. I'm going to miss you so much tonight."

"Me too." The words caught in my throat. Seeing how good he was with Bella, and how much he looked like he wanted to be here, was all too much to take. I was in a definite danger zone, and falling hard for this guy.

"I'll call you later." Lucas said before we turned to walk our separate ways.

"He's so nice, Mommy." Bella beamed and a comfortable warmth surrounded my heart. Lucas was turning out to be an unexpected kind of wonderful.

"Yes, baby. He sure is."

chapter 17
Lucas

"YOU SURE YOU'RE not going to get sick of me? I'm usually not here this early." Sam teased as we traipsed around Union Square.

Bella's grandparents wanted to take her on Friday night instead of Saturday morning, so Sam came over earlier than usual. We shopped at the Farmers Market on Fourteenth Street for a dinner she wanted to cook for us tonight. I shook my head, like I could ever get sick of her. Whenever she'd stayed at my apartment, I hated when she had to go home.

I pulled her towards me and wrapped my arms around her.

"Now I'm *really* going to hate when you leave on Sunday. You're spoiling me with all this extra Sam time." She giggled at me as I gave her a soft peck on the lips.

"Don't distract me! I have a list!" Sam yanked me by the hand to all the different booths, collecting a huge assortment of vegetables. It was cute how she always liked to be healthy, but I hoped we'd be stopping for some kind of meat somewhere.

We never came out and said we were exclusive, but she was all I wanted—and there was no way in hell I would ever share her. Technically, she was still married—and I hated it. As we strolled around hand in hand like a normal couple, I didn't need any kind of a label for what we were doing. As long as we were together, that was enough for me.

"O'Rourke? Is that you?" I turned and spotted an olive skinned muscle head running towards Sam.

"Jason? Oh my god, what are you doing here?"

Sam rushed over to him and he lifted her up in a big hug. I was a little pissed off until I recognized who it was. Jason was a freshman the same time Sam was, and I remembered them meeting in the Freshman Seminar class I taught and becoming close friends. I also remembered Jason having a boyfriend in that same class. He was the only guy I didn't mind touching Sam like that.

"You look awesome, girl! Even in the sweltering July heat! I've been meaning to contact you since I moved back. How's the family? Marc and Bella good?" I cringed at hearing Marc referred to as Sam's family.

"Bella's good. She's five now, believe it or not. She starts first grade this September. Marc, well . . ." Sam scrunched her face at Jason. "Marc's gone. We broke up and he's working in Chicago."

"Wow, has it been that long since we spoke? I'm, well, sorry—"

Sam laughed. "Don't pretend you're sorry. It's okay. I know you didn't like Marc and I don't blame you. I was stupid for a long time before I finally got a clue and threw him out."

"Sounds like a story I'd like to hear over dinner soon. I just moved to Chelsea last month, and I'd *love* to hear how you tossed him out on his sorry ass." Sam chuckled and swatted Jason on the arm. He looked over Sam's shoulder and finally noticed me standing there.

"Lucas? Hey, I remember you, how's it going?" Jason reached out to shake my hand.

"Good! Nice to see you, Jason." I wrapped my arm around Sam's waist as I shook his hand. Jason looked between us. His eyes grew wide as he smirked at Sam.

"You're with *Lucas,* now?" Sam rolled her eyes and gave Jason a dirty look. It was adorable how she still got embarrassed about having a crush on me. I tried not to laugh and make it worse.

"Yeah, you and I have a shit ton to catch up on. Same cell, right?"

"Yep, give me a call and we'll make plans." As she gave Jason a goodbye hug, he whispered something in her ear and she smacked him on the back. I knew he was probably teasing her about me.

"You know it! Good to see you again, Lucas." Jason waved as he strutted away, disappearing into the sea of organic farmers.

Sam finished shopping and we headed back to my apartment. I didn't want to upset her, but I couldn't resist messing with her on the walk back.

"So, how many people knew about the crush you had on me? I'm a little hurt I was the last to know." I made a sad face and she scowled at me.

"*Please*. Spare me. You knew from that first day I met you at Daina's. Can you let me keep a tiny bit of dignity? Jason was a good friend, and nice enough to listen to me ramble on about a lot of things. He even told me once I should tell you." She huffed and shook her head.

I stopped walking and pulled her back.

"I really wish you had."

Sam's shoulders slumped, and she lowered her head.

"We've been over this. Telling you back then would have probably done more harm than good. We were in completely different places in life. It would have gotten awkward, and maybe even cost us our friendship—which I would've hated. Stop feeling bad about it."

I nodded and we kept walking. After stopping to get chicken—*thank God*—we headed back to my apartment and didn't speak much the rest of the way.

Sam insisted on cooking alone in my kitchen. I came in to get a beer from the fridge, and she didn't turn to look at me. I wished I had left it alone and kept my mouth shut.

"What's different now?" Sam asked as I left the kitchen, not looking up from what she was stirring.

I stopped and narrowed my eyes at her. "What do you mean? Different about what?"

She turned from the stove to face me and folded her arms.

"All that time, you knew damn well how I felt about you. I was right there for the taking for three years. I meet up with you years later, and everything is different. I guess I don't understand why for as long as I knew you, I was nothing more than a friend, and then one night at a bar changes everything. When you think about it, it really doesn't make a lot of sense."

It *didn't* make sense when you thought about it. I never expected to feel so much for Sam now, and I *definitely* didn't expect to feel it so fast.

I shrugged. "I suppose you could see it that way. Truth is, there were times I saw you as more than a friend, more than I let on. That night you came to see me present at that Finance Club seminar, I caught the way you were looking at me—like I was a superhero, and you were amazed by me. It humbled me to think you saw me that way. When we had coffee afterward and I walked you to the train, I almost kissed you."

Sam's eyes grew so wide they almost bugged out of her head.

"I thought I imagined that. You really wanted to kiss me?"

I nodded slowly. "I sure did. But, you were right. We were in totally different places, and I had just applied for a ton of jobs on the West Coast. All the other girls I dated were for fun, nothing serious. If I kissed you, you would have expected more, and I couldn't hurt you like that. I wasn't capable of 'more' in those days. I didn't have real superhero status just yet."

I gave her a sad smile and strode to where she was leaning against the counter. I put down my beer and took her face in my hands, making her look at me.

"When I walked into the bar to meet you that night, you were so beautiful. Striking, in fact. I couldn't take my eyes off you the entire night. You had such a sad and tired look in your eyes, and I wanted to take it away, to make you see what I saw." I tucked a piece of hair behind her ear and she closed her eyes.

"I made all kinds of excuses to see you again, texted you all the time, forced you to come to Shake Shack with me." Sam laughed and ran her hand along my jaw.

"I was too stupid and selfish not to notice how incredible you were all those years ago. But, I meant what I said. I got a second chance with you, and I want 'more' with you *now*. I want it *so* much." I grabbed her by the nape of the neck and covered her mouth with mine. I tried to say with a kiss what I wasn't ready to say out loud yet.

Sam pulled back and gazed at me with a dizzy look in her eyes.

"Good answer." She gave me another quick kiss on the lips. "I spent all day planning this dinner and don't want to screw it up. I'll call you when it's ready, okay?"

I pulled her closer and kissed her forehead.

"I can't wait. Be quick about it, though, I'm starving." I smacked her on the ass and heard her laughing as I went back into the living room.

I wasn't going anywhere this time.

chapter 18

Samantha

"SAMANTHA CHRISTENSEN. HOW can I help you?"

"Hi Samantha! I'm looking for someone in your marketing department. She's a sexy as hell brunette with legs that go on for days and a rack from heaven."

I shook my head and smiled. Since work kicked my ass this week, Lucas and I didn't have a chance to see or even speak to each other. Even our usual nightly phone conversations—that now lead to fantastic phone sex—before I went to sleep were limited this week. Julianna's older brother showed Bella and Julianna *The Nightmare before Christmas* over the weekend and Bella was scared to sleep alone. I was cranky, overworked, and missed Lucas like crazy.

Sometimes, being an adult with responsibilities and obligations kinda sucked.

"You're such an ass. It sounds like you may miss me."

"Maybe. Any chance you could leave a little early today for a late lunch? My friend Mike opened his deli on Twenty-Ninth and Third and I promised I'd stop by this week. And if I don't see you soon, I'm going to lose my fucking mind."

I laughed. Lucas was too damn adorable sometimes. "How could I refuse such a great invitation? As a matter of fact, I've been here before eight o'clock all week and was planning on leaving a little early since it's Friday. Does three work?"

"Three is perfect! Can I have a selfie to tide me over until then? Maybe close the door of your office and take one of your—"

"Really, Lucas? Are you *that* hard up?"

"Sweetheart, you have no idea how *hard* . . . I am see you soon."

Mike's Deli was a small space that looked like a typical deli. There was a small seating area with wrought iron tables and chairs towards the back.

When I walked in, Lucas was at the counter talking to a man about his age who was concealing a pudgy belly behind a white apron. Mike, I assumed. Lucas usually dressed casual unless he had a meeting but today he wore a black suit with a white shirt and black tie. It's true what they say about how suits are to women what sexy lingerie is to men. I loved seeing him in a suit. He always looked good enough to eat.

Lucas greeted me at the door with a hungry kiss. I was a little embarrassed but so glad to see him that I didn't stop him.

"Mike, this is Samantha. Sam, this ugly guy in the apron is Mike."

"Nice, Luc. Samantha, it's a pleasure to meet you." Mike kissed the top of my hand, and I giggled at him. He seemed like a nice, teddy bear of a guy.

"Get your own girl." Lucas took our sandwiches and then pulled me by the hand to one of the tables.

It was way past lunchtime, so the deli was empty. I was unwrapping my sandwich when Lucas pulled my chair closer to him. I jumped and cringed at the harsh screech of chair legs scraping against the hard tile floor. He buried his face in my neck, running his lips and tongue over every sweet spot. I pulled my shoulder up to push him away, but he was determined and wouldn't stop.

"Lucas, please stop it." I tried to whisper so no one could hear us, even though it was only Mike in the deli. "You're turning me on and there is nothing we can do about it in a public pla—*agh*." I swallowed a moan. Lucas's mouth felt so damn good. I had to fight the urge to move my head so he could keep devouring my neck.

"I missed you so much this week. And this dress is driving me crazy . . ." He kept kissing in between his words. Other than our make out session in front of Starbucks, we had managed to keep the PDAs to a respectable minimum.

"You don't like my dress? I had meetings this morning and everyone *loves* this dress." I couldn't resist teasing him. My dress was black matte jersey with cap sleeves and an empire waist. It made my waist look small and fell above the knee. It was form fitting but not tight, and although I never could avoid looking top heavy, I didn't show an inappropriate amount of cleavage.

Lucas growled and pushed my hair to the side to get better access to the back of my neck, giving me open mouth kisses there I felt all the way to my toes. "I love your dress, too. If you presented something to me looking like this, I'd buy whatever you were selling in a heartbeat. So fucking sexy . . ." His hand rubbed my thigh, and slowly inched all the way up until his thumb was on the edge of my panties. I had tingles between my legs, but I picked up his hand and took it off my leg.

"Lucas, Mike is right over there! We aren't exactly alone, and you're embarrassing me. Stop. *Please.*" I straightened out my dress and tried to hold it together. I was all wound up at this point and my heated cheeks made me certain I was turning bright red as usual. I looked up and Mike was laughing at us from behind the counter.

"Hey, don't stop on my account! Place is always empty at this time anyway, and Luc, my office is right in the back if you guys need privacy." Mike threw a wink in our direction. I put my face in my hands, mortified I was in my mid-thirties and got caught making out as if I was a teenager. I was so humiliated I wanted to crawl into the corner, and yet so turned on I wanted to fuck Lucas on this little table right next to my turkey sandwich.

"See, Mike understands. I haven't seen my girl in almost a week. It's no wonder I can't keep my hands off her," He brought his lips back to my neck and whispered in my ear. "Or out of her . . ." His hand went to the same place on my thigh it was before I removed it. I tried to pull it off again, but it now gripped tight. His girl? Had Lucas called me his girl? We were careful not to put a label on what we were doing, but hearing him say I was his girl? As pathetic as it was, my eighteen-year-old heart sang—and if we didn't have an audience he could have spread me on top of the cold cut counter and do whatever the hell he wanted to me. I put the intrusive thought from my head. While I may be Lucas's girl, I was technically still Marc's wife.

It seemed like Lucas had ten pairs of hands and was out of control. I tried to scoot my chair away from Lucas, but it was too heavy. I got up to pick it up and move it over when Lucas grabbed me by the waist and pulled me onto his lap. He kissed me hard and I tried to resist, but with every swirl of his tongue and movement of those very talented lips, I gave in. I forgot I was in a deli, and was completely and totally lost in kissing him. In fact, I was so preoccupied I didn't even hear the door open.

"Samantha?!"

Carmine, my least favorite of Marc's friends, somehow walked into this tiny deli in lower-midtown Manhattan and found me on top of a man who wasn't Marc. Carmine was short, chubby, and always a little sleazy looking. He always loaded his black hair with tons of product, so it looked like a greasy mess.

I'd hardly spoken to Marc since he left, other than a few text messages about when he would be sending money home. He wouldn't answer why he hadn't signed the papers, and I kept tabs on him through his mother. We were absolutely not together anymore, so I wasn't sure why I felt like I got caught doing something I shouldn't.

I slid off Lucas's lap and sank back into my chair. "Hi, Carmine. How are you?" Carmine loved to gossip and was the world's biggest loudmouth. My relationship with Lucas had just been outed—big time.

Carmine smirked. "Not as good as you, that's for sure. I didn't know you and Marc had an open kind of marriage. Oh, oops. He did know you were married right?" He used air quotes when he said 'open.'

The playful Lucas from a few moments ago was gone. He kept his arm around me, but his hand was balled in a tight fist. His mouth was set in a hard line, and it looked like he was grinding his teeth to keep his temper in check. Carmine looked me over from head to toe, and it made me queasy. "Maybe I should ask Marc how to get onto his wife's rotation."

Lucas shot out of his chair so fast it clattered to the floor behind him. He flew across the deli and went to grab Carmine's collar but before he could reach him Carmine backed away, and I ran over to hold Lucas back. Carmine always loved to start with people, but he never had the guts to finish.

"Say something like that to her again, and see what happens," Lucas yelled to Carmine through gritted teeth. I never saw him lose his temper before, but he looked ready to kill.

I stepped between Lucas and Carmine. "We're getting divorced. Lucas, this is Marc's friend, Carmine. Carmine, this is my boyfriend, Lucas Hunter." Carmine was running back to Marc about all this immediately, if not sooner. Marc knew Lucas from when we were all in school together. Knowing I was seeing Lucas was going to get under Marc's skin in a big way. He refused to speak to me, so the 'I'm seeing someone' conversation had never had a chance to come to fruition. I didn't think Marc would be jealous, but I was sure he'd be embarrassed to find out this way. Carmine would tell all the guys a colorful story about the compromising position he'd found Lucas and me in. Looking stupid in front of his friends was a fate worse than death for Marc.

"Funny, Marc never mentioned you guys getting divorced when I went up to visit the guys last weekend." I wasn't sure if he was trying to cause trouble, or if Marc was keeping our current marital status under wraps. Either way, I sure as hell wasn't going to let him brand me as some kind of adulteress and make Marc out to be a victim.

"Oh, so he didn't mention he was served with papers in Chicago? I threw him out before he left. I can see why it probably wouldn't come up in conversation." I looked right at Carmine and said with a smile big enough it hurt my cheeks. "Throwing your asshole friend out was the absolute best thing I ever did. His daughter and I are *so* much happier since he's gone. Since I know you're going to run back and tell him everything, please feel free to quote me."

With that, I took Lucas's hand and led him back to the table. I was pretty damn proud of myself.

Carmine looked a bit taken aback. I never spoke to Marc's friends, let alone put them in their place. I wanted to be disassociated from everything having to do with Marc, other than my daughter. Today was as good a day as any to start.

"Hey, no harm, no foul right?" Carmine put both his hands up and backed away. "You two have a nice lunch. Nice to see you, Samantha." He gave me a sickening smile and walked out, without getting anything to eat.

"You okay?" I asked Lucas. He nodded without looking at me.

"What about you?" He turned to look at me with his jaw still clenched. I could still feel anger radiating off him. I was a little shaken up, sure. But I was fine, even though I had a feeling a shit storm was coming. But, I could take it, and I felt ready for it—and hoped Lucas was, too. I nodded and gave him what I meant to be a reassuring smile.

"Mike, Sam has to use the bathroom. Can I take her in the back?"

I was confused. Maybe he was still upset and wanted to talk it out in private.

Mike nodded. "Sure, go ahead. She can use the one by my office."

"Thanks, Mike!"

Lucas took me by the hand without a word and led me through the swinging doors that lead to the deli's back rooms. He pulled me into the bathroom and locked the door. I was about to ask him what was going on when he pulled me against him and crashed his lips onto mine. He lifted my dress and put his hand inside my panties.

"I need you, *please.*" Lucas whispered against my lips. He pushed my panties down my legs and over my shoes, knelt in front of me and lifted one of my legs over his shoulder. I tried to say we couldn't do this here, but once his tongue found my clit and he slipped two fingers inside, my head dropped back and I couldn't say anything. I grabbed the back of his head and pulled him tight. When I tugged at his hair, he let out a moan and licked and sucked harder, grabbing me by the hips to pull me even closer to his mouth. My insides clenched and I fought hard to will it off. I wouldn't be able to stop myself from screaming once I came. My entire body went rigid, but I forced myself to speak.

"Lucas, please, you're going to make me come. Please . . ." I wanted to say 'please stop' but it wasn't coming out at all. Lucas straightened, unbuttoned his pants and let them fall to his knees. Then he backed me against the sink and, spreading me wide open, entered me hard and quick.

"I love being buried inside you." He had a possessed look in his eyes I had never seen before as he thrust harder and harder like he couldn't get deep enough. I realized then what he was doing—he was claiming me. The mention of Marc rattled him, and this was his way of taking back what was his.

The entire time, he never took his eyes off mine. We were in a public place with most of our clothes on, but I never felt more intimate or exposed.

I was already close, and with the force he was using to plow into me, it wouldn't take long for me to come.

"Lucas . . . I'm going to . . . Oh God, Lucas!" I bit into the shoulder material of his suit jacket so I wouldn't scream.

"That's it, baby. Give me everything . . . I love making you come . . ." Lucas followed immediately, growling my name like a prayer and pulling my head into his chest as he filled me up. It was like he wanted me to take every last drop, like he was marking me.

After we stopped panting, Lucas put his finger under my chin to lift my face, and gave me a sweet, gentle kiss.

"My girlfriend is so pretty." He ran his finger down my cheek and gave me a big smile.

My heart melted, but my stomach dropped—maybe I assumed when I shouldn't have.

"Lucas, I didn't mean to . . . I mean I'm not pressuring you or . . . anything. It's that—"

Lucas put a finger on my lips and laughed. "My girl likes to ramble, and she can't see what's been obvious all along." He took my face in his hands and gave me light kisses on my cheeks, my eyelids, and my forehead.

I wanted to tell him how much I loved him—that I never thought I could feel as much for anyone as I did for him. But I couldn't. Not because I was afraid I wouldn't hear it back, but because I didn't want him to think it was a knee-jerk response to an encounter with one of Marc's friends.

Instead, I put my arms around his neck and told him, "Thank you, for making me feel alive, and happier than I have ever been in my entire life." He smiled and leaned his forehead against mine.

"Right back at you, Baby Girl."

chapter 19
Lucas

"C'MON GUYS, DINNER is ready!" Sam called out from the kitchen.

Bella and I finished watching *Frozen* in the living room. I promised her when I took them for ice cream last week we could watch it when I came over. It wasn't awful, and I was surprised that fucking song they played every five minutes on the radio didn't annoy me.

I supposed most guys would be put off by a woman with a kid, but Bella was easy to love—like her mother. The more time I spent with Bella, the more I could tell she was a mini Sam. Bella was a shy and timid little thing, until you made an effort to know her. Now, whenever she saw me, her eyes lit up and she ran over to give me a hug. I loved it, and now had a big soft spot growing for this little girl.

Bella took my hand and led me to the table. This was the first time I'd been to Sam's house—the house she used to share with Marc; something I tried like hell not to think about. All the other times I saw Bella, we'd met up somewhere. Marc was a jackass for not appreciating how good he had it, but no one was happier than I was that he was gone.

"Did you like the movie, Lucas?" Bella asked me once we sat down. I could tell by the way she was bouncing she wanted me to say I loved it. I couldn't look into those big light brown eyes and disappoint her.

"It was awesome, and I knew Prince Hans was a douche—I mean not really a nice guy." I looked over at Sam as she was bringing food over to the table and mouthed 'sorry.' She laughed and shook her head. Sam had on tight black yoga pants and an even tighter gray Yankees T-shirt. I loved how she filled that shirt out, and that defecting to Queens didn't make her a Mets fan. She turned around and bent over to get dinner out of the oven, and I had to look away. I shouldn't have been thinking about all the bad things those tight pants made me want to do to her right after discussing a Disney movie with a five year old.

"See, Mommy? I told you Lucas would love it." Bella told Sam as she put dinner on the table. The big smile spread across Bella's face was worth the white lie. "This is my favorite dinner. Mommy got it from Rachael Ray's show and she makes it all the time."

I raised an eyebrow at Sam. "I didn't know you were a Rachael Ray fan."

She narrowed her eyes at me and folded her arms. "Why is that so surprising? She has good ideas for quick dinners, which is good for a working mom." I felt like I just got scolded. It was kinda hot.

I held my hands up in defeat. "Relax, I wasn't hating on Rachael. Dinner looks delicious."

Sam was still scowling at me but said, "thank you" and strode back into the kitchen.

Bella whispered to me, "Don't say anything bad about Rachael Ray. She gets mad."

Not only was Bella adorable, she was turning out to be a valuable little insider. What else could I get her to tell me about Sam that I didn't already know?

I looked around the table and was shocked at how normal this felt—having dinner with the two special girls who were now in my life. Being at home with them made it feel a lot more real than sitting at a restaurant table.

"I saw *Star Wars* yesterday at Julianna's house. Nicholas wanted to watch it. Lucas, did your mom get your name from Luke Skywalker?" I only hoped the droids didn't give her nightmares like the last movie Julianna's brother had them watch.

"No, sweetie, Lucas is from *way* before Luke Skywalker." Sam told her but was eyeing me with a smirk.

"Not much before, Sam." I narrowed my eyes at her. She was going to pay for that later. "My mom got my name from my uncle. Do you know where your name comes from?"

"Yep. Mommy got my name from a girl in a book."

"That's cool, Bella. Do you know what book?"

"Sure, *Twilight*." I dropped my fork and looked across the table at Sam. I had to bite my lip to keep from laughing.

"Okay, Bella. I think Lucas has learned enough about you and Mommy tonight. Let's be quiet and eat." Sam wouldn't look me in the eye. I couldn't wait to tease her and she knew it.

After dinner, I wasn't sure if I was supposed to leave or stay after Bella went to bed. I didn't want to assume anything. Bella and I got along great, but I wasn't sure if Sam was comfortable with her daughter waking up and seeing me during breakfast. I decided to follow her lead.

"Bella, say goodnight to Lucas." She scurried over and tackled me with a big hug.

"Sweet dreams, Butterfly." I kissed her on her cheek and she ran to her room.

I took that as I was at least staying until later, if not overnight. I walked into the kitchen to start drying the dishes.

I heard the bedroom door shut and Sam joined me a moment later to put the dishes away. I walked over to her and leaned against the refrigerator.

She tried to look mad but she was fighting a smile.

"Got something to say?" She cocked an eyebrow at me and tapped her foot, waiting for what was coming. Sam was so adorable when she got feisty.

"I'm embarrassed." I said with a shrug and exaggerated sigh. Sam shook her head at me and went back to gathering the dishes.

"Embarrassed for *me*. I mean, the woman I'm in love with named her daughter after a vampire movie. What do I tell people?" Dishes crashed to the floor as Sam dropped them and spun to look at me.

"What did you say?" She looked pale and her eyes were wide with shock. *All right, then. Rachael Ray* and *Twilight were off limits. Got it.* I walked over to her and put my arms around her waist.

"Aw, Baby Girl, I was kidding. I actually think it's cute. I didn't mean to make you mad." I tried to pull her closer to me, but she wouldn't move.

"Think about what you just said." I ran what I said over in my head. *That's* why she was freaking out. *Talk about a slip.*

She turned away from me and held onto the edge of the kitchen sink for dear life. I was so in love with her I couldn't see straight. She was my first thought when I woke up, and the last thing I thought about at night. And in the time between, I still couldn't get her out of my head. I looked at her and saw marriage, kids, and my future. She was *it* for me, but I could never tell her. I was afraid Marc would come back and steal Sam away, that he would guilt Sam down the line into taking him back. I knew they were separated, and I thought Sam loved me too, but I could never get past that. Until he signed those papers that thought would always be in the back of my head. Since that night in the bar all those months ago, Sam owned me. Body and soul. And it fucking terrified me.

I made Sam turn around and took her face in my hands. It was now or never.

"Look at me, Samantha. Look. At. Me." When Sam looked up, her eyes were filled with tears. Not knowing if this was good or bad, I took a deep breath and kept going.

"I love you. I love you because you're the most beautiful person I've ever known, inside and out. I love you because you're brave and smart and funny as hell without realizing it. I love you because you're fierce, protective, and loyal—why you're such an amazing mother. I love you because of the way you look at me—like I'm a superhero who can do anything. I love you because I can't picture my life without you."

As I finally told Sam how I felt about her, the tears she'd been holding in her eyes fell nonstop. A few moments passed that seemed more like hours, and Sam was still crying so hard she couldn't speak. She buried her face in my chest, sobbing so hard she was shaking.

"Sam, you're scaring me. Please, fucking say something. Anything." *I couldn't have read her that wrong, could I?* My grip on her arms got tighter as I panicked.

"I—" she looked up at me, swallowed a sob and tried to catch her breath so she could talk. "I love you so much. I've always loved you. It's—" She stopped again, still crying but gave me a big smile. "It's always been you, Lucas. Always you."

I breathed a huge sigh of relief as Sam beamed at me through her tears.

"Thank God!" I pulled her close and kissed her. I could taste the salt on her lips from all those tears, which only made me kiss her harder. Not taking my mouth off hers, I lifted her up on the kitchen counter and she wrapped her legs around my waist.

"Don't ever scare me like that again!" I said against her lips, making her giggle.

Sam pulled back from the kiss and looked up at me. She smiled and ran her hand down my cheek.

"How could you possibly think I didn't love you? I love you more than I've ever loved anyone." She lay her hand on my chest, over my heart, "You have the most beautiful heart, Lucas. You made me believe I deserved better than what I was settling for. And Bella is finally coming out of her shell, and starting to learn how a real man is supposed to act. You saved both of us. You're our Superman."

I laughed and shook my head. All I wanted was to be her hero, every day, for the rest of her life. That, I wasn't sure she was ready to hear yet.

I leaned my forehead against hers.

"Would it turn you on if I started wearing a cape? Not the tights, though. A man should have a little pride." She laughed and grabbed my face, pulling her lips towards mine.

I loved kissing her, how she melted in my arms every time I touched her. I would never, *ever,* get enough of her. I trailed kisses down her neck and grabbed the hem of her T-shirt to lift it over her head; she had a white lace bra underneath. When I kissed my way down her chest and bit one of her nipples through her bra, she let out a sexy little moan.

"You're so damn beautiful. I love you so fucking much." I gave her slow, open mouth kisses along the tops of her breasts, pulling down her bra straps so I could get better access and work my way lower.

"I love you too." Sam grabbed the back of my head to pull me closer. I slid my hand inside her yoga pants and groaned. She was soaked.

"Pants off. *Now.*" I whispered in her ear and sucked on her earlobe.

Sam giggled. "Bossy Lucas is so hot." She lifted her hips off the counter and I pulled her pants down, revealing a white lace thong I'd never seen on her before. She caught me staring and gave me a devious little smile.

"Oh, you like my new panties?"

I didn't think that little bit of material could qualify as panties.

"Yes, I like them a lot." I nibbled on her bottom lip, making her giggle again. "I'll like them a lot better when they're lying on the floor."

When her pants were finally off, she spread her legs to show me a very obvious wet spot through the tiny triangle barely covering anything. The blood drained out of my head directly into my pants.

"You like to tease? I'll show you what happens when you tease." I pulled her towards me and kissed her again, hard. I loved tasting her, everywhere. I took her hips and pulled her close to me. I rubbed my now throbbing hard-on against her core and she whimpered.

"Feel that? That's what you do to me. Is this what you want?" I rubbed against her harder. We needed to take this to the next level soon as I was hanging on by a thread.

"Yes please, Lucas," She unzipped my jeans and wrapped her hand around my cock and stroked it, inching her hand up and down at a slow pace that drove me out of my mind.

"Fuck, Sam . . . if that's what you want, it's all yours. Take it, baby." I needed to be inside of her, as deep as I could go—and was very ready to take her right there on the counter.

"Pants off, Lucas. *Now.*" I laughed as she pulled down my jeans.

"Your wish is my command—"

"Mommy! Darth Vader is in my room."

Sam jumped off the counter and scooped her clothes off the floor.

I let out a frustrated groan as I squatted to ride out the worst case of blue balls I'd probably ever had. "Is it bad to want to beat the shit out of a ten-year-old boy? She's not allowed to watch anything other than Disney movies or cartoons."

"I'll be right in, Bella!" Sam couldn't stop laughing. Apparently, she thought watching me uncomfortable and frustrated was the funniest thing in the world. Finally, she sobered. "I'll be right back. Think you can stay the night?"

"I think I can manage that." I stood, pulled her close and licked the seam of her lips. I did it again and when she tried to kiss me, I pulled back.

"See, you're not the only one who can tease," I slapped her on the ass and she jumped. "Go! I'll be here when you get back."

She rushed upstairs to Bella's room and I picked up the mess from the dishes she dropped. I wanted Sam so much. I wanted a life with her, and didn't want to only stay the night. As far as I was concerned, she was mine and my heart was all hers.

But the fucking state of New York said she was still his.

chapter 20

Samantha

LUCAS LOVED ME. I still couldn't believe it. Last night I got Bella back to sleep and we finished what we started in the kitchen—twice. I couldn't remember ever being as content or happy as I was in that moment. Bella loved Lucas too, and it was so great to watch them together. I didn't feel weird or guilty that she would find him still here when she woke up. He was still asleep beside me, his arm wrapped around my waist like ivy. I snuggled closer into his chest and he pulled me towards him.

"Good morning, Sam. I think I created a sex monster. You still want more?"

"I was trying to cuddle. I wouldn't want to tire out a man your age." It was always so easy to bait him. He rolled until he was on top of me.

"Does this feel like I'm tired out?" Lucas was definitely sporting morning wood, and when he ground it against me I let out an involuntary moan.

"Ha, that's what I thought." He trailed his tongue across my collarbone, over my breasts, taking a nipple into his mouth and gently biting it. It would be so nice to wake up to that every day.

The phone rang, and it was too early to be anything but bad news. I looked at the caller ID and it was an area code I didn't recognize. I reached over to pick it up, a thousand scenarios going through my head to justify a call this early on a Sunday morning.

"Hello?"

"You miserable, fucking whore."

Marc. My guess was he talked to Carmine. I was a bit

disappointed; the deli incident was a couple of weeks ago, so Carmine missed a step. I had expected this call the following morning.

"Wow, I haven't spoken to you in months and the first thing you say is 'you miserable fucking whore?'"

"What?! Who is that?" Lucas sat straight up and grabbed for the phone, but I waved him off. This was my fight and he didn't need to be involved. I mouthed *Marc* and his jaw clenched.

"Hang up!" Lucas told me through gritted teeth.

"Well, what do you call it when your wife is making out on top of a guy in a deli in the middle of the afternoon? And of all people, you're fucking Lucas Hunter? You always had a thing for pretty boy, so I shouldn't be surprised." Carmine may be late, but at least he was accurate.

"We're getting divorced. You were served with separation papers months ago that you never signed. I changed the locks and took all your clothes to your parents' house. This isn't your home anymore and I'm *not* your wife—so who I spend my time with is none of your business."

"Oh Jesus, another tantrum when you get your panties twisted. Look, for now I'll accept you were lonely and always wanted to screw this guy. Stop it, and we'll talk when I get home."

I think I saw red, or looked like those cartoons where smoke billows out of a person's ears. Going to a lawyer and drawing up separation papers was me having a tantrum? Even now, he didn't take me seriously.

"Marc, there is nothing to talk about, I'm in love with someone else. There is nothing to come back to. You don't call to speak to your daughter, and you obviously can't stand me. Why the hell would you come back? You never wanted to be here and aren't *wanted* here! This isn't your home anymore."

Marc let out a long sigh. I could picture him rolling his eyes like he usually did.

"I won't have you all over this guy in public, embarrassing me. You know the shit I had to deal with from the guys after Carmine told Rick what happened. How fucking dare you act like this while I'm away! Stop acting like a whore and remember you're still my wife. I don't want him at my house either."

"How dare I act like this? We aren't married, and really haven't been for a long time. Sign the fucking papers and you won't have to deal with me anymore."

The maniacal laugh I heard on the other end of the line made my stomach turn. *And here was the shitstorm I was expecting.*

"Fuck you, Samantha. I'm not signing shit. For what? So you can play house with pretty boy?"

I ran my hands through my hair, wanting to yank it out. Marc didn't love me, but now that people knew I'd moved on, he was embarrassed and wanted to spite me. I chuckled at the fucked-up-ness that was my life.

"You don't live here, and I've been paying the mortgage on my own for a very long time. What the hell makes you think you can have any say in what I do or who I'm with in *my* own fucking house? You have no right to call me a whore!"

"Give me the goddamn phone!" Lucas yelled as he yanked the phone out of my hands.

"Listen to me, you fucking asshole. If you *ever* call her a whore again, I will beat the shit out of you like I should've done when you were a punk back in college." He hung up and threw the phone across the bed.

"There has to be something I can do—go around him somehow. I'll call Robyn and figure out something. He's not bullying his way back home or into my life because he's fucking embarrassed." I tried to get a hold on my anger. Marc would *not* get the best of me.

"You can always move, you know." I could tell Lucas hated being in this house, knowing I lived here with Marc, but I wasn't going to be intimidated out of my own home.

"This house is mine. There has to be a way to get his name off of it. I know Robyn; I'll tell her to figure something out and she will. I can't let him get to me."

"I meant what I said. I will knock his teeth down his throat if he ever calls you a whore or talks to you like that around me again." I loved when alpha Lucas came out—the hot, possessive way he would take his claim and protect me made me fall for him over and over again.

We would get through this. We loved each other, and I wasn't going to let Marc's attempt to punish me ruin any of that.

"I know. And I can't tell you how unbelievably hot that makes me . . . like really, *really* hot." I trailed my eyes up and down his body and licked my lips.

Lucas raised his eyebrows and moved closer to me on the bed. "How hot? Tell me."

I pushed Lucas back so he was laying down. My lips began their descent down his chest, nipping at his abs as I got lower. Lucas moaned and grabbed my hair, pulling a little harder as I worked my way down.

"Mommy!"

"She's got great timing, doesn't she?" Lucas shook his head and laughed.

"She's up extra early today too, the phone must've woken her up or she must somehow know you're still here. Want some breakfast?"

"I can make us all breakfast. You have the stuff for French toast, right? Or does Rachael Ray not use bread or eggs in her recipe?"

I threw a pillow at him. "Yes, I have the stuff for French toast, jerk."

Lucas laughed at me as he put on his T-shirt and jeans from last night.

"Hey, Lucas?" He turned to look at me as he was leaving the bedroom. "I love you."

A slow smile spread across Lucas's face. He strode back over to me and bent over the bed to kiss me.

"I love you too, Sam. So much it makes me a little crazy." He gave me another soft kiss and walked out the room, yelling Bella's name.

chapter 21

Samantha

SUMMER SEEMED TO fly by. Lucas, Bella and I became our own version of The Three Musketeers. Lucas would come home from work with me on Friday and spend the entire weekend with us. We'd go to the zoo, the beach, and even went away on a long weekend to Lake George. It had been just Bella and I for a long time, way before Marc and I officially separated, but having Lucas with us never felt weird at all. It actually felt very right. After seven months it felt like he'd always been here. I didn't like remembering how life used to be without him.

After that one phone call, I realized Marc wasn't planning to sign a thing. Robyn said we could go another route. On the grounds of abandonment—since technically Marc left and worked out of state—she could draw up divorce papers. And if he still didn't respond by then, after a certain amount of time she could make an affidavit and process the divorce without him. We both agreed it was better not to badger him at this point, and to make it work to our advantage that he was completely ignoring me. I tried to get it out of my head, as I was worried about enough today.

"Should be a good day, it'll be just us so we'll have the pool all to ourselves." Lucas's mother asked us to her house for a Labor Day barbecue, and he was excited to take us there.

"Yeah, hopefully." I stared out the window as Lucas drove us upstate. I'd known Lucas's mother and his sister, Jessica, for years from being friends with Daina. I even used to call his mother "Aunt Jenn."

"Stop being nervous. It's not like you haven't known them all these years. They've always liked you, and now they'll love you like I do." Lucas grabbed my hand and ran his thumb along my wrist as he was driving.

"I'm not just 'Daina's friend' anymore. I'm your girlfriend." I also had a daughter from a marriage I couldn't quite call previous yet. Whether they knew me or not, I hoped they weren't put off by the obvious baggage I brought into this relationship.

Lucas's father died when he was young, leaving Lucas as part of a little family of three. Lucas was the oldest, but was babied by both of them.

Lucas had tried to teach Bella how to swim all summer. She was still a little frightened but Lucas assured her it would be only us today in his mom's huge in-ground pool and he would be right there the whole time, as usual. He was so good with her, knowing how to encourage her without pushing, and never becoming annoyed if she got scared. In the short amount of time Marc spent with Bella, he never had any patience for her. Lucas was always exactly what both of us needed.

We arrived at Jenn's huge house and walked around to the back.

"Hey, guys! I wondered when you'd get here." She gave Lucas a big hug and he twirled her around. She was a little bit of a thing next to her son's over six feet of height.

"Traffic was miserable, as usual." He turned toward Bella and me and said, "You remember my girls, right?" *His girls.* He'd started calling us that on our mini-vacation and I loved it.

"Yes, of course I do!" Jenn walked over to give me a big hug. "I'm so glad my son finally brought you up to see us. You look beautiful, but you always were such a pretty girl. Probably one of the reasons Lucas doesn't stop talking about you." I breathed a sigh of relief. Jenn seemed happy to see me and have us here.

Jenn knelt down in front of Bella, who now held onto Lucas's leg when she got shy. "The last time I saw you, you were a little baby. Lucas talks about you a lot, too." Bella peeked out from behind Lucas and spoke a barely audible "hi."

"Lucas told me to blow up all the rafts since you guys would be swimming today." Bella peeked out over Jenn's shoulder at the pool in the back, and then looked up at Lucas.

"We can go in now if you want." Lucas gave her a big smile and she nodded.

"Hey, big brother!" Jessica rushed over to Lucas. She looked just like her brother. Her hair was a darker brown, but she was still a knockout—same light blue eyes and perfect features. Lucas pulled her into a big hug. Jessica turned to Bella and me and gave us a small, somewhat forced, smile.

"Hey Samantha, glad you could make it. Bella, you've gotten so big since I last saw you. You definitely are mommy's mini-me. Lucas never shuts up about either one of you." I could've sworn that I saw her eyes roll. Jessica was never as warm as Lucas and Jenn were, but something was off with her today. Lucas went back to helping Bella put on her water wings and took us both by the hand over to the pool. I told myself I was reading into it and tried to relax by the pool.

Lucas hopped in the water and stretched his arms out for Bella to swim to him.

"Come on, Butterfly! You can do this." She had the cutest look of determination on her face as she dog paddled over to him. She reached Lucas's arms and he picked her up out of the water.

"See, Butterfly? I told you that you could do it!" Bella beamed over at me.

"Did you see me, Mommy? Can I take off my water wings?" Lucas raised his eyebrows at me and I reluctantly nodded. That made me a little nervous but Lucas would never let anything happen to her. It was wonderful seeing my daughter having fun and learning not to be so shy or afraid. Lucas would make the best dad. I got a sudden shiver thinking of having babies with Lucas in the future, but I stopped myself from daydreaming. My divorce from Marc needed to be final before we made any real plans together.

Jenn called us out of the pool to eat when she was done grilling. Lucas handed Bella to me to dry her off and put her cover up on. Lucas came up behind me and gave me a kiss on my neck.

"You look so fucking sexy today. You're driving me crazy." he whispered in my ear. I had on a strapless one piece. Bathing suit season was hard when you were big chested, and I thought this one showed the least amount of boob for a day with my boyfriend's family. I turned around, shaking my head at him.

He wrapped his arms around me when I stood up, and gave me a light kiss on my lips. I gave him a look I hoped said "let's not make out in front of everyone." He held me tighter and buried his head in my neck to take a bite of my earlobe, making me giggle as I pushed him away. I stopped when I noticed Jessica glaring at us over Lucas's shoulder. It was a concerned look, like she didn't like what she saw.

The rest of the day went by smoothly. When we were inside the house getting ready to leave, Jenn asked Bella if she wanted to check out the bunny rabbit next door. Next to butterflies, she loved bunnies so she happily went back into the yard.

"I spoke to Daina last week. She said she met up with you guys in Lake George a couple of weeks ago." Jessica hadn't really spoken directly to me all day. I realized she and I were alone in the kitchen.

"Yeah, we had so much fun! Little Jake is getting so big."

"She also told me Marc is refusing to sign the separation papers." *And here we go.* I should learn to trust my instincts.

"He's being difficult, as usual. My lawyer says there are ways we can go around him to file for divorce if he doesn't want to sign."

"But *why* is he being difficult? Sounds like he's trying to hold on to you." She crossed her arms and leaned back against the stove. I was being interrogated.

"Trust me, Jessica. There is nothing at all to hold on to. There is no way—in *hell*—I would ever get back with Marc. I'm in love with your brother. End of story."

I could have killed Daina. She didn't mean any harm and was

probably on a 'Marc is an asshole' rant, but right now it wasn't making me look very good.

Jessica huffed and shook her head. "Samantha, I like you. I really do. I don't think you'd ever intentionally hurt Lucas, but this whole situation doesn't sit right with me. He's gotten too attached to both of you. I saw it today. Every time I speak to him, it's Sam this, Bella that. You're not even legally separated yet. Don't you think you should back off from my brother until whenever—or *if*—your marriage actually ends?"

"Who the hell do you think you are to tell her to back off?"

Lucas must have heard us talking and stormed into the kitchen toward his sister.

"You don't know anything about Sam's marriage to Marc, or what we have together. I told you before, when it comes to us mind your own business! I love her, and she loves me, and that's all you need to know." So this wasn't a new subject of discussion with them. *Great. Exactly what I was afraid of.*

I was blind-sided, but I understood her. If Lucas were my brother, I'd be a little concerned about what he was getting himself into. Would I have sandbagged my brother's girlfriend? Probably not. But I still couldn't blame her for looking out for him.

"Lucas, hey it's fine," I rubbed his arm, trying to calm him down. "I get why she's concerned—"

"No, it is definitely *not* fucking fine. I have the car loaded. I'll go out to get Bella because we're leaving."

Jessica grabbed Lucas's arm before he got to the door. She looked remorseful, and her voice came down an octave.

"I'm sorry for upsetting you, Lucas. I'm just worried about you. I don't want to see you hurt."

"And I told you I know what I'm doing and to stay out of it." He pushed past her and out the back door. Jessica put her head down and left the kitchen. I hated seeing a close family fighting because of me.

Lucas didn't say much in the car. We drove most of the way home in silence. Bella passed out by the time we left their driveway just as I expected after a busy day. We were almost home when I finally couldn't take it anymore.

"I know why your sister's worried. I would be too, if you were my brother."

Lucas shrugged but still looked tense. "She's a pain in the ass, but I know she thinks she's looking out for me. I wish she would stay out of it."

"So, why do you seem so upset?" I rubbed the back of his neck as he was driving. He clenched his jaw and let out a frustrated sigh.

"I hate knowing that fucker won't sign the papers. I didn't need a reminder that you're still legally married to that asshole."

We pulled into my driveway and sat in the car for a few minutes. It was dark and the street seemed quiet. I unbuckled my seat belt and climbed over to Lucas, straddling him in the driver's seat. He looked at me strangely, and I took his face in my hands.

"There is no chance I will *ever* get back with Marc. We are over, and have been for years. He can play games with the papers if he wants and I'll find a way around him. I love *you*. Always *you*. Got it?" I sank down a little and rubbed myself against him. His body seemed to feel better as he was already hard beneath me. He chuckled and ran his fingers through my hair.

"Got it. I love you, too. Always you." Lucas pulled me close and brought his lips to mine. There was so much in Lucas's kiss—love mixed with a little desperation. My divorce needed go through ASAP, as all this stress was majorly screwing with Lucas's head.

"I got a little scared, too. I didn't want to think about what I would do if you really did back off." Lucas looked away, and I took his face in my hands again to make him face me.

"There is no way I could ever back off. I've waited for you for most of my life. Nothing and no one could ever take me away from you." I gave him a soft peck on the lips, and he pulled me into another deep kiss.

"Let's get inside before we give the neighbors a show."

Lucas nodded with a smirk. "If you insist."

We got Bella out of the car and put her right into bed. As far as I was concerned, Lucas, Bella, and I were a family. Papers were exactly that, *paper*. What was in my heart was mattered. And in my heart—there was only Lucas. I needed to find a way to make him believe that.

chapter 22

Lucas

W HY DID I still pay rent at my apartment? It was a waste since I was with Sam and Bella almost every night. Every time I went home without them, everything seemed way too quiet and just—off. It didn't feel like home without my girls. My sister was right. I *had* gotten attached to both of them, and it didn't look like Marc was signing those fucking papers anytime soon. A couple of months had passed since Jessica told Sam to back off. Even though our fight blew over, she was still constantly on my case—telling me I should keep a little distance, but I couldn't. I decided it was better to risk getting my heart ripped out than spending every moment missing the hell out of them when we were apart.

I walked out of Sam's bedroom and found Bella on the couch staring blankly at the TV.

"What's the matter, Butterfly?" Bella shrugged at me as I sat next to her.

Sam answered for her from the kitchen as she made us breakfast. "All her friends are going to a dance tonight and she isn't."

"Dance? She's five-years-old! Do they all have dates too?"

Sam laughed. "Yes, with their fathers. Every November, her Daisy troop has a father daughter dance at her school. That was the one thing Marc took her to last year because he was friends with a couple of the dads. I offered to take her, but she said no because all her friends would be with their daddies."

"Why can't I take her?" It came out before I realized it.

"You would?" Sam and Bella both asked me at the same time. Bella gazed at me with big sad eyes that screamed "Please, Lucas!" I didn't know what I had to do at this dance, but I couldn't disappoint her.

"Why not? How 'bout it, Butterfly? Would it be okay if I took you—?"

"Yes!" Bella shot up and knocked me over with a hug. I chuckled at how excited she was.

"Thank you for saying yes. So what do I have to wear for our date tonight?"

"Mommy, I'm going on a date with Lucas." Bella scurried over to her mother in the kitchen. I could never understand why Marc completely ignored his daughter. If she was mine, I would spoil the shit out of her.

"I know! I'll miss you guys tonight." Sam lifted her up and came into the living room.

"Bella, I think you can wear your blue dress." She turned to face me. "All you need is a button-down shirt and pants, nothing too fancy."

"Could you paint my nails for tonight, Mommy? Please."

"Sure! You know where the nail polish is. Go pick a color."

"Yay!" Sam put Bella down and she rushed into Sam's room. What a difference from the mopey little girl she was when she woke up.

Sam put breakfast on the table and strutted over to the couch, planting herself on my lap.

"You're not jealous are you? We could still go on a private date tonight—*later*." I whispered in her ear and bit her earlobe. A little moan escaped Sam as I moved my lips over her neck.

Sam giggled and put her arms around me. "Thank you. This means a lot to her."

"You don't have to thank me. Anything for my girls." I pulled her closer and put my mouth on hers. I groaned when she licked the seam of my lips and bit my bottom lip. I was hooked on her and she knew it.

"Mommy, is this color good?" Sometimes it was a little too easy to forget we weren't alone. Sam nodded as she climbed off my lap.

"Perfect!" Sam replied as Bella skipped to the table. Sam

shrugged at me with a devious little smirk. We were *definitely* having that date later.

"YOU KNOW WHERE the school is right, babe?"

"Yes, Sam. I've picked Bella up with you a couple of times."

"Okay, just making sure. Bella! Come on, time to go!"

Bella came out of her room in a short-sleeved blue dress with rhinestones along the hem and a pair of black Mary Janes on her feet. She looked like an adorable little princess. I knelt down in front of her.

"Wow, Butterfly! You look beautiful! Ready to go?" Bella flung her arms around my neck and giggled.

"Don't wait up, Mommy!" I told Sam as I led Bella out to the car.

The dance was in the cafeteria of Bella's school. It looked like a typical dance with streamers everywhere and a DJ of sorts who hooked up an iPod to speakers. Dads were congregated on one side while the girls were running all around. Bella let go of my hand when she saw her friends, and I headed over to the refreshment table for a bottle of water.

"So you're Lucas, I take it?" I was surprised one of the fathers knew who I was. "John Ericson, Julianna's dad." I'd met Julianna quite a few times and even picked Bella up from their house, but never met her father before.

"Lucas Hunter, nice to meet you." I shook his hand. He seemed like a decent guy, so I was hoping he wasn't one of Marc's friends.

"We didn't know Bella had a voice until this year. She talks about you all the time when she's over the house. It's nice to see. I hated how her father used to grunt at her when he'd pick her up. You must've been just what she needed." I hated how it was common knowledge that Marc treated his wife and daughter like garbage, but I was glad to hear I might be turning it around.

A stocky guy in a sports jacket came up to John. He had headphones on and looked like he was listening to the game on his phone.

"I hate these fucking things. My ex-wife was on my case to bring Sarah. Did you hear Marc Christensen moved to Chicago? I was wondering why I hadn't seen him around. Maybe his hot wife is available now; what was her name again? Yes, Samantha! I would *love* to tap that. A pretty face with a rack like that shouldn't go to waste." John grimaced as he turned to look at me. Yes, that was a friend of Marc's, all right.

I extended my hand to him. "Lucas Hunter, Bella's date and Samantha's boyfriend. I assure you Samantha and her rack are *very* unavailable." I shook his hand a little harder than I had to.

"Nick Matthews, good to meet you." Nick put his head down and slithered away. I laughed, like he ever had a chance with my girl. I decided then that I'd go to more school functions, as I was sure a lot of other dads noticed more than Sam's rack.

"Lucas! Can we dance?" Bella ran over and John took Julianna over to the makeshift dance floor. "It's okay if you don't, Daddy always hated to dance."

"Absolutely, Butterfly! Let's go!" One Direction was playing, and it was actually a song I recognized since Bella made us play it in the car over and over again. I knew all the words to *The Best Song Ever* and twirled her around like all the other dads.

"Are you having fun, Lucas?"

"I'm having the best time ever!" She laughed and ran back to her friends.

As I strolled off the dance floor, someone tapped my shoulder. I turned around to see an older woman with dark hair and kind eyes. I assumed she was one of Bella's teachers.

"You must be Lucas. I'm Joanne Nelson, Bella's troop leader. Samantha called to let me know you would be bringing her tonight. And after hearing about you for so long, I was anxious to match a face with the name. It's good to meet you." I shook her extended hand.

"Guilty as charged. It's nice to meet you, too. This is a nice little party."

Joanne smiled. "I'm glad Bella got to come. She has made such a turnaround from last year. She was so shy, and now we have to tell her to be quiet sometimes. I have something to show you."

I followed Joanne to the back of the room where the bulletin board was decorated with artwork from the girls. She took down two pieces of multi colored construction paper. The first one she handed me was a picture Bella must've drawn with two stick figures colored at the bottom with blue crayon. Under the drawing Bella wrote "Lucas teached me to swim."

"We asked the girls to draw the best part of their summer at the beginning of the school year. Bella was the only one who didn't have to think about it."

There was a definite change in Bella from when I first met her. Sam said Marc was always snapping at the both of them when he was home, so Bella was always introverted for the most part. I loved thinking I may've helped bring her out of the shell her dick of a father scared her into.

Joanne handed me the other picture and smiled. "I figured you'd want to see this, too. We asked the girls to draw a picture of their favorite person who wasn't their mom or dad and to tell us what made them great."

Written across the top of the picture was "Lucas." I chuckled at the brown crayon spikes that she gave me for hair and boxy jeans she colored in for me. What I read at the bottom made a lump form in the base of my throat so large, I found it hard to breathe for a minute.

"Lucas is the best. He never yells and takes me to swim and for ice cream. We watch princess movies and play games. I like it when he is at my house."

When I was about ten, right before my father got sick, Mom took Jessica and me to visit him at work. He had pictures that we had drawn or colored hung all across his wall. I asked him why he hung them up instead of awards like we saw in other offices that day. He told me the best thing he ever did was have two great kids that loved him so much. I never quite understood what he meant—until now.

"Could I . . ." I was a little speechless and couldn't finish the sentence.

"Keep them? Sure. I bet Bella would like to hear how much you liked her pictures." Joanne nodded and walked away.

I stared at the drawings in my hand, and could hear my sister saying, "See, I told you that you got too close," but there was no going back for me. Bella had changed me as much as I changed her. I liked when I was home with them, too, and I wished I never had to leave.

Bella rushed over to me with a big smile on her face.

"Lucas! Mrs. Nelson said she gave you my pictures! See! One is you and me and one is just you. Your hair isn't really brown so I put yellow in it, too."

I laughed and knelt down to look her in the eyes. "You did a great job! Mrs. Nelson said I could take them both home so I can hang them up. I think one will go in my apartment and one will go in my office."

Bella's eyes opened wide. "You like them that much?"

I nodded. "Of course I do. You made them!" Bella tackled me with a bear hug and I gave her a kiss on the cheek.

"I'm so happy you came!"

"Me too, Butterfly."

AT THE END of the night, Bella was quiet as we left the school and I strapped her into the car. She still hadn't said anything as we drove away.

"What's the matter, Butterfly? Didn't you have fun?"

"Yes." I could barely hear her. I didn't know what could have happened. She was having a great time until right before we left.

"You're gonna leave."

"What? Who told you that?"

"Sarah. She said you're not my real dad and you're gonna leave. And I don't want you to leave. I don't want to be sad."

We pulled into Sam's driveway, and I got into the back seat next to her. I studied the fallen expression on her face. I wanted to see the happy little girl who belted out her favorite song and ran around with her friends.

"Do you know why I call you 'Butterfly'?" I asked as I tucked a piece of hair around her ear.

"Yeah, because I like butterflies."

"That's not the only reason. When I was a kid, I used to love to chase butterflies, especially the really pretty and colorful ones. I didn't see many since I lived in the city like you do, but when I saw one, it always made me happy. And that's how I feel every time I see you. Happy." I kissed her forehead. "That's why I'm not going anywhere." The corners of her mouth turned up into a smile.

"Am I pretty like a butterfly?"

"You're the prettiest butterfly I know. Now let's get inside before Mommy starts to worry about us." I pointed to my cheek and she gave me a kiss.

I unbuckled her from her seat and she raised her arms for me to pick her up. Poor thing was exhausted from all the dancing. She wrapped her arms around my neck and buried her head in my shoulder.

When I wasn't looking, Bella had flown right into my heart—and no matter what happened, she would never leave.

chapter 23

Samantha

LUCAS AND I were on my couch enjoying a lazy Saturday night. At the last minute, Marc's mother asked me if she could switch weekends. We really didn't have any solid plans so, although it seemed sort of fishy, I gave in without a problem.

There was a loud bang at the door, sounding like someone trying to break in. I shot up to check, but Lucas stopped me and jetted to the door to look through the peephole.

"You've got to be fucking kidding me." He shook his head, and my stomach sank.

"What? Who's at the door?" Lucas moved aside so I could take a look.

Marc. Trying to use his key. Robyn was right on the money when it came to douchebag husbands deciding to come back home because they felt like it.

"Seriously?" This explained why his mother wanted Bella tonight. Marc probably told her we needed to talk alone. But we were so *not* alone. There was a third person in this situation, and I had a bad feeling tonight would not end well.

I opened the door—and found the husband I hadn't seen or really spoken to in an entire year. He looked exactly the same, although I could swear his black hair was starting to recede a little bit and he looked a little heavier than when he left. He had to be living the ultimate bachelor's life in Chicago. The one thing I didn't see on him was an attitude. He gave me a shy smile. Did he really come here thinking we would reconcile? He was about to find out that was not happening. Ever.

"Can I help you?"

"Something's wrong with the lock, babe. My key doesn't work."

Babe? Oh, *hell* no.

Lucas was standing behind the door but pushed it open. I could tell he was agitated by Marc coming here, and hearing Marc speak to me like we were still a happily married couple infuriated him.

"That's because when you left a year ago—she changed the locks, *babe*."

Lucas answered for me through gritted teeth. The only time I'd ever seen Lucas this tense was in the deli when we ran into Carmine. Lucas was holding onto the doorknob so tightly his knuckles turned white. I was afraid my normally cool and level-headed boyfriend was about to commit murder.

Marc smirked at him. "I see pretty boy is still around. Congrats on being part of his little harem." He shook his head and laughed. Maybe Lucas wasn't who I had to worry about, I'd strangle the son of a bitch myself.

"Yes, and he's not going anywhere, so I'm not sure why you're here. I told you when the job in Chicago was over, you don't live here anymore. Unless you have the signed papers in your pocket to hand over, you can leave."

"Look, Samantha," Marc walked in past the both of us. I looked over at Lucas and shook my head. His jaw was shut tight and he didn't take his eyes off Marc.

"We both said some things we're sorry for, and you've had time to get this," He motioned back and forth between me and Lucas. "out of your system. So, I'm ready to come home."

I thought my head would explode. *Ready to come home? Get Lucas out of my system?* Then, it hit me. This was going to be the only time I may be able to really talk him into signing. We'd been separated long enough that Robyn was able to draw up divorce papers. I had my own copy he could sign tonight. Did I think I could actually reason with him? I wasn't sure, but there was also a lot I still felt I needed to say to Marc. If he still wouldn't sign the papers, Robyn had other plans. It was worth a try.

The hard part was asking Lucas to leave so I could talk to Marc alone.

While Marc made himself right at home again, sitting on the couch and flipping channels like he never left, I pulled Lucas into the kitchen.

"You stay in here." Lucas kept his eyes on Marc as he spoke to me. "I'll deal with throwing that asshole out. That arrogant fucker thinks he can come back here like it's nothing. You're with me now, and if I have to bash it into his skull he'll realize that tonight."

I took a deep breath. Lucas wasn't going to take this well at all.

"Lucas, I need you to stay calm. I'm going to talk to Marc— and I'm asking you to let me speak to him alone. Maybe I can get him to sign the papers tonight if I can make him see that it's really over."

"*What?* You can't be fucking serious! He's had the papers for months and didn't sign them. You think you can magically convince him tonight? How?"

"In his stupid little head, he thought it was me having a tantrum, and I wasn't serious. Now, I have the chance to tell him exactly *why* he got served with those papers."

"Fine, I don't think you're going to get anywhere but I'll go in the bedroom." Lucas shrugged and turned away. I grabbed his arm, silently praying he wouldn't flip out.

"If you're here, I know you, you'll make sure you can hear the entire conversation and it'll turn into a pissing match between the two of you. You can't be in the house when we talk. Please, babe, I'm asking you to trust me." I reached for his hand and he yanked it away.

Lucas ran his fingers through his hair, looked up at the ceiling and laughed. It wasn't a happy laugh, that's for sure.

"Right. That's why you need me to leave. I knew this would happen. He'd come back at some point and make you listen to his bullshit. I love you, so much it fucking tears me up inside, but you were never really mine were you?" I thought his voice might've cracked at the end. My marriage to Marc was Lucas's Achilles Heel, his weakness. I knew that, but I hadn't understood the magnitude of it until that point.

"Lucas, I love you too, so much. You know that. I'm trying to make this easier for us. Robyn's trying to go around him, but it's much harder and takes longer. This is the quickest way to get what we want. If it doesn't work, then it doesn't work. We'll wait out the other option. I know you're angry and hurt and frustrated as hell right now, but this has nothing to do with buying into Marc's bullshit. This is about a fresh start. For us."

Lucas didn't look convinced. "Go talk to your husband. I'll leave so you can be alone. Work out whatever you need to." I had never heard Lucas sound so cold before. I grabbed his hand.

"Please don't leave like this." I pleaded with him but his icy stare didn't waver.

"Good-bye, Samantha." He pushed past me and stormed off without a glance, slamming my front door behind him. I wasn't choosing Marc over him, but I could tell by his reaction that was exactly what he thought. I wanted to run after him, throw my arms around him and make him believe me, but this was my best chance to finally be free of Marc. It was more important than ever to get his signature on those papers tonight.

I walked into my bedroom, grabbing my copy of the papers in my top dresser drawer. I took them out, found a pen, and walked into the living room.

I picked up the remote from the seat next to Marc and shut the TV off. I sat on the other end of the couch, and looked at the man I once thought I loved enough to marry. He wasn't always the creep he was today. I couldn't forget the awful way he spoke to me over the past few years or the rumors and signs I chose to ignore. I needed to move on from Marc Christensen. Whether he signed or not, I was going to make sure that happened right *now*.

"Pretty boy left, huh? Just as well; you couldn't be enough for a guy like him, long term. He's probably still got women following him around everywhere he goes. I'm sure he's not gonna be sleeping alone tonight. I could never stand that self-righteous prick, but I did envy how he always seemed to be knee-deep in pussy."

In just a few words, Marc told me I wasn't good enough to keep a man like Lucas, and made me think of women like Nicole and the girls in school who always seemed to fall at his feet. Marc's harem comment wasn't inaccurate in the least bit. *What if he didn't forgive me? No.* Marc wasn't getting in my head tonight. Lucas and I would be fine. It was Marc I needed to deal with.

"I told him I wanted to speak to you alone. He's very protective of me—and Bella—and, well, he really hates you. That's why he left angry. We're in love, and would probably be married by now if you realized when you're dead, you're supposed to lie down."

Marc rolled his eyes and looked at me. "I know this is all because you got mad I left. It's really okay. I don't hold it against you. You always were sensitive like that. It's annoying as fuck, but I get it." He reached for the remote to turn the TV back on. I took a deep breath. As much as his backwards thinking made me want spit in his face, I couldn't lose focus of what I was trying to do.

"No Marc, I wasn't mad you left. I was happy. Ridiculously, stupidly happy. Ecstatic even. I didn't have to worry about what kind of mood you'd be in when I came home from work, and I didn't have to hear all the rumors about who you were really with when you said you were out with the guys all night. Don't mistake my silence for ignorance—just because I looked the other way doesn't mean I didn't know what was going on.

Marc looked at the floor and put his face in his hands. He wasn't making excuses or blowing me off. I'd finally found the guts to bring up the elephant in the room that I'd ignored for longer than I wanted to admit.

"Marc, what did I ever do to you to make you hate me so much?"

Marc let out a long sigh, and scratched the back of his head. The obvious indifference he walked in with was replaced with apprehension.

"I wasn't ready for this, Samantha." His words came out in a rush.

"Ready for what?"

"*This.* Marriage. A baby. All of a sudden, there were all these . . . expectations. It was all about the baby, you being tired, giving me an attitude when I wanted to see my friends. You weren't the Samantha I first knew. It was always nag, nag, nag. Maybe once in a while I'd have too much to drink and things went a little too far. If you'd made yourself available to me more, I wouldn't have had to go elsewhere." I shook my head—acting like a wife and mother was grounds for *looking elsewhere* in our marriage? He had to be kidding me.

"So, whose fault is it you felt you had to sleep around? Mine, Bella's or both? We talked about kids when we got married. Bella was unplanned but she wasn't a total surprise. You felt pressured? Well, I felt alone. Since Bella was born, I've been a single parent. Do you know she hasn't asked for you since you left? Not even once in a year. You're her father, and she never missed you. I'm ashamed it took me that long to tell you to leave. Not for me, but for her, too."

Marc leaned back on the couch and put his hands on his knees.

"What do you want from me, Samantha? I'm trying to be a stand-up guy here."

I handed him the papers, and clicked the pen I had in my hand.

"You want to be a stand-up guy? Let me move on. We're over, Marc. I know you know that. In fact, you only got pissed when you heard I was with someone else because of *how* you heard. You were embarrassed. Now you know how it feels. Sucks doesn't it?"

He took the papers and the pen from my hand, and looked them over. I held in a breath, was he really going to do it? *Please,*

Marc. Sign the damn papers.

"The red X's at the bottom are where you sign and date it."

"Would I still get to see Bella?"

It surprised me that he even asked about his daughter, considering he hadn't contacted her once in all the time he was away.

"I would have full custody, I wasn't anticipating a fight from you. I am asking you for child support. But seeing as you haven't sent me a cent since you started working again, I'm not holding my hopes up terribly high. If you're serious about actually spending time with her, I wouldn't keep you from seeing her. But, you need to be consistent. It's all or nothing. You see her when you say you will, or you don't see her at all. I would rather Bella have no father in her life than a bad one. Understand?"

Marc nodded, looked for his name, and signed. My signature was already there, so as soon as Robyn got into the office on Monday, Marc and I would be on our way to divorce.

"I guess you're staying with your parents." I wasn't sure how I felt about Bella seeing the father who had been absent all this time sleeping in the same house she was. I didn't want her to get confused, or have Marc ignore her. She was only five, but I had first-hand experience knowing those types of awkward moments could mess with a child's head long after they became an adult. I also was a little miffed at Marc's mother for being sneaky about why she wanted Bella tonight. I had no problem getting into the car and bringing her home.

"Yeah, for now. I may go have a drink with some of the guys on the way home, so I won't see Bella until the morning."

I didn't like it, but he was still her father. If I made a big deal about allowing Marc to see her it may make things worse. She had her grandparents in the house, so she wouldn't be alone with him.

"When you talk to her, do not make promises to her you don't intend to keep. Mark my words, you do that even once, you will never see her again."

"Agreed." Marc nodded and got up from the couch to make his way to the door. There was no screaming match, no blow out—we quietly ended something that was done and over a long time ago. It was exactly what my goal was tonight.

I opened the door to let Marc out. He turned around to speak, but he looked like he didn't know what to say.

"Samantha, for what it's worth—I'm sorry."

"Yeah, me too. Good luck, Marc."

I didn't know the right thing to say to someone after you've agreed to divorce. I did wish Marc luck. Maybe someday he would grow up and realize having to act like a man wasn't a punishment, and being a father was a privilege. But he wouldn't make Bella and me suffer anymore as he was figuring it out.

It was time for my next problem—Lucas. I sent text after text with no response, and my calls went straight to voice mail. I crawled into my cold, empty bed that still smelled like Lucas. I nuzzled into his pillow with my phone in my hand, waiting for a buzz that would tell me we were still okay. We had to be.

chapter 24

Samantha

M Y STOMACH HAD been in knots all night long. Lucas wouldn't pick up his phone, I didn't know if it was off or if he was deliberately ignoring me. Every text I sent still went unanswered. Something wasn't right.

Bella was still over her grandparents' house and I didn't need to pick her up until the afternoon. If Lucas didn't want to answer me, I was going to make him. I was up early since I didn't sleep all night. I put on my black satin dress under my coat—maybe a little too fancy for a Sunday morning, but it was a special day and Lucas always said that dress was his favorite.

This was ridiculous. Things were finally good. Marc signed the papers, and when I texted Robyn she said the divorce may be able to go through in just couple of months. My life with Marc was now on its way to being legally over, and my life—*our* life together—could officially begin. I wanted that more than I'd ever wanted anything. And although he was still upset with me, I was sure Lucas wanted it, too.

I climbed the outside steps to ring his bell, but the door was open so I breezed right in, and took the inside steps up to his apartment. I knocked on the door, hoping he was here and mad at me—not hurt or God forbid worse. I breathed a sigh of relief when I heard him unlock the door.

Lucas looked like hell. Gorgeous hell—but hell nonetheless. I noticed dark circles under his eyes that were brought out by his unusually pale face, and his hair was sticking straight up. I had to hold in a laugh at how silly he looked. He was shirtless but still had his jeans on, which I found a little odd. Lucas was looking at me strangely, like he wasn't sure if he was glad to see me or not. We stood there for a few seconds, enough time to make it awkward.

"Hey. Can I come in?" He still said nothing in reply and pulled the door open wider and stepped back to let me into his apartment.

When I got to the kitchen, I took off my coat and draped it over one of the dining room chairs. I reached into my purse to pull out the envelope with the divorce papers. I handed them to Lucas and he looked confused.

"What's this?" His voice was scratchy as he pulled the papers out of the envelope and squinted at them. As I took a closer look at his face, Lucas looked a little green. I realized he was hungover, which explained why he wouldn't answer my calls or texts—he was too busy drinking all night. Today was supposed to be a good day, one where we could forget the past and move forward. I decided that Lucas hanging out at the bottom of a bottle while I was scared he might be somewhere bleeding in a ditch was all part of the past.

"My signed divorce papers. Marc finally did it! I'm free! And I'm—well *we're*—all yours. That is, if you still want us . . ."

A slow smile spread across Lucas's face, and even though his eyes were still glassy, they lit up. He put the papers on the counter and darted across the kitchen to me, taking my face in his hands.

"Do I still want you? Are you fucking kidding me? You're all I'll ever want or need. I love you so much. All mine. Finally, all fucking mine." He kissed me so hard I almost fell backwards before he put his arms around me and lifted me up. I snaked my legs around his waist and giggled as we kissed. I ran my hands through his disheveled hair, waiting for him to carry me into his bedroom so we could really celebrate.

"Luc, I think your hot water shut off—Oh sorry!"

I stopped kissing Lucas and turned my head. Nicole . . . the woman my boyfriend used to have casual sex with, was standing in nothing but a towel in my boyfriend's kitchen—at nine o'clock on a Sunday morning. Little by little, my brain and my body were piecing together what I was seeing—and both went into shock. The air in the room suddenly got very thin, and I was light-headed. *This couldn't be happening.* This wasn't my Lucas. He couldn't have been so angry with me last night that he had sex with another woman.

I glared at Lucas; silently pleading with him to tell me this wasn't true, that it was some silly misunderstanding. He shut his eyes tight, and slowly put me down.

"Sam, I know this looks really bad, but it's not—"

"Did she sleep here, Lucas?" I knew the answer already, but still dreaded hearing the confirmation.

Lucas took a deep breath. "Yes, but we didn't—"

I grabbed the envelope with the papers off the counter and my coat and flew out the door. I didn't look at Lucas or speak. He followed me down the steps, screaming my name. I wouldn't turn around and fall apart in front of him. My legs wobbled and my hands shook but I tried to hold myself together enough to get down the stairs without falling.

I almost got all the way out to the curb, hoping for the appearance of a cab I could jump into and go home to mourn what I thought my new life was going to be. Lucas caught up with me and grabbed my arm.

"Samantha, please listen to me! Nothing happened, let me explain!" In all the years I'd known Lucas, I'd never seen him so panicked. I imagine getting caught in the act rattled a person.

As I tried to jerk my arm away from him, I lost my balance and fell down the last two steps. I tried to break my fall with the palms of my hands, but I ended up scraping them and both my knees like I've seen my daughter do a hundred times. Then it registered. *Bella. Oh My God.* She didn't blink an eye when her father left, but losing Lucas would devastate her. Bella and Lucas had become close over the past few months, and once again her mother's shitty decision-making when it came to men would hurt her. *What the hell was I supposed to tell her?*

Then the sobs came. I sat on the concrete with my head in my hands and started to wail like a child. I couldn't get up.

"Shit, Sam! Baby Girl, are you okay?"

God, please no. Calling me Baby Girl now was like sticking a knife directly into my already broken heart. Lucas lifted me off the ground to help me stand. He wrapped his arms around me and kissed the top of my head. I always loved when he did that, but now it hurt like hell. It was torturous, but I let myself feel him one last time. I wanted to remember the way he smelled, how his arms felt like home—but he wasn't my home anymore, and it killed me to know that.

"Let me clean you up. You're bleeding. Come upstairs and we can talk. *Please.*" I pushed out of his hold and looked at his face. His beautiful face. His blue eyes were still glassy, but they were red now. I didn't want to believe what I saw. I wanted to look at the unshed tears growing in Lucas's eyes and think it meant he really loved me, and he would never *ever* hurt me.

I had ignored Marc cheating on me for long enough. As much as I loved Lucas—more than I ever loved Marc–I couldn't be that woman again. I owed it to myself, and I owed it to my daughter to face things, and even to walk away if I had to. No more pretending it wasn't happening because that was the easier choice.

I saw an empty cab coming up the block and raised my arm to hail it. I must've fallen hard as blood trickled down my wrist when I held my hand up. The cab slowed to a stop and I headed to the curb where it waited. I willed myself to stop crying at least until I got inside.

Lucas grabbed my arm again, shaking his head. "You can't leave like this." His voice was cracking. "I need you, I love you. You *know* me, Sam."

I shook my head sadly. "No. No, I don't." The words came out shaky but I managed to say them. I tried to pull away and run to the cab, but he wouldn't let go of my arm. The cabbie honked impatiently.

"Please, let me go." My words came out in a whisper as my jaw trembled. I couldn't hold off the crying any longer. I needed to leave.

"No!" Lucas yelled as a tear ran down his cheek. "You're mine, Samantha—and I'm yours. You, me, Bella. We're a family. My family. This is not what you think it is. I would never hurt you like that. I love you so much. *Always* you. You're my life, my everything, my entire fucking world. I'll never let you go. I can't. I won't."

"Sir, is there a problem?" A uniformed police officer walked over to us. He must've seen Lucas grab me, and gave us a concerned look.

"No, Officer. I was getting into a cab. Everything is fine." My voice broke on *fine* as I tasted the tears that escaped from my eyes. My eyes met Lucas's one final time. He was crying now, too—and it made me stop for a minute. *No, I needed to leave.*

"Good-bye, Lucas."

"No!" Lucas grabbed my face in his hands; the panic and anguish on his face startled me. His hands shook as he pleaded with me. "You can't tell me good-bye. I can't be without you. Please just fucking listen to me!" Tears poured down his face as I jerked out of his grasp. He tried to grab my shoulders but the officer pulled Lucas back.

We stared at each other for what seemed like forever. *How was I going to walk away from Lucas?* He mouthed "please" and held out his hand to me. My legs didn't want to move. Everything in me wanted to take his hand and fall into his arms again, forgetting last night and this morning ever happened. I wished for some kind of reset button I could press so we could just start over. The thought of leaving him for good made it hard for me to breathe. *Could I do that?* I loved our life together so much, now and what I always thought we could have when I was finally free of Marc. Maybe I didn't have to throw it all away. Maybe we could get past this . . .

I reached for his hand. Lucas let out a deep breath and swallowed hard as he came closer.

"Luc, you okay?"

Nicole, now dressed, sauntered over to Lucas and touched

his arm. The second his hand touched mine I pulled it away, shaking my head.

Fuck reset.

I narrowed my eyes as I glared at Lucas, knowing this would be the last time we spoke.

"You told me good-bye last night. I'm just saying it back." I nodded at Nicole. "Enjoy your new old life, the one you had before some plain Jane and her kid wasted your time."

Lucas jerked his arm away from Nicole and ran toward me.

"Sir, I'm not going to tell you again. Step back." Lucas ran his hands through his hair as the officer pulled him away. I spun around and ran for the cab, still hearing Lucas scream how much he loved me and begging me to turn around.

"Queens. Go over the 59th Street Bridge and I'll get you from there. Go!" I screamed at the driver, hoping it would make the cab go faster and make Lucas disappear from my view sooner. He glanced at my swollen eyes and tear-stained face and shrugged as he pulled away.

My head dropped to my hands and I finally let it all out. I cried for me, I cried for Bella, and I cried for Lucas. I would always love him. He was the one who gave me the courage to leave a miserable life and believe I deserved better. But right then, I didn't want better. I wanted Lucas.

chapter 25
Lucas

A half hour earlier

I WOKE UP to pounding on my skull. Even my eyelids hurt as they fluttered open. I looked around, and I was on my couch. Memories started to return—getting off the train from Queens and not wanting to go home; everything would feel like Sam in my apartment. I had pictures of the three of us all over the place, and could still smell her in my bedroom and on my sheets from when she stayed over last weekend.

I wanted to crawl out of my skin thinking of her alone with Marc. I dug my phone out of my pocket to see if she'd contacted me, and it was dead. I got up, slowly as the more upright I stood the worse the pounding got, and plugged my phone into the charger on my end table. After my third glass of Jack, my recollection of last night got hazy. I didn't even remember how I got home.

"Look who's up!" A woman's voice was coming from my kitchen. I slowly turned my head, and saw Nicole drinking from one of my coffee mugs.

Fuck, please tell me I didn't do what I think I did last night.

"Calm down, Lucas. I can see your eyes bugging out of your head. I ran into you at Shamrocks last night. You were at the bar, drunk off your ass, and got into an argument with the bartender because you wouldn't leave after last call. I got your address off your license in your wallet and walked you home. Miraculously, we made it up the stairs before you passed out on the couch. I slept on the other side of the sofa since it was so late. I figured you wouldn't mind."

I was grateful I'd woken up at home and not on the street, but if Sam ever found out Nicole stayed here overnight she would lose it. I still thought of us as together, because I couldn't consider the alternative. Not knowing what happened between her and Marc last night was killing me.

"Thanks for doing that. I was out trying to forget something."

"Trying to forget Sam? Sorry Luc, even as drunk as you got, that didn't happen. All the way back here, all I heard over and over was how beautiful she was, how much you loved her, how could she buy, I think you said 'Marc's' bullshit. Before I pulled you out of the bar, you started to cry about how much you needed her. I felt awful for you."

I must have been a real fucking sight last night. I needed coffee, badly. I staggered into the kitchen and bumped into Nicole, making her spill coffee all over my shirt. I wasn't fully awake yet, and still wobbly. The room was starting to spin.

"Sorry, Lucas. I saw you had a Keurig so I helped myself. Would you mind if I took a shower before I left?" I hoped I looked pathetic enough last night to discourage her from trying anything. She did get me home, so I didn't want to be rude. But I needed to talk to Sam, and Nicole needed to be out of here.

"Sure. There are towels behind the door. I need to leave soon, so I'm going to have to ask you to make it quick." My phone was coming back to life and I could hear it blowing up.

"No problem. Thanks!" She ran into the bathroom, and I walked back into the kitchen.

I took off my coffee-stained shirt and threw it on the back of one of the kitchen chairs. I rubbed my temples to ward off the pain. Last night was not my finest hour. I felt awful for the way I left Sam's house, but I was angry. When it came to her, I didn't think rationally. I was all caveman where she was concerned, and I wanted to beat Marc senseless for even thinking he could come back to her.

I heard a knock at the door, and trudged over to answer it. I opened the door and there she was—*Sam*.

We had a couple of moments of awkward silence before she

asked if she could come in. I moved out of the way to let her enter, and my breath caught as she took off her coat. She was wearing my favorite dress. I loved the way she looked in it so much that whenever she wore it, it was always a matter of time before I had it crumpled on the floor or pulled up to her neck.

Sam reached into her purse and she handed me an envelope. I opened it and unfolded the papers inside. My eyesight wasn't the best in my hungover state, but could make out names—Marc Andrew Christensen, Samantha Elizabeth O'Rourke, Isabella Rose Christensen. I skimmed through the rest of them and got to the last page, where I saw two signatures and dates.

My eyes met Sam's, and she beamed.

"My signed divorce papers. Marc finally did it! I'm free! And I'm—well *we're*—all yours. That is, if you still want us . . ."

Sam was all I ever wanted, and she finally belonged to *me,* without anything or anyone standing in my way. I ran over to her and kissed her. Sam giggled as I lifted her up and she wrapped her legs around my waist.

"Luc, I think your hot water shut off—Oh sorry!"

I was so happy, I forgot to mention to my girlfriend that there was a woman in my shower. My hot water did turn on and off at times, but I got the feeling she came out in a towel with an ulterior motive—to try to entice me to do something. That would never have happened, the only woman in the world for me was already in my arms.

Sam's entire body went rigid as she glared between me and Nicole. I could tell right away what conclusion she'd come to. The look on her face said it all, like her heart had broken right in half.

I closed my eyes and put her down. I would tell her the truth, and she would believe me—she had to.

"Sam, I know this looks really bad, but it's not—"

"Did she sleep here, Lucas?" Her voice was cold, and it scared me.

I took a deep breath, praying the day I finally got *all* of her wouldn't be the same day I lost her.

"Yes, but we didn't—"

I didn't even get to finish the sentence as she bolted out the door. Whatever I said, or pleading I did, to make her believe me, would be useless—but I still went after her. She couldn't leave. I couldn't lose her. Not now—not when we finally had everything.

When I caught up to her outside, I noticed her big sad eyes—the same eyes she had at the bar all those months ago. She looked at me like I was no better than Marc. Couldn't she see how much I fucking adored her? How much I needed her? No, this was *not* happening. I wouldn't accept it.

Samantha hailed a cab coming up the block. She started to walk over and I grabbed her arm.

"You can't leave like this." I panicked. I was afraid if I let go of her arm, she would disappear forever. "I need you, I love you. You *know* me, Sam."

She shook her head. "No. No, I don't." I saw the tears roll down her face. I wanted to wipe them away and fix this. *Why wouldn't she fucking let me?* I couldn't picture a future without her and Bella. My girls were slipping right through my fingers and there wasn't a goddamn thing I could do about it. Sam told me in a small voice to let her go, and I snapped.

"No!" My own tears streamed down my cheeks as the horror of losing the only woman I'd ever loved sunk in.

"You're mine Samantha—and I'm yours. You, me, Bella. We're a family. My family. This is not what you think it is. I would never hurt you like that. I love you so much. *Always you.* You're my life, my everything, my entire fucking world. I'll never let you go. I can't. I won't."

I was about to get down on my knees right there on the sidewalk and beg.

"Sir, is there a problem?" A cop in uniform walked over, looking at my grip on Sam's arm and most likely thinking I was trying to hurt her.

"No, Officer. I was getting into a cab. Everything is fine."

Samantha looked back at me. "Good-bye, Lucas." I shook my head at her. No fucking way was this good-bye. It couldn't be.

'No!" I grabbed her face, desperately trying to somehow get through to her. "You can't tell me good-bye. I can't be without you. Please just fucking listen to me!" I was close to full on sobbing but didn't give a shit. I needed to make Sam see how much I loved her—she had to believe me. I reached for her, but the cop grabbed me by the shoulders and shoved me away. It was January and I was outside with no shirt. I must've looked and sounded like a lunatic.

Our eyes locked, and I silently pleaded with her to stay. I mouthed, "please" and saw her stumble. I reached for her hand, and she looked down at the ground before gazing up at me and reaching back. I let out a deep breath, so relieved that I hadn't lost her. We'd talk. We'd fix this. There were no more obstacles or legal bullshit to keep us apart. This woman was *mine,* and I was going to be fucking damned if I let her get away.

"Luc, you okay?" Nicole appeared at my side, touching my arm like she was comforting me. Sam jerked back from me, and my stomach twisted knowing she was about to walk out of my life. She glowered at me, anger now overtaking the sorrow in her eyes.

"You told me good-bye last night. I'm just saying it back." Sam nodded towards Nicole. "Enjoy your new old life, the one you had before some plain Jane and her kid wasted your time."

How could she think that? Sam and Bella were everything to me. I'd never fucked up anything so royally in my entire life.

Sam bolted to the cab and got in. The driver drove away so fast the tires screeched.

I was screaming like a mad man, "Stop! I love you! Please talk to me!" But the cab was already halfway down the street. Now that Sam had left, the cop gave me a stern look and moved away.

I wiped the wetness off my face and turned to Nicole.

"What the fuck was that? Why would you touch me like that in front of her? That's the woman I love who now thinks I had sex with you—please just go." I put my face in my hands and rubbed my eyes. I'd never had the urge to hit a woman before but was dangerously close.

"Lucas, I'm sorry if I caused any trouble—"

"Thank you for seeing me home last night, but you need to leave, *now*." She nodded, and moped away. I wished she'd left me on the fucking street.

I ran back up to my apartment and checked my phone. There were a ton of unread texts and voicemails—all from Sam. I didn't blame her at all for thinking what she did. I stormed out of her house, wouldn't answer her all night, and then she came over my apartment to find a naked woman in my kitchen. *How the hell was I going fix this?*

I was desperate, and I needed to find a way to make her listen to me—and I could only think of one person who might be able to help.

"Lucas? Why are you calling so early? Is everything okay?"

"Daina. I need you to help me . . . please."

chapter 26

Samantha

ONCE I GOT back to my house, I was a zombie. I cried so much in the cab that I was dehydrated and dizzy. My phone was going off with text after text from Lucas, and with calls—which I sent straight to voicemail—in between. I would never shut my phone off when Bella wasn't with me, so I had to look at one painful message after another.

Lucas: Sam, please talk to me. I swear nothing happened.

Lucas: Please listen to me. I love you. Don't shut me out.

Lucas: I can't lose you. I'm losing my mind. Please answer me.

Lucas: Did you get home OK? At least give me that.

Really? *Give him that?* Did he give me any peace of mind last night? All my calls and texts went unanswered, and now I knew why. The asshole could suffer as far as I was concerned.

Marc's mother sent me a text asking if she could keep Bella another day, since it was she was off from school on Monday. I was still pissed at her for not telling me Marc was back, but I couldn't face Bella yet. I needed the extra day to deal with my misery so I could pretend to have a brave face. I couldn't think about how I would tell her Lucas and I weren't together anymore. Every time I thought about it, I broke into tears.

I was home alone for a few hours before I decided to completely embrace my torment. I took one of Lucas's shirts out of his drawer—yes, he had a drawer—and put it on. It smelled like him, and I wrapped my arms around myself. I crawled onto my bed and, as I did last night, laid my head on his pillow and let the sobs roll yet again.

My doorbell rang, and I didn't feel like dealing with anyone. I let it ring, but whoever it was didn't seem to want to leave. When I heard pounding, I finally got up to open the door. There was Daina, shaking her head at me.

"You look lousy, doll. Can I come in?" Lucas must have called her right after I left. I was too weak to fight so I opened the door for her to come in.

She took my hand and led me over to the couch. She wrinkled her nose at the pathetic mess I was sure I looked like.

"I want to take your heads and knock them together. You love each other so much, and look at you. All because you're both so damn insecure."

"Daina, he cheated on me! He got pissed at me last night when I asked him to leave so I could talk to Marc, and I found him with Nicole this morning. I can't do this again. Bad enough Marc finally confirmed he slept around for years. I won't be that woman again. *Ever.*"

"Samantha, do you really think I would be here if I thought Lucas cheated on you? Cousin or not, anyone who hurt my best friend would have their balls in a vice. The only thing he's guilty of is letting Marc get under his skin. When he left your house last night, he stopped at a bar near his apartment and got shitfaced. He couldn't make it home by himself because he was so drunk. As luck would have it, Nicole saw him in the bar and took him home. Her story was it was late so she slept on the couch, but who the hell knows if she was planning something or not."

"You believe that bullshit, Daina? She was naked in a towel in his kitchen."

"She asked him if she could shower before she left, and he felt bad since she took him home. He told her she had to make it quick because he was leaving."

I shook my head and turned away from her. Some best friend she was; blood really *was* thicker than water.

She grabbed my shoulder and forced me to turn around.

"I *know* Lucas. And you do, too. Think about all these months you've spent together. Do you really think he'd do something like that to you? I admit, it probably looked awful and most people would have thought the same thing you did. But think about how he's treated you—from the beginning. He was never that type of guy. He's not Marc."

The worst part of all of it was this wasn't Lucas *at all*. Was I really surprised to discover Marc was cheating? Not in the least. But Lucas always made me feel loved and protected—even back when we were pretending to be friends. Could he have been telling the truth?

"Lucas's only fault is he turns into this alpha moron when it comes to you. He was a broken man when I spoke to him this morning. I haven't heard my cousin cry since my uncle died, and he was bawling to me today. He loves you and Bella so much— why do you think Jessica went after you that day? She knew you had the power to gut him if you went back to Marc. Don't throw him away, Samantha. At least give him the chance to explain. I think if you really listen, you'll know he's telling the truth. I'm going to leave you alone now. Please, give him a chance."

We stood up from the couch and she gave me a big hug. Daina was the sister I never had, and she never would have come here to speak to me if she thought Lucas was lying.

I changed into an old T-shirt and jeans—I could wallow in Lucas's clothes later—and went for a drive to think. I drove to the park I usually take Bella to and sat on one of the benches.

I took out my phone, and decided to listen to Lucas's voice-mails. I wanted to see if Daina was right. I would know if he was lying or not.

"Sam, please let me explain. *Nothing* happened. I went to Shamrocks to drown my sorrows in Jack because I was scared to death Marc was going to convince you to take him back. I should have trusted you, and I'm so sorry I didn't. Nicole was there and took me home since I was too drunk to walk home myself. I slept on my couch—alone. I didn't know she was here until this morning. She asked if she could take a shower before she left, and I should have told her to leave. I could never be with anyone else. You have to know that. Please, Sam. Talk to me."

"Sam, I wish you would call me back. A text, anything. It killed me to see you like that today. I'm your Superman, remember? I'm supposed to be the one to save you. And you wouldn't let me. I was the bad guy today instead of the hero. I'm so sorry, Sam."

"Ever since you left, I keep thinking about what today would have been like if you hadn't found Nicole here. I would have kept kissing you, carried you into my bedroom and made love to you for hours. You know what that dress does to me. After we were finally done—for the moment anyway—you would lay your head on my chest, I'd play with your hair and watch your eyes flutter, and we'd talk about the future. Maybe we'd talk about looking for a new house that would have only our memories in it. You would tell me what sappy book character you'd want to name our first baby after. I need you to tell me we still can have all of that. That it's going to be you, Bella, and me against the world. I love you, Samantha. Always you. For the rest of my life."

Could someone pass out from crying too much? I was sobbing again, but there were some good tears this time. Lucas was telling the truth. I knew it, like Daina said I would. I believed Lucas now, but did I forgive him? Not quite. We loved each other, but last night was a perfect example of how the same issues kept popping up over and over again between us. I wanted us to have a real chance, but we couldn't move forward if we didn't deal with the past.

chapter 27
Lucas

DAINA TOLD ME to wait until she spoke to Sam before I went after her. As the day went on, I couldn't take it anymore. When I got to her house, her car wasn't there. I used my key and let myself in.

The house was eerily quiet. I called her name as I walked from room to room. I got to her bedroom and noticed the side of the bed I slept on had the sheet taken down, and one of my T-shirts was laid across the bed. I smiled to myself, thinking of what I was doing back at my apartment. I spent most of the afternoon with my face buried in one of my old shirts that Sam liked to sleep in. I could still smell her perfume.

Daina was right. We were two fucking idiots.

I sat on the edge of the bed and put my face in my hands, pinching the bridge of my nose. This wasn't how today was supposed to be.

We promised Bella she could get her ears pierced if she learned how to swim by the end of the summer, and even though she still needed my help, it was a good enough effort. Sam was too much of a worrywart to take her to a store at the mall, so we took her to a small jewelry store not too far from where they lived in Queens. Bella took the piercing like a trooper and couldn't stop admiring herself and her tiny diamond studs in the mirror. The shy little girl I met all those months ago was becoming a tough little cookie.

I picked Bella up once she was done and started tickling her. She put her hair behind her ears and asked me "Do I look pretty, Lucas?"

"No, Butterfly, you look beautiful!" I gave her a kiss on her

cheek.

Bella looked confused. "That's better, right?"

I laughed at how adorable and innocent she was. "Yes, Bella, that's much better!"

I looked over my shoulder and realized we'd lost Sam. I found her over in the corner where they kept the more expensive pieces. I was still holding Bella when I walked over to her. Whatever she was looking at, it distracted her enough that she didn't notice me sneak up behind her.

Still holding Bella with one arm, I slid my other one around Sam's tiny waist.

"See anything you like?" I whispered in her ear. She jumped and laughed as she rubbed my hand.

"It's nothing. We can go."

"What were you looking at?"

She pointed to a case of rings. They looked like engagement rings, but they were different colors. Some were brown and yellow, and one was pink. I'd never gotten far enough with a woman to research diamonds, so I didn't know what the colors meant.

"I read a book about a rock star giving his fiancée a pink diamond ring, but I never actually saw one before. It's really pretty. But like I said, it was nothing. We can go."

I always teased Sam, calling her a sentimental mushball because she loved her romance novels and cried so easily.

"If you say so." I put Bella down and followed Sam out of the store.

"Wait a minute, I think my phone fell out of my pocket. Can I meet you guys at the car? I think I dropped it over in the corner."

"Sure, babe. I'll get Bella strapped in and we'll wait there for you."

I pretended to look. Once I saw them leave the store, I ran over to the case where the rings were and called over a salesgirl.

"I want to put down a deposit on this ring." I pointed to the pink one Sam was looking at. "My girlfriend is in the car and I don't have a lot of time before she starts to wonder where I am. Can you run my credit card quickly?" I didn't even ask how much it was. When I saw how Sam was looking at that ring, I knew it had to be hers.

The salesgirl gave me a dreamy look. "That is so sweet! Sure, I can do this quickly. Can you get one of her rings without her knowing so we can size it?"

I smirked at her. "So you want me to steal from her? Sure, I can do that."

She giggled and ran off with my credit card. The car was parked right in front of the entrance so I kept watching the door to see if she was coming back in.

The salesgirl came back with my receipt to sign. "Congratulations, sir. And good luck!"

"Thanks." I stuffed the receipt in my pocket and jogged over to the car.

Did I just buy Sam an engagement ring? I should've been freaked out about it, but I wasn't. At all. Marc was still being an asshole about the papers, but Sam was looking into other ways to file for divorce without his approval. I hated that she was still married to him, but she belonged to me. And I belonged to her. To both of them. I felt a peace and contentment I never had before knowing I made it official—or at least I hoped I did. She still had to say yes. I was proposing to her the second her divorce was final.

I walked out of the store and watched Sam as she strapped Bella into her car seat. I was so in love with her. It still took me by surprise sometimes. A year ago, the words 'husband' and 'father' would have made me break out into a cold sweat. Sam and Bella changed all that. They were my family; I just needed to make it legal.

"Everything okay? Did you find it?" For a second, I forgot what my cover was.

"Yep, exactly where I thought it was." I pulled her into my arms and kissed her. It was the type of passionate kiss I usually *reserved for behind closed doors, but I couldn't help it. Sam forgot herself, too—a sexy moan escaping her as she grabbed the back of my head to deepen the kiss. Thank God Sam's SUV had tinted windows in the back and a sun visor so Bella couldn't really see anything. When we stopped, we were both a little breathless.*

"What was that for?" Sam smiled and looked at me with those big light brown eyes I loved so much.

"I'm in love with you, Samantha. Crazy, head over heels in love. Not sure if I told you before." I gave her a sideways glance with a wink, and watched her smile grow wide. I wanted to make her smile like that every day.

"Yeah, I think you did tell me that. I'm pretty crazy in love with you, too." She gave me a soft kiss and snuggled in to my chest.

I kissed her on the top of her head. "I think it's time to get my girls home." She nodded and we got into the car.

Home with my girls. That's where I wanted to be—for the rest of my life.

Sam's ring had been burning a hole in my drawer for three months. As soon as her divorce went through, I was making her mine—permanently. She was my future, and I was getting her back today.

My phone buzzed in my pocket. It was already half dead since I'd spent most of the day checking it every five seconds to see if Sam had called or texted back. I had a voicemail and a missed call.

"Lucas, it's me." There was a long pause. It was Sam. "I believe you, and I want all those things too. But we need to talk. Too many things happened over the last twenty-four hours. Call me back."

I dropped my head between my legs. I never felt such overwhelming relief in my life. She believed me. She still sounded angry, but I would do whatever I needed to—grovel, beg, cry. I fucked up, but we could fix this.

"Hey." I turned around and saw Sam standing in the

threshold of her bedroom. I was so into listening to her message I didn't even hear the front door unlock.

"Hey," I whispered. Sam looked drained. Her eyes were red and puffy, probably due to lack of sleep and crying over my stupidity over the last day. It twisted my insides to know I was the one to break her like this.

"Are you hurt? That was a bad fall." I stood up from the bed and reached for her hand. Her palm was raw and bruised. I brought her hand to my mouth and kissed the healing cuts and scrapes, attempting to erase all the pain I had caused. She shut her eyes, as if my lips on her skin were causing her physical pain. *I did this to her.* A lump formed in my throat.

Sam shrugged. "I'll live. I've done worse." Her voice was scratchy and strained. This wasn't the Sam I was used to seeing—the one who lit up whenever she saw me, laughed and giggled at my dumb jokes, and melted from my kisses. Sam had put me on a pedestal the entire time I'd known her, even all those years ago. The disappointment and sadness in her eyes as she looked at me now killed me. I was about to head straight to the begging as this was bringing me right down to my fucking knees.

I pulled her over to the bed to sit next to me. I cupped her cheek and she leaned into my palm. That was progress at least.

"I'm so, so sorry. I never should have run out like that."

"How could you possibly think I would ever consider taking Marc back? After all this time, you have that little faith in me?" I could tell by the clipped tone to her voice that while she believed me, she was still angry as hell.

"You have a child together, and you fell for his line of crap once—I've always been afraid he'd come back and take you away. I—"

"You what? Thought when I told you I loved you I was lying? I let you get close to my daughter and almost move in because you were a casual in-between fling until I got back with Marc?" I reached for her hand, but she pulled it away.

"You didn't trust me either, Sam. I realize how it looked, but you know me better than that. Have I ever given you reason to think I would hurt you? For the past year, I've never looked at anyone else. I only saw you. How could you not know that?"

"I tried to tell you how I felt about you back in college—twice. Both times you had a beautiful woman in tow, and you didn't even notice I was there. I went to your apartment today to tell you I wanted to spend the rest of my life with you, and there was a naked woman in your kitchen. In the blink of an eye, I was back there again. Pining for a man who had better options than mousy little me." Sam's voice was steady, but tears ran down her face.

"You're the most beautiful woman I've ever known. You were never mous—" Sam rolled her eyes and held up her hand.

"The way you left last night, you were cold as ice. I was trying to do the right thing for us, and you walked out my door like you were walking out of my life."

I took a deep breath. I wasn't the only one with a knot in my stomach for the past year, waiting for everything to turn to shit.

"It made me sick thinking of you alone with Marc—"

"I don't want Marc, I want you! Since I was eighteen years old all I've ever wanted was you! But you didn't believe me. You ignored my phone calls and texts. I spent the night awake and scared shitless that something happened to you. Marc finally confirmed last night that he spent almost our entire marriage sleeping around, and I come to your apartment this morning to find you with Nicole? What was I supposed to think? Is this what you're going to do every time you get pissed at me? Get drunk and end up with a woman you used to fuck in your apartment? What would have happened if I wasn't there this morning?"

Sam's voice cracked as she stood up and turned away from me. Her shoulders were shaking with sobs that she was trying to hold in.

I got up, wrapped my arms around her waist and kissed the back of her head. It was one thing to assume Marc was cheating on her, but another to know it for sure. Seeing Nicole at my apartment was a one-two punch to the gut.

"You didn't deserve any of that." I whispered in her ear.

"From Marc, or from me. You're beautiful and amazing and I love you *so* much. I was so afraid of losing you that it made me nuts. I would have never touched Nicole or anyone else. The only woman for me is you. The only woman I've ever loved is you. *Always you.*" I moved her hair to the side and feathered kisses across the nape of her neck and behind her ear. Sam didn't turn around, but she relaxed in my arms.

I stepped in front of her so we could face each other. I took her face in my hands and wiped her tears away with my thumbs.

"I need you to forgive me. Tell me you're mine again. Please, Sam. Say you forgive me for being a crazy jealous bastard and you'll take me back."

I saw a hint of a smile on her face.

"I never stopped being yours. I'll always belong to you. No matter how stupid you are." Sam rolled her eyes again and smirked at me.

I laughed and pulled her closer.

"I'll take it. I thought about having to live without you and I didn't know how to breathe."

Sam was still crying, but nodded. I kept wiping away the tears and lifted her head up to look at me.

"I have never been more scared in all of my life as I was thinking I lost you. Please. I need you. I need to touch you and kiss you. I need to know you're real."

I gave her a light kiss on her forehead, on her still-wet cheeks, and on her lips. She was stiff, but I felt the tension leave her body as the kiss deepened.

"I love you so much." Sam ran her hand along my jaw, then grabbed me by the back of my head and crashed her lips onto mine. Her hands slid down my back and she grabbed onto my ass.

"Easy there, tiger," I laughed against her lips, expecting her to giggle, but instead she kissed me harder. Sam found the hem of my T-shirt and pulled it over my head. She ran her nails down my chest to the waistband of my jeans. Goose bumps broke out across my skin. I noticed a hungry look in her eyes as she started fumbling with my zipper. I grabbed both her hands.

"Hey, I'm not going anywhere—ever." I tried to reassure her by wrapping my arms around her. "Today, you're all mine and I'm going to claim every single fucking inch of you."

I backed her up against the bed until she fell back. I crawled on top of her and lifted her shirt, slowly kissing up her stomach, all the way to her chest until I raised her shirt over her head. I ran my tongue along her collarbone as I pulled down her bra straps. Sam started to moan and writhe under me. I took one of her nipples in my mouth, sucking and pulling it with my teeth until it became a rigid peak. As Sam started to whimper, I tried everything I could to hold it together. After the day we'd both had, just touching her had me close to blowing in my jeans like a teenager. I reached behind her to unsnap her bra and pull it off. I gave her other nipple the same attention and put my hand down her pants. *Fuck.* She was so wet, she was dripping onto my fingers.

"I need to taste you," I whispered in her ear, making her squirm even more.

I unbuttoned her jeans, and she lifted her hips so I could pull them off along with her panties. When I looked up at her, she had her hand over her eyes like she was embarrassed.

"What's wrong?"

"Not very sexy, right?"

Her knees were covered with bruises, and I smiled at the Barbie Band-Aids she had on the scrapes.

"It was all I could find." She shrugged and ran her fingers through my hair. I took her hands and kissed the cuts on her palms again.

"You're unbelievably sexy. The Barbie Band-Aids only make you hotter. I was barely holding on before, but *now*, Jesus . . ." I kissed Sam's knees and she laughed. I spent most of the day scared to death of losing her, but I didn't want to dwell on all the drama that went on between us today. I wanted to come home— and home to me was being buried inside her.

I licked a path from the inside of her thighs to the wet and swollen flesh at her core. I gave her one long and slow lick and then grabbed her hips as I devoured her. When I circled her clit with my tongue, she lifted her hips and pulled at the hair on the back of my head. It was so fucking hot watching her lose all control.

"Oh my god! That feels so good." I wrapped my lips around her clit and sucked hard. When Sam's moans turned into screams, I licked and sucked even harder.

"God? Who's between your legs, baby? Who's about to make you come?" I lapped at her clit as I slid two fingers deep inside. Once her legs started to shake, I knew she was close.

"Lucas, please . . . I . . . oh my god, Lucas!" She arched her back as she went over the edge. She looked so fucking gorgeous as her entire body quivered. I loved knowing from now on, I was the only man who would ever watch her come.

She gave me a dazed but satisfied smirk.

"Jerk."

I laughed as I took off my jeans and boxers, positioning myself on top of her.

"I love when you come in my mouth." Her legs fell apart as I thrust inside of her. She felt amazing—so wet and tight. I kept my mouth on hers as I moved deeper, and the groans I heard made me move faster and harder. Her body went rigid underneath me, and that was all I needed. We came together, and I collapsed next to her.

I ran my fingers through her hair and pulled her close so her head was on top of my chest. We were both physically and emotionally spent. We had lost each other, but we were right back where we were supposed to be.

"You okay?" I asked Sam. She lifted her head to face me with a sleepy smile on her face. Two orgasms had reduced her to a little puddle of Sam.

"I feel . . . claimed." She giggled while I kissed her swollen lips.

"Get used to it."

All she needed now was a new last name.

chapter 28

Samantha

WOKE UP exhausted. The past twenty-four hours had been grueling, to say the least. I prayed the worst was behind us. Both of us made stupid choices and wasted too much time being scared, waiting for the other shoe to drop.

I buried my face in my pillow, not having the strength to actually lift it up. Soft, warm lips ran up my naked back and wet kisses trailed across the nape of my neck. I moaned as I squirmed from the delicious torture. I lost track of how many times Lucas and I "made up" last night. I turned over to see a playful look on Lucas's face.

"Morning, beautiful." Lucas hovered over me and kissed my forehead and cheeks before moving to my lips. I wouldn't have minded staying in bed all day, but I had a little girl to pick up— and didn't want to leave her in that house any longer than was necessary.

"It's nice waking up like this. I may never let you leave." I buried my face in Lucas's neck and enjoyed the groans he made as I kissed behind his ear.

"Keep doing that, and I won't go anywhere." I giggled as I buried my head in his neck.

"Then, don't go. Stay with me." I froze, realizing that without realizing it, I just asked Lucas to move in.

Lucas pulled back and looked at me with narrowed eyes.

"Did you just ask me what I think you did? Stay with you, meaning live here with you?"

The adrenaline coursing through my veins woke me right

up. After all that happened between us over the past day, I was certain Lucas and I were permanent. He pretty much lived here anyway. We spent maybe two nights per week apart, if that. But, maybe making it official by actually moving in was rushing it a bit.

"Yes . . . I mean no." I sat up and put my face in my hands. Lucas squinted at me, confusion all over his face.

"What I meant was that I love having you here. I love sleeping in your arms and waking up with you, and want this to be your home so you never have to leave. But, if you aren't ready for it or don't think it was a good idea, it's alright. I'm not mad or anything, I just thought—" Lucas put his finger on my lips and laughed.

"Do you have any idea how adorable you are when you ramble? I would love to move in. I hate being away from you. I never suggested it because I thought you weren't ready for it. I'm all in. You're it for me. I never want to wake up again without you next to me."

I felt like standing on my bed and jumping up and down, but figured I had enough bruises from falling this week. Instead, I jumped on top of Lucas and attacked his mouth. He chuckled against my lips and flipped me over so he was on top of me. His expression was serious.

"I love you so much." Lucas weaved his fingers through my hair and pulled me back into a kiss. Things got heated quickly as he kissed a path from my neck, down my collarbone and stopping at my breasts. He gave me a hungry stare as he bit my nipple and then sucked it into his mouth.

"Mmm, Lucas. I think we need to get out of this bed or we'll never leave."

Lucas smirked at me and cocked an eyebrow.

"I don't like to go anywhere until I eat breakfast." His mouth continued its descent down my body until he got to the apex of my thighs. My head fell back, and I figured a few more minutes wouldn't hurt.

Mornings were going to be awesome from now on.

"BREAKFAST" LASTED LONGER than I thought. We didn't make it to Marc's parents' house until noon. I was a little apprehensive picking Bella up knowing Marc was probably there. We ended things as amicably as we could, but this was the first time I'd see him after officially ending our marriage.

When Jeannie answered the door, she gave me a look I couldn't quite describe, but it made me uneasy. Maybe she was like her son and thought I was just having a tantrum and never truly believed I would go through with the divorce. Whatever the case, we were over—and now everyone knew it, and had to deal with it.

"Hey, Jeannie! Is Bella ready to go?"

"Yes, she's been packed since this morning. I'm surprised you're here so late." Jeannie never complained if I was late picking up Bella, so the curt tone in her voice was odd.

"I'm sorry, I didn't realize you needed me to pick her up by a certain time."

"No, it's fine. I guess you were with your new boyfriend— Lucas, is it? Bella has been talking about him since Saturday and kept asking when you were coming to pick her up so she could see him before he goes home."

Usually when Bella stayed with her grandparents, Lucas wasn't at the house. I stayed with him at his apartment. So I supposed knowing Lucas was there, Bella wanted to get home to see him. This was probably the reason for the cold shoulder I was getting from my soon to be *former* mother-in-law.

"Mommy!" Bella came running out from behind her grandmother and almost knocked me over.

"Hey baby! Did you have fun with Grandma and Grandpa?"

"Yep! We went to the movies yesterday. Daddy said he was tired and he had a headache, so we couldn't make too much noise in the house." Marc's swinging bachelor life continued. I had hoped he'd spend at least *some* time with Bella. Even to sit and talk to her for a minute. He was still a big child, but he wasn't my problem anymore.

"Is Lucas in the car?" I caught Bella by the hand as she almost took off to run to the curb. Lucas must've seen her; he got out of the car and met her on the sidewalk.

"Hey, Butterfly! I missed you!" She ran into Lucas's open arms and he scooped her up.

"Do you have to go home yet?" Bella clung to Lucas's neck as he kissed her forehead.

"Nope. I can stay with you as long as you want." Lucas looked over at me and smiled. I wasn't the only one who would love Lucas officially living with us.

"Yay! I saw a movie yesterday, can you take me to one today?"

"We'll see, Bella." He strolled over to Jeannie with Bella in his arms, extending his hand. "Hi, you must be Mrs. Christensen. I'm Lucas Hunter, nice to meet you." Jeannie glared between Lucas and Bella and hesitantly took his hand to shake it.

I reached for Bella's backpack near the door. "Since you had Bella this weekend, we made plans for next Saturday. We can make up a new schedule." Jeannie huffed at me and gave me a shrug in response.

Jeannie was still staring at Bella and Lucas. He hadn't put her down yet and was whispering in her ear, making her laugh.

"I guess that's fine. We can work out a schedule if Bella is still allowed to come here."

I narrowed my eyes at her. Jeannie wasn't the friendliest person but she was never this cold. I was confused. "Of course she is, why wouldn't she be?"

"Oh you know. Things change." She nodded over at Lucas. Who would think Marc's mother would be the one most bothered over the fact I'd moved on. Jeannie looked perturbed by the easy rapport between Lucas and Bella. She had to know her son had no relationship with his daughter. *Hey lady, point the finger at your son, not at me.*

We headed back to the car. Jeannie made me feel uneasy,

but if she had issues with Lucas, that was her problem.

"I thought you said she was nice." Lucas pursed his lips and shook his head as we got in the car and drove off.

I shrugged. "She's been okay. I don't think she appreciated hearing Bella ask for you all weekend or how close you both seemed. Bella was definitely never with Marc the way she is with you. You guys have your own little thing together, that's for sure."

Lucas glanced at Bella through the rear view mirror.

"Sounds like Mommy is a little jealous, Butterfly." He turned around and gave her a wink and a big smile.

"Lucas likes you too, Mommy. Don't get mad." We both laughed at my daughter's attempt to make me feel better.

Lucas reached for my hand as he was driving and kissed my wrist.

"Yeah don't get mad, Mommy. I like you, too."

AFTER DINNER, BELLA begged us to rent a movie, but couldn't keep her eyes open. I carried her into bed and read her half a story before she passed out.

I strolled back into the living room and cuddled next to Lucas on the couch.

"I love that you don't have to go home." He laughed and pulled me onto his lap.

"That's because I'm already home. My home is where you are." He ran his hand down my cheek and rested his forehead against mine.

"You always know the right thing to say. Wanna do it on *our* couch?" Lucas burst out laughing.

"*Do it?* Come here, you horny little teenager . . ." I yelped when he pulled me under him and hooked my leg over his hip.

My cell phone rang, and I was about to send it to voicemail when I noticed it was Robyn calling.

"I'm sorry, babe, its Robyn." I sat up on the couch.

"Hey girl. Everything okay?"

"I didn't want to call you at night, but I figured you'd want to know right away. Before I left work, I got a call from Marc's lawyer. Samantha, he's filing for joint custody."

chapter 29

Samantha

NOT A DAMN thing about any of this made sense. The first weekend Marc was back, he went right back to partying—not even spending time with Bella when they were in the same house. I told him I wouldn't stop him from seeing her, as long as he didn't pop in and out of her life. I didn't think that was the reason he was now asking to share custody. Marc's ego was bruised because he was the last person to know I was seeing someone, but other than that he didn't care. That night he finally signed the papers, there was no plea from him to save our marriage or take him back. My head hurt from trying to figure out why we were in this mess.

I called in sick to work. I couldn't act like there was nothing wrong and my entire world wasn't crumbling because someone was trying to take my little girl. Robyn said she'd come over after work and we'd come up with a game plan. I was desperately hoping she was the brilliant lawyer I believed her to be and she would say something to give me some reassurance or peace of mind.

Lucas had a meeting he couldn't get out of, but told me he was coming back home right afterwards. He was trying his best to comfort me, telling me we had nothing to worry about. I had a feeling he was as anxious as I was, but didn't want to show it.

I spent the entire day cleaning, organizing, and doing any kind of mindless house work to keep busy. Pretending in front of Bella was the worst part. Unfortunately, kids are always smarter than you think. She kept asking us why we were so quiet during dinner. Lucas and I didn't say much, just kept looking at the clock and counting the minutes until Robyn walked through the door and told us she could stop Marc from getting half of my daughter.

The doorbell rang and we both jumped.

"Why are you guys being so silly?" Bella wrinkled her nose at us.

"Adults act weird, Butterfly. I told you that, right? Why you should stay a kid." Lucas picked her up from her seat and tickled her under her arm. She squirmed and giggled, and it tugged at my heart.

I sprinted to the door, and when I opened it, I was out of breath.

"Hi, Samantha. I've wanted to come over to see you guys for a while, but under better circumstances." Robyn gave me a warm smile. She must've been in court today. Her long black hair was pulled back in a bun and she had on a navy jacket and skirt. I smiled at seeing "lawyer Robyn" for the first time, and observing my friend look the part made me feel a little better.

"Hi, Robyn." I gave her a big hug.

"Stop worrying," she whispered in my ear. "No one's taking Bella, please trust me."

I nodded and invited her in, introducing her to Lucas.

"Maybe we should go into the kitchen to talk." I noted to Robyn, before getting Bella settled on the couch with a movie.

Robyn nodded. "Probably a good idea." She followed me into the kitchen.

"The new man is *hot,* Samantha. Dayam girl!" Robyn whispered as she fanned herself. I laughed for the first time in a day. "How are things going?"

"Really well. He's moving in with us." Robyn gave me an odd look, like the one I give Bella when she asks for a second ice cream. I had the feeling she was going to tell me that wasn't a good idea.

"Lucas needs to be a part of this conversation, then."

Lucas strolled into the kitchen. "I thought my ears were

ringing." He gave Robyn a big smile and sat down next to me at the table.

"How long have you been together now?" Robyn asked as she was taking out papers in her briefcase.

"I guess, a little over a year." I looked at Lucas and he nodded.

Robyn looked between us with a perplexed expression on her face.

"I knew Lucas before. We—"

"Wait a minute!" Robyn's eyes bugged out of her head. "This is *Lucas* Lucas? Daina's cousin, the college advisor, the—"

"The huge crush. Yep, that's me." I smacked Lucas's arm, making him laugh at my obvious discomfort.

"Hmm, Samantha, I'm going to have to ask you a few questions you may not like. I don't want you to get offended. Marc left a year ago right? Were you, *together,* at any time before that?"

I shook my head. "We only started dating after Marc left. Before that, we were just friends."

"How did you reconnect? Didn't Lucas move away while you were still in college?"

"Facebook, believe it or not. We "friended" each other and met up for a drink when he moved back."

"When was that?" Robyn was taking notes now and it was bothering me. I couldn't see what this had to do with anything.

"Last October, I think. Why are you asking me all this?" I was getting irritated. We were wasting time.

Robyn put her hand over mine. "Samantha, we all knew Marc. Tim and I hated watching how he treated you. I'm not asking you these questions to judge you. You look happy, and I'm delighted. You deserve that more than anyone. But I need to know if you were with Lucas while you were still married. If Marc's lawyer plays dirty and tries to use it against us, I can handle it much better if I already know."

"We were friends for three months before—"

"Was there any overlap at all between the time you were married to Marc and when you and Lucas were more than just friends?"

I put my face in my hands, thinking of that one night at Lucas's apartment before Marc left. Marc could sleep around and party all throughout our marriage, but I was about to be punished for my one indiscretion—and it pissed me off.

"Samantha, please, as your lawyer I need to know—"

"Two days before Marc left. So yes, there was an overlap. Now what?"

Lucas pulled me closer to him and rubbed my back.

"Calm down. She just needs to know so she's prepared." Lucas whispered in my ear as he tried to soothe me, but it wasn't working. I was equal parts infuriated and scared out of my mind.

Robyn was expressionless, all business.

"Did anyone see you together? Were you ever in public?"

"No, we were at his apartment one night and I came home early the next morning. Marc was packing for Chicago when I got home. We had a fight and I threw him out. Two days later, I called you to draw up separation papers." I crossed my arms and hid my hands so they wouldn't see them shaking. My stomach dropped as I realized karma may be coming to collect.

"I don't think it will be hard at all to prove your marriage soured long before that point. And Marc never contacted Bella the entire time he was away? Never sent you any child support?"

"Nothing. He did ask about Bella the night he signed, and I told him he could see her, he just needed to be consistent. I didn't even press for child support. I don't know what's making him do this."

"I do." Lucas huffed, shaking his head.

"You do?" Robyn and I asked at once.

"Marc's mother didn't like the fact you and I seemed serious, and *really* didn't like how close Bella and I looked when we picked her up from their house. She's pissed her son has no relationship with his daughter so she's trying to force it, and make sure she doesn't get left behind when we start our own family." I noted Lucas said 'when' not 'if,' and even in my scattered state, my heart warmed.

"Now that I think about it, you may be right. He barely spoke to her this weekend, still has no interest in her and is just following what his mother wants. Jesus, this is frustrating! We can't prove this and stop it?" I pleaded with Robyn, who now had sympathy in her eyes.

"Right now, my advice is to let her go over there without fighting it. She'll only be there every other weekend for the time being. And—this is very important—do *not* get into an argument with Marc or his mother. If there is an issue, call me right away and I'll take care of it with his lawyer. I know the next few weeks are going to be hard, but if it's really Marc's mother behind all of this, it will come out soon enough. In the meantime, I'll do a little digging and see if I can speed that up."

Robyn turned to me, and this time had a sad look on her face.

"As far as Lucas moving in, he still can, but if he has an apartment, he should still keep it in case anyone checks. We don't want to give them ammunition to use against you."

I nodded, putting all my faith in my friend, who I prayed was as smart as I always thought she was.

AFTER BELLA WENT to sleep, I decided to take a nice long shower. I had painful tension in my neck and my eye was twitching. Robyn had told me not to worry, and Lucas was optimistic— at least in front of me—and tried his best to set my mind at ease. Neither were very successful in making me feel better. I tried to remember that it *was* only every other weekend right now. As much as I wanted to rip the hair out of Jeannie's head for putting us through this, I did take a small amount of comfort in knowing she would take care of Bella.

I stood under the showerhead with my eyes closed, letting the hot water hit the back of my neck to maybe provide some needed relief. I'd been running on pure adrenaline for two days between finally getting the papers signed, Nicole-gate, breaking up, Lucas moving in, and now prepping for a custody battle. Now feeling the after effects, my body was beaten and tired.

I also couldn't shake the feeling that this was my fault. I happily let Jeannie have Bella all those weekends so I could enjoy alone time with my boyfriend. It gave her a false sense of entitlement to my daughter and a say in how I lived my life.

My eyes were still closed, my muscles relaxed from the steam of the hot water. The shower curtain opened, making me jump.

"It's only me." Lucas stepped in to the shower and put his arms around me.

I hadn't even heard the bathroom door open. "Sorry, babe. I'm so out of it. My neck hurts and I think my eye is starting to twitch. It's been a long couple of days." I rested my head on Lucas's chest as he massaged my shoulders.

"No one is taking Bella away from us. Both my girls are staying with me, so there's no need to worry about anything." Lucas's hands moved up from my shoulders and massaged my neck, right where the knot was. I moaned at how good it felt.

"I wish I was as sure as you are." Lucas kissed my forehead as his hands slid down to the small of my back, pulling me closer.

"Trust me. We're going to be fine." Lucas pulled back and put his finger under my chin. His sandy brown hair looked almost black now that it was damp. My eyes trailed the water that dripped from his neck, down his chest, over his abs, and lead to his bulging hard-on, dripping off the tip. Lucas caught me looking and smirked.

"What did you expect? My sexy girlfriend is naked and wet, probably everywhere." He pulled me closer and sucked on my bottom lip.

"We can't even have you officially move in. God, Lucas, I fucking hate this–"

"Stop." He put his finger on my lips. "Marc is not taking anything away from us, or getting between us ever again. Whether it's official or not, I'm here to stay and not going anywhere. Do I have to claim you again to prove it?" He crashed his lips onto mine, and I moaned into his mouth as he worked my tongue into submission.

"Maybe." He chuckled against my lips.

He trailed kisses down my neck, cupping both my breasts and ran his thumbs over my nipples. I bit my lip so I wouldn't cry out and wake Bella.

Lucas sucked on my earlobe and whispered in my ear, "Spread your legs for me."

His hand slipped down between my legs. He traced circles around my clit with his thumb, making my head fall back. I whimpered as he plunged two fingers inside and then inched them out slowly over and over again until I couldn't take it anymore. I bucked my hips against his hand trying to make him go faster, and he covered my mouth with his to muffle my screams. I was dizzy as the entire lower half of my body started to throb and I scratched my nails down Lucas's back as I came, trying to level myself so I wouldn't fall.

"I could watch you come all day long." Lucas looked at me with hungry eyes. He gave me a devious smirk and lifted me up, pinning me against the shower wall.

"Hold on tight."

I wrapped my arms around Lucas's neck as he thrust inside me. As he moved deeper, his pace became quicker. I shut my eyes and closed out the rest of the world as Lucas hit every right spot.

"I love you so much."

"I love you, too. Every single part of me is yours."

Lucas groaned and plowed into me even harder. I fell off the edge a second time, and Lucas came so hard he was shaking afterwards. He lowered me gently to the tile floor and leaned his forehead against mine until we both stopped panting.

"I think somebody likes being claimed—a lot." He kissed my forehead and I giggled.

"I think I'm in love with you. Crazy, head over heels in love with you." I cupped his cheek and ran my thumb over his lips. He bit my thumb and winked at me.

"I can relate to the crazy part. Let's dry off and go to bed."

We stepped out of the shower, taking a little too long to dry each other off. I loved Lucas so much it brought me to my knees. I had a nagging premonition that I was about to be punished for it.

chapter 30

Samantha

A WEEK OF almost no sleep was taking its toll on me. I navigated through my day in slow motion. The first weekend of our joint custody experiment was upon us, and the closer we got, the more anxious I became. I wished Starbucks made coffee IVs as I had to over-caffeinate myself in order to deal with clients. I didn't dare talk about how I felt at home. Lucas was always trying to set my mind at ease, which never worked—and if Bella saw me upset she would know something was up. Not sure I could pretend everything was okay for much longer before I passed out from exhaustion.

My phone dinged in my purse and I dug it out.

Lucas: I miss your face. How about some coffee?

Me: You just saw my face this morning. I'm afraid if I have any more coffee today I'll never blink again.

Lucas: You need a break. I'll buy you an ice cream.

Me: Ice cream? I'm not Bella.

Lucas: No, you're not. Bella loves when I buy her ice cream and doesn't give me an attitude. It's a beautiful day. I want to see my girl. I'll meet you in front of your building in 15 minutes.

I let out a long sigh, and threw my phone in my bag. I didn't have the energy to argue and work was on the slow side this afternoon. I used to live for afternoon dates with Lucas. Now I was so drained and on edge I couldn't even enjoy that anymore.

By the time I got downstairs, Lucas was holding two ice cream cones with a smug look on his face. I laughed to myself as I strode over to where he was leaning against the building.

"One for me, one for my girl. Let's go across the street and find a bench."

It really was a nice day, the first sunny February day above fifty degrees and Madison Square Park was bustling with activity. In addition to not sleeping, my appetite had been crap over the past week, so I didn't feel so guilty indulging. I planted myself on an empty bench, licking my chocolate ice cream cone as I stared into space. Lucas snickered as he sat beside me and put his arm around my shoulder.

"I should buy you ice cream more often—even though I'm getting a little jealous of that cone right now." He nudged me in the side and I shook my head.

"Yes, because you're *sooo* deprived at home. Thanks for the treat." I kissed his cheek and leaned back against his chest. Being close to Lucas made my body relax a bit.

"You're welcome." He snaked his arm around my waist and kissed my temple. "You going to tell me what's bothering you, or do you want me to guess?"

My eyes grew heavy; I could've slept on Lucas's chest right on the bench. It reminded me of a happier time in my life. No custody fights, no worrying about my daughter—just Lucas and me. Following that sweet memory was the bitter realization of how enjoying that too much may have gotten me into this mess.

"I gave Marc's mother too much access to Bella. I let her think she has a say and a stake in how she's raised. I was selfish— out enjoying romantic weekends with my boyfriend and never thinking about the consequences."

"Hey," Lucas lifted me off his chest and turned my head so I faced him. "Spending weekends at my apartment is not why this is happening. You *never* put me before Bella. All those months at the beginning, I hardly ever saw you on weekends. You wouldn't leave her with anyone. You let Bella stay with her grandparents, who came to you and asked, and who you had no reason to believe would turn on you like this." Lucas took my hand and interlocked our fingers. "Do you regret any of that time with me?"

I sat up straight, shaking my head.

"No! I loved every second I spent with you. Waking up in your arms, having private dinners and staying in bed all day. I crushed on the Lucas I knew all those years ago, but during all those weekends with you, I got to know the amazing man you are—and I fell so hard for you." I smiled as I trailed my hand down his cheek." I never thought I would have to choose between being a good mother and being in love." I ran my fingers along Lucas's jaw, and he leaned into my hand.

"You *don't*. This would have happened regardless of whether you let Marc's parents take Bella a couple of weekends a month. Marc's mother is a scared and jealous woman who is afraid of losing access to her granddaughter. She's the selfish one, not you." He gave me a quick kiss and started eating his ice cream again. Mine became a melted mess but I slurped up what was left.

"I loved those weekends, too. That was a big reason why I couldn't go back to my apartment the night Marc came back. I'd look around and see us everywhere, making dinner together in my kitchen, your beautiful body sprawled across my bed, my head between your legs on the couch . . ." Lucas buried his head in my neck and gave me slow kisses behind my ear.

"You can't talk dirty to me when I'm eating ice cream." I shut my eyes as Lucas pulled me closer.

"Why? You afraid it's going to melt?" I chuckled and pushed him away.

"Those are good memories. Don't let any of this take that away from us. You should spend your energy thinking about where you'd like to move when all this is over."

I put my hand over my eyes and tried to massage my temples.

Every conversation led to this topic lately.

"Lucas, I know you hate the house—"

"I don't *hate* the house. I just would like a place that was all ours, not where you used to live with Marc. Don't you want to move back to the Bronx where your family is? Or maybe somewhere else? The one good thing about having a career in finance is that I knew exactly how to invest and save all these years. And now that I just made partner, I can buy us a huge house anywhere you'd want to go."

I really didn't have the energy for this today. I could see his point, but Bella and I liked our house. I paid for it, so to me it was all mine. We liked the neighborhood, and Bella liked her school. I stood to throw out the rest of my ice cream soup in a trash can next to our bench and turned back to Lucas.

"I don't have much family left in the Bronx, my mother lives in New Jersey. That's why I didn't see the big deal in buying a house in Queens where Marc lived."

"Usually the guy moves to where his girl lives, no? At least that's what I would do." I looked up and groaned. He was never going to let this go.

"That's because you're an abnormally nice guy. Most guys are a lot more selfish."

"Did you just call me weird? I think you did." Lucas gave me a sideways glance from where he still sat on the bench, making me laugh.

"No, I said you were abnormal because you were so nice. Maybe I did call you weird, because before you, a truly nice guy was very odd to me. Although with the movie star looks and panty-dropping smile, I'm sure getting women to not follow *you* everywhere was tough." Lucas choked on the last of his ice cream and burst out laughing.

"*Panty-dropping?* Did you just say I had a panty-dropping smile?" Lucas grabbed me by the waist and pulled me onto his lap. He ran his hand up my skirt, making me squeal.

"What are you doing?" I tried to squirm out of his hold but he tightened his grip.

"I smiled a good three times just now, checking to make sure you had panties on before you went back to work." I tried to grab his hand but he wouldn't budge. It felt so good to laugh, especially after spending the entire week dreading impending disaster.

"I'm glad you told me. There could be panties down all over the city because of me."

I fisted the material on his jacket and pulled him closer. "There better not be." Lucas answered by grabbing the back of my head and giving me a passionate kiss.

I giggled and rested my forehead against his. "Thank you." Lucas shrugged in reply.

"It's what I'm here for. Ice cream and getting your panties to drop. Now you've given me two good ideas for later." I tightened my arms around him and buried my head into his neck.

I was lucky to be happy with Lucas, and I refused to feel guilty about it anymore. I still dreaded what was ahead of us, but I was happy we were in this together.

chapter 31
Lucas

AFTER TWO MONTHS of going back and forth between her home with us and Marc's parents' house, things weren't getting any easier. In fact, I was pretty damn sure they were getting worse. The custody arrangement changed to every weekend after about a month. Robyn was trying to get the hearing moved up but couldn't do anything about it at the moment. Bella was happy when she got home on Sunday nights, but as the week progressed she got quiet and withdrawn. When Marc came to pick Bella up on Fridays, she would give us the saddest look before she left, tearing both our hearts out.

We weren't stupid—Marc's mother had been the one taking care of Bella. I could guarantee he was still the same douche he'd always been and was staying out all night. Even though I was positive she was the evil mastermind behind this whole mess, Sam was confident Bella was safe with her grandmother. Miserable like Sam and me—but safe.

Last night wasn't just miserable. It was fucking awful.

"Shh. Bella, please. Don't cry, baby."

Sam knelt down to hold Bella in her arms, rocking her back and forth in an effort to calm her down. Big tears streamed down Bella's face as she clung to her mother for dear life. I looked into my girl's watery eyes and knew it was a matter of time before she broke down, too.

I joined Sam and Bella on the floor and rubbed Bella's back as I put my arm around Sam. Both my girls were upset and I had no idea what I could do to make it better. I looked over at Marc, who couldn't have cared less. He was leaning against the wall with his arms folded, rolling his eyes as Bella's wails got louder. *Putting my fist through his face wouldn't help anything, but it would've made me feel a hell of a lot better.*

I remembered what Robyn told us about being amiable and cooperative—and while pummeling the bastard would feel really fucking good, it would only hurt us in the long run.

"Bella, come on. Enough already. Grandma is going to get pissed at me if we're any later." Marc let out a long sigh and shook his head at his daughter.

He tried to pull Bella's arm off Sam, but she wouldn't budge. Sam attempted to remove her daughter's grip from around her neck, but it only made her cry harder.

"Butterfly, come with me. I want to talk to you."

I pried her away from her parents' tug of war and carried her into her room. I put her down on the bed and took a seat on the floor in front of her.

"Talk to me, Butterfly. Tell me what's wrong."

Bella's face was red and blotchy, and her eyes were swollen. She cried just like her mother, and it tore up my insides the same way.

"Why can't I stay with you and Mommy? Don't you want me around anymore?"

Bella was only three and a half feet tall but managed to gut me in under a minute. This back and forth was getting to all of us. She didn't belong there, she belonged here—with us. This poor little girl was in the middle of a power struggle and was suffering because of it.

"That's not true. Of course we want you. Right now, Grandma, Grandpa, and your Daddy want to spend time with you, too. Sunday night we'll come to pick you up, and we can go anywhere you want. Sound good?" I kissed her forehead and put my arms around her.

Her crying looked like it slowed a bit, and I breathed a sigh of relief.

"They won't be there. They're going away."

Bella looked down at the floor, and instead of sad, she looked scared.

"Who's going away, Butterfly?

"Grandma and Grandpa. Tomorrow morning they're supposed to see Aunt Mary and they come home Sunday. Daddy
doesn't like me. He yells at me a lot."

Bella was going to be alone with Marc. No wonder he was
in such a rush to get her back to his parents' house. His mother
probably wanted to see her before she went away for the weekend.

I didn't like this. At all.

There wasn't a goddamn thing I could do. Keeping her here
would be a violation of the custody agreement, and knowing
that wretched woman, she would use it as leverage to keep
Bella for longer. My hands were tied, and Bella was looking
at me for an answer I didn't have. It would have hurt less to
plunge a knife into my own chest.

I took her Hello Kitty pad and pen from her nightstand and
tore off a piece of paper. I jotted down my cell phone number,
folded up the paper and put it in her hand.

"Listen to me. If you need me, call this number like we
showed you. I don't care what time it is. I'll come get you. Okay?"

Bella made a fist around the paper and flung her arms
around me. I held her as tight as I could.

"I love you, Lucas." Bella's words were a faint whisper as
she buried her head in my neck. If only I really were Superman,
I'd fly her and her mother far away from this horrible situation
to where no one could hurt them. Right now, reassuring them
both was the best I could do, even if I didn't believe it myself.

I pulled back and rested my forehead against hers.

"I love you, too, Butterfly. Remember what I told you."

She nodded and I took her hand, leading her back into the
living room.

Sam was sitting on the couch, but got up as soon as she saw
us.

"You okay, baby?" Bella gave her a little nod and glanced
at her father.

"Finally! Get your coat on Bella. We have to go."

Marc threw Bella's coat at Sam. I was still holding Bella's hand, but shook from the rage I was trying to hold in. After Sam helped Bella with her zipper, she gave her a quick kiss on the cheek. Marc took Bella's hand and yanked her towards the door.

"You going to be all right, just you and Bella now that your parents are away?" Sam's head jerked up to stare at me with a horrified expression on her face.

"Bella and I will be just fine, pretty boy. None of your concern."

Sam moved to wrap her arms around her daughter one last time. As Bella left, she glanced back at me and I nodded. If she called me, I would get right in the car and bring her home. Legal consequences be damned.

As the door shut behind them, Sam couldn't hold her sobs in any longer. I hurried over to her and she collapsed in my arms. I trailed kisses across Sam's forehead and down her tear-stained cheeks. She threw her arms around my waist and cried into my chest.

I hated the thought of Marc taking care of Bella alone—given his track record of ignoring his daughter—and it had to be tearing Sam up. All I could do was hold her and say everything was fine, when we both knew it was anything but.

Neither one of us could sleep. We spent the night on the couch watching TV. Sam was in my arms all night, while I clutched my phone in my hand.

After a long and sleepless night sick with worry over Bella alone with her father, Sam and I decided to go to the gym. That was always her way of therapy, and pretending a punching bag was Marc for an hour or two didn't sound like a bad idea. She wanted to try a yoga class afterwards to relax. After two hours of weights, cardio, and punching a hole in said punching bag, I told her I'd wait for her in the coffee shop across the street.

I bought an iced coffee and sat at a table in the back. I was sweaty now and sore all over, but didn't feel any better. I tried to think of excuses to check on Bella after Sam got out of class.

I noticed a stocky guy leaning over the counter by the barista, obviously flirting. The girl was giggling and touching the guy's arm. From where I sat, she could have been no more than twenty. The man went to the refrigerator next to the register and took out what looked like a juice box.

No fucking way; that couldn't be Marc.

Sure enough, Marc dropped the juice box in front of Bella, who was sitting at the table behind him with her head down. He had his back to his daughter the entire time. Anyone could have taken her and he wouldn't have known until it was too late. I couldn't tell if she was sleeping on the table. Knowing Marc, he'd dragged his daughter out of bed in an attempt to get into the barely legal barista's pants.

Fuck this.

I got up and crept over to where she was sitting. Marc didn't notice me approach, which infuriated me. No doubt he was a big jerk, but this kind of negligence even I didn't expect.

"Hey, Butterfly!"

I tapped Bella's shoulder and she slowly lifted her head, like it was too heavy for her shoulders. She was flushed with a sweaty forehead, but she looked like she was shivering. It was a chilly morning, and all she had on was a windbreaker.

"Lucas, you came! I wanted to call you but Daddy wouldn't let me have his phone." Her voice was raspy and soft.

The look of happiness and relief on her face broke my heart. The Hello Kitty paper with my number on it was crumpled in her hand.

"What's wrong?" I pushed away the hair that was sticking to her forehead, and her head was burning up. She was sick, and yet Marc brought her out in the cold anyway.

"Marc!" I yelled to him as he was whispering in the girl's ear. He turned around laughing but rolled his eyes when he saw me.

"What do you want, pretty boy?" He turned to the barista with a sickening grin. "He can never stand anyone else talking to a cute girl. Always has to get everyone's sloppy seconds—"

"Your daughter is sick, you asshole. Did you notice she was

burning up with a fever?"

Marc squinted his eyes at me and shook his head.

"She's fine, she's just like her mother and never wants to go anywhere." He turned back to the barista, and I saw red. I stormed over to him and grabbed him by the shoulder.

"Go feel her fucking forehead! And roll your eyes at me again."

I took another step towards him and got in his face. "I *dare* you."

Marc huffed. "Excuse me, Candie. I'll be right back."

Marc followed me over to Bella and reluctantly felt her forehead. His face fell, and he stepped back.

"She wasn't like that when we left. She must have just gotten sick. Great, the one weekend your grandmother isn't here. Ugh! We'll go home in a little while." He turned to walk back to the counter and I grabbed his arm.

"Your daughter is sick. She can barely lift her head up and needs to see a doctor. Are you that fucking stupid?" I was doing the exact opposite of what Robyn told us to do, but as far as I was concerned, that all went out the goddamn window if Bella was in trouble.

Marc pulled his arm away.

"I said give me a little while. God, you still bitch like a woman."

He headed back towards Candie, and I'd had enough. I took my jacket off, wrapped it around Bella, and picked her up.

"Come on, Butterfly. I'm sorry my jacket is sweaty. We'll go wait in the car for Mommy and go to the doctor."

I bolted towards the door when Marc grabbed my arm.

"Who the hell do you think you are? This is *my* kid not yours. Same as it's *my* wife that you're sleeping with in *my* bed. Why don't you get your own damn life and stop taking my leftovers."

If Bella wasn't in my arms, Marc would've been on the floor, bleeding and possibly missing teeth. But she was, and I didn't want to scare her.

"They're yours in name only." I kept my voice as flat as

possible. "A real father wouldn't ignore his sick daughter. He would be worried as hell and running to the doctor, not trying to score with an underage waitress. Samantha and Bella are mine, more than they *ever* were yours. Even this bullshit custody fight your mother started won't change that. If you'll excuse me, my butterfly needs a doctor."

I stormed out the door and carried Bella to the car, texting Sam with one hand to let her know where we were.

"Lucas?" Bella sounded so weak, and it was scaring the shit out of me.

"Yeah, Butterfly?" I sat with her on my lap in the driver's seat, trying to warm her up before I strapped her in the back.

"You saved me. You're just like Superman."

I tightened my arms around her and kissed her still burning forehead.

"I'll always save you. No matter where you are." She gave me a little smile and closed her eyes, cuddling into my chest.

Sam's class would be over in five minutes, and I knew as soon as she read my text she would run here. If I knew where her doctor was, I would have taken her myself.

I had loved Bella for a long time—how could I not?—But I couldn't remember exactly when things changed. All I knew was the little girl in my arms was my life now, as much as her mother was—and I would be just as broken if I ever lost her.

chapter 32

Lucas

I COULDN'T UNDERSTAND how Sam was so calm. We sat in pediatric urgent care—thankfully a two-minute drive from the gym—for over an hour. I was getting more and more pissed off as the nurse called in kids who didn't look nearly as sick as Bella. She was sitting on Sam's lap, half sleeping on her chest with flushed cheeks.

I marched up to the check-in counter to ask the nurse what the hell was going on.

"Excuse me. Can you please check when Isabella Christensen is supposed to get called in? She has a high fever and has been here for a while." I watched her check the sign-in sheet with a lack of urgency that grated on my already frayed nerves.

"Should be about fifteen minutes, sir. There are two children before her."

"Two children before her? I have a sick kid here. Can't you move her up?"

"Sir, they're all sick kids. We'll call her when they're ready."

"Babe, please come sit back down." Sam patted the chair next to her in the waiting room. She had a patronizing smile on her face. *Why wasn't she as freaked out as I was?*

"This is bullshit. I just saw a kid walk in with ice wrapped around his thumb. Bella's actually sick and they still haven't called her name." I shook my head and put my head in my hands, ready to bang it against the wall.

Sam rubbed my back and leaned over to kiss my shoulder.

"Aren't you cold? You can run home and get another jacket. Doesn't look like you're getting this one back anytime soon." Bella had my jacket wrapped around her like a blanket.

I wiped the hair off Bella's face. Her forehead was still hot and damp.

"I'm fine." I told Sam, still looking at Bella. I was still agitated from my altercation with Marc, and the snail's pace the doctor seemed to be going at didn't help.

"Not that I don't love staring at your muscles, but we don't need you sick, too."

I wore a sleeveless shirt, and actually *was* cold—but I wasn't going anywhere until a doctor said Bella was all right.

"Why are you so calm? I love you, but you're getting on my nerves."

Sam laughed and rubbed my back.

"I'm ninety percent sure this is strep throat. Bella just told me it hurt to swallow. For the past couple of years, she's gotten it right after Christmas. I'm surprised it took this long, I was hoping maybe she avoided it this year. They'll swab her throat and give her some antibiotics. She'll be better in a week or so."

I shrugged. I was probably overreacting, but seeing Bella sick and Marc completely ignoring her still infuriated me. I wasn't going calm down until the doctor looked her over.

"You know," Sam kissed my cheek and whispered in my ear. "Kids get sick. Especially when they go to school and share new germs with each other. It's scary and hard not to panic every time. You're new at this, but you'll get used to it."

I turned my head and gave her a soft peck on the lips. Sam was right, I needed to learn to keep cool in times like this, and not act like a nutcase. I needed to find a way to reel it in.

"I actually love that you're this worked up. Marc never came with us to the doctor. He was always more annoyed at the inconvenience whenever Bella got sick, as you may have noticed today. Bella never had a real dad who worried about her so much before."

I looked over at Sam and noticed her eyes were a little watery, it usually didn't take much to make my girl cry. She rested her head on my shoulder and whispered in my ear.

"Do you want to come home with me?"

I laughed and kissed her forehead, then shrugged at her. "Sorry, I already live with someone."

Sam giggled. "She must be pretty."

"No." I kissed her cheek and whispered in her ear. "She's *beautiful.*" I took her hand and intertwined our fingers.

"I texted Robyn and let her know what happened with Marc. She wants to talk to you to get the details. Could you give her a call once the doctor calls Bella in? I know you want to see the doctor too, but I can handle it." She winked at me and I laughed. Our roles were reversed for the day. Usually, I'm the calm one and she's the worry wart.

"Isabella Christensen."

I breathed a sigh of relief. Sam handed me her phone before she carried Bella to one of the exam rooms. I strolled outside to tell our lawyer I did the exact opposite of her advice. I felt like I was reporting to the principal's office for bad behavior.

"Samantha? How's Bella?"

"Hey, Robyn. It's Lucas. Sam told me to call you."

"Oh, hi. Yes, I felt it was better getting all the details straight from you. Tell me what happened."

I took a deep breath and prayed I hadn't made this already horrendous situation we were in even worse.

"Not much to tell. I was sitting in a coffee shop and noticed Marc flirting with one of the girls who worked there. Bella had her head down on a table like she was sleeping, and he had his back to her the entire time. I went over to her and realized she was sick. I told Marc she needed a doctor and he blew me off, so I carried her out and waited for Sam in the car. I also . . . had some words with Marc."

"What words?"

I cringed and put my hand to my forehead. "I called him an asshole and told him he was fucking stupid."

I braced myself for her reaction, and was surprised to hear her laugh.

"That sums up what my husband and I always thought about Marc. You're a good man, Lucas. You saw Bella was in trouble and got her the help she needed. I *did* tell you to avoid fighting with Marc or his mother, but you did what you had to do. I'm going to put a hold on the joint custody agreement, citing what happened today. Bella won't have to go back to Marc until we have a hearing. I've been working on a plan to get Marc to admit his mother is behind his request for joint custody, and I think I'm ready to show it to the judge. Focus on getting Bella better, and I'll take care of the rest. We're in a good place, so stop thinking you fucked it all up."

I laughed. Sam was right about Robyn. She looked and sounded like Snow White, but she seemed like she knew what she was doing. The confidence in her voice made me feel optimistic for the first time in over a month. I hoped her plan was a good one, because we needed this all to be over.

THE DOCTOR CONFIRMED that Bella had strep throat. After some pink medicine and some Tylenol, she passed out in her room. Sam and I tiptoed in to check on her. I knelt next to her bed and felt her forehead, cool for the first time today.

Sam came up behind me and ran her fingers through my hair. Still kneeling on the floor, I wrapped my arms around her waist and pulled her down to me.

"You know what I need around here?" I whispered so I wouldn't wake Bella.

"What's that?" Sam ran hand down my cheek.

"Another man in the house. I already have my work cut out for me, keeping boys away from *you*." I tucked a piece of hair behind her ear and glanced at my little butterfly, asleep in her bed. "This one looks more like you every day, and as you like to point out—you're with an *older* man. I need a little help here."

"Are you saying you want to have a baby?" It was dark, so I couldn't tell what her reaction was.

I slowly nodded my head. We'd never really talked about

having kids. Sam was a fantastic mother, but I never considered the possibility that she only wanted one child. It wasn't a deal breaker if she did, but I'd been thinking a lot about seeing Sam's belly grow with my baby inside. I was surprised at how the more I thought about it, the more I wanted it.

"Not right this second, obviously. Someday. But if you don't I understand. And I'm happy with you and Bella—" Sam put her finger on my lips.

"You're cute when you ramble. I would love to have a baby with you. Although, I'm not sure if the women of the world are ready for Lucas Hunter's son."

I pulled her close and kissed her. Sam pulled back from my lips and leaned her forehead against mine.

"We could have another girl, you know. What would you do then?"

"I would love another girl. I'd just accept the fact I was probably headed towards an early grave."

Sam chuckled and shook her head at me. I stood, pulling her by the hand along with me.

"I love you so much." I crashed my lips onto hers, and heard the cutest little moan escape when I bit her bottom lip.

"Let's take it outside." Sam took my hand and led me out the door.

If all went according to plan, in a few months, Sam and I would be married—provided she said yes, Bella would be staying put, and maybe we'd have a new little person on the way not long after. Everything would be pretty damn close to perfect.

chapter 33

Samantha

AS WE WAITED for Robyn outside the family court building, my stomach was in knots. She was able to get an earlier court date than expected, which was great if things went our way, and awful if they didn't. At least until the hearing, we had sole custody and didn't have to worry about Bella on weekends. I really didn't want to go back to our previous arrangement. Even more than being afraid of her getting sick or being in trouble because of Marc's negligence, Bella was getting older, and becoming more aware of her father's indifference. Having personal experience—and unresolved issues—with a father like that, I wanted her as far from Marc as possible.

Lucas held my hand, running his thumb back and forth over my palm. He was tense too, but trying so hard to hide it. Robyn approached us wearing a confident smile and led us inside. Before we reached our assigned courtroom, she turned to us with a stern expression.

"I do all the talking unless I tell you otherwise or the judge addresses you directly. Don't let Marc get the best of you and make you leave a bad impression in front of the judge. Lucas, if you're asked to recount what happened in the coffee shop, just give a short story without calling Marc a douchebag or . . . what did you call him?'

"Asshole." Lucas and I both said together, giving all three of us a much-needed laugh.

"Yes that. I believe I have a plan that will shut this down today. So, whatever happens, trust me and let me handle everything. Agreed?"

We nodded and entered the courtroom.

I'd only ever seen an actual—not TV—courtroom during my two brief stints at jury duty. Judges intimidated the hell out of me, and just being in the courtroom increased my anxiety level exponentially. I took a deep breath as Lucas and I sat next to Robyn at a sturdy wooden table up front.

Marc was seated across from us with his lawyer—and his mother. I scowled at the back of Jeannie's head but then looked away before she saw me. She was probably here to police her son and make sure he didn't say anything stupid.

The judge walked in and I barely paid attention to the introductions. My heart was pounding in my ears as Robyn addressed the court.

"Your honor, we are here to ask that Marc Christensen's petition for joint custody be denied. He's proven that he's not building a relationship with his estranged daughter at all, and has, in fact, demonstrated negligence that could adversely affect his daughter's welfare."

"How dare you! Samantha's boyfriend is the one who is endangering her welfare, snatching her away from her father like that." Jeannie's face was red as she glared at Lucas. "She's estranged from her father because of *him!*"

Their lawyer pulled Jeannie into her seat. I'd never seen her so unglued. She was always a bit stern and cold, but now she was in full Disney villain mode. All she needed was the fur coat made of Dalmatian hides.

"Control your clients, please." The judge didn't look happy as he reprimanded her. I guessed that was one point for us.

Robyn turned to us and raised her eyebrows, silently reiterating what *not* to do. Then she returned her attention to the judge.

"Your honor, what Mrs. Christensen was referring to was an incident in which her son took his daughter to a coffee shop while she was sick with a high fever, and then ignored her while he flirted with an employee. Mr. Hunter removed her and took her to a doctor. I have further evidence of negligence beyond that incident that I'd like to share with the court."

My blood ran cold. *Bella's been in some kind of danger with Marc before? Had Robyn been investigating the house on weekends and saw something?* No, I was sure she would have told me. My breath caught as I waited to see what Robyn meant. She did seem sure she could 'shut this down' today. Lucas took my hand under the table and laced our fingers together. I gripped his hand as I braced myself.

She opened her laptop and walked it over to the judge. She was logged onto Facebook, which I found to be odd.

"Every single weekend that Mr. Christensen had custody of his daughter over the past couple of months, he was actually out the entire weekend. There are posts and check-ins at various bars, clubs and parties, often both days and almost always both nights of the weekend. You can open the tracking information in each photo to view the date, time, and place it was taken. Since he's returned from Chicago, he hasn't acted like a father wanting to be close to his daughter. It's obvious he hasn't attempted to spend any time with her while she was supposedly in his care."

"Are you fucking serious? You're tracking me on Facebook? This has to be some kind of violation." I almost felt bad for Marc's lawyer as he dragged Marc back to his seat.

"I'm not going to warn you again." The judge looked pissed as hell as he glared at Marc and his mother.

"If it's on social media, anyone can see. All rights to privacy are lost when someone posts their every move. The one thing to note that's *not* on his Facebook page are any pictures of his daughter since he's been back. In fact, the only mention of her over the past three months was the night before Bella got sick in the coffee shop. He updated his status to read, 'I'm on kid duty. Looks like the weekend is going to suck for me.'"

"Why are you going after Marc? She's the one who practically has a live-in boyfriend while she's still married to my son. I have no words for this situation."

Jeannie was out of control, and after everything she'd done

it would've been sweet to see her hauled off in handcuffs.

"I have a couple of words." Lucas whispered in my ear. I turned around and he winked at me. I managed a smile and squeezed his hand.

The judge looked irate. I didn't know if Marc's Facebook was going to be what cracked the case open or if it even had any validity in court, but Robyn's plan was certainly getting under Marc and Jeannie's skin.

"Fuck this!" Marc yelled and looked over at me. "She can have sole custody. I'm not going to answer to anyone for what I do on my own time. It's a free fucking country." He turned to his mother.

"I'm taking the full-time job in Chicago. I went along with this because you begged me to, but I'm not dealing with this aggravation. You want to see Bella, work it out with her yourself." Marc grabbed his jacket and stormed out of the courtroom.

Robyn slid into her seat next to me. Marc was a hothead, and hated to be told what to do. He never wanted custody. Once he realized the inconvenience Bella would be to his lifestyle, he threw his hands up and walked away. His mother did boss him around sometimes, but in the end, Marc looked out for Marc. Robyn played him perfectly.

"Holy shit, you're good." I whispered in Robyn's ear.

She shrugged in response. "It's what I do. I fight for the happy ending that people deserve. Sometimes, you need to be a little creative." She squeezed my hand and turned to face the judge.

"Sole custody of Isabella Christensen remains with her mother, Samantha Christensen. Marc Christensen's appeal for joint custody is dismissed." The judge frowned at Jeannie.

"Grandparents are supposed to protect their grandchildren, not hurt them for their own selfish reasons. You should apologize to the little girl who has been made to suffer needlessly because of your actions. Any visitation rights to Isabella that you will have in the future will be at her mother's discretion."

It was over.

I left the courtroom lighter, like a brick had been lifted off my chest. I hugged Robyn with tears in my eyes. I had no idea how to thank her.

"No need to get weepy." Robyn teased as she grabbed my shoulders. "I told you I would shut things down today. Now go home and tell Bella she can look forward to weekends again." I laughed as I wiped my eyes.

Lucas slid his arm around my waist and kissed my forehead.

"My little mushball." I jabbed him in the side with my elbow and he laughed. I could see the relief in his face, too.

"Work has been texting me so I need to call and see this is about. And you," He picked Robyn up by the waist and kissed her cheek. "Thank you so fucking much."

As Lucas walked away, my tough as nails lawyer giggled like a schoolgirl and blushed.

"You're a lucky woman, my friend." Robyn put her arm around me as we stepped outside.

chapter 34

Samantha

THREE MONTHS LATER, things had settled into a wonderful normal. Robyn worked on finalizing my divorce, making sure that Marc was required to pay child support. I didn't care, I'd always provided for my daughter just fine by myself and wanted no more delays. My marriage had been over for a long time and I needed to get the state of New York to agree. It was time to move on—officially. Robyn insisted that even though I may not need it, I was still entitled to it. If Marc didn't want to actually pay, she said she could arrange to have the money come directly out of his paycheck. I made a note to never get on Robyn's bad side.

Lucas drove Bella over to Julianna's for a sleepover. I sat at my kitchen table, looking through the real estate section of the Sunday New York Times Lucas now felt compelled to buy every week. I perused through the new listings each week to appease him for the time being.

My cell phone rang, and I saw Robyn's name on the screen. I rolled my eyes at what the next possible issue could be.

"Hey, lady. What now?" I couldn't hide the irritation in my voice at what could be up this time.

"That is not a very happy greeting considering what I have to tell you."

"Don't tease me, Robyn. Did it happen? Am I divorced?"

"Signed, sealed, and delivered. I checked today. You're free!"

"As in done, final, as in—"

"Legally okay to finally marry the man of your dreams? Yep,

all clear as of this moment."

My mind was spinning. I was afraid to believe it. After almost a year and a half since Lucas and I reconnected, there were finally no more barriers or complications.

"Well he has to ask me first. Thank you. I keep saying this but I have no idea how to repay you for all you've done."

"Stop, please. Thank me by getting married ASAP and having lots of blue-eyed babies."

"Maybe we'll name a couple after you—I'm sure Lucas wouldn't mind."

"Lucas wouldn't mind what?" I jumped as Lucas snuck up behind me.

"You didn't hear the news? I'm single!" Lucas froze in place, having the same reaction I did when Robyn told me. A slow smile spread across his face as he pulled me up to stand.

"Single? The hell you are!" He snatched the phone from my hand. "Robyn, she'll have to call you back." I heard Robyn laughing as he ended the call.

Before I could say anything, his mouth was on mine. It was the kind of searing kiss that made my knees weak and my panties damp. He was so damn good with his mouth. We broke apart, my eyes still closed.

Lucas trailed kisses down my neck, and I yelped when he bit my ear lobe.

"This calls for celebration, don't you think?" He whispered in my ear as he continued to nip and lick his way across my collarbone.

"Yeah, I can start dating again." He stopped kissing me and slapped me on the ass.

"You're a bit of a smartass, aren't you?" I giggled as Lucas pulled me closer.

"I can make us a nice dinner. We have the house to ourselves tonight." I ran my hand along his jaw.

"I would take you out, but I'd be pawing at you all night long and we'd end up running back home anyway." His lips went back to my neck, and a moan escaped me as I laughed.

"And that's different from any other night we've gone out, because?" He swatted my ass again and cocked an eyebrow at me.

"You'll see."

WE ENDED UP just ordering in and watching movies on the couch. It felt so good to be able to breathe. I was free from my marriage to Marc, and really wanted to make things permanent with Lucas. All he had to do was ask.

I rested my head on Lucas's chest while he played with my hair.

"You aren't upset we didn't go out?" Lucas asked as he rested his chin on the top of my head.

I looked up at him and shook my head.

"No, I like to be groped in the privacy of my own home." I expected him to laugh, but he just nodded.

"Hey, you okay?" Lucas looked tense for some reason. I would think he felt the same weight lifted off his shoulders that I did. He could give up his apartment and officially move in. I was afraid maybe he was having second thoughts.

"Know what I was thinking?" Lucas asked. "That night I met you at the bar. God, you were stunning. You were always beautiful, but there was something about you that night. It was always there, I was just too stupid to see it all those years ago. I had a feeling I was done for by the time I walked you to the train. I spent the next three months trying to be your friend when I was falling for you a little more every day."

I sat up next to him and kissed his cheek.

"I was done for the day you walked into Daina's yard on the Fourth of July." Lucas smiled and looked away.

"When you told me that day in Starbucks that you wanted to take a chance on us, I knew. I knew then you were it for me. I couldn't imagine being away from you or with anyone else—ever.

I would never let you go. I got to know Bella, and then I fell in love a second time." He smiled at me and my eyes filled with tears.

Why is he bringing all this up? Unless he's . . .

"I belong to you, I always have." Lucas stood up from the couch and reached into his back packet. He pulled out a black velvet box and got down on one knee. My heart went into my throat as tears streamed down my face.

"And I want everyone to know that you belong to me. I want to spend the rest of my life with you. I want you, Bella, and me to be a family—an official one. I love you. It was always you. Samantha, will you marry me?"

He opened the box, and I recognized the pink diamond ring he caught me drooling over at the jewelry store. I sobbed so hard, I opened my mouth to speak and nothing came out. What were the chances I'd actually get the one thing I wanted most for my entire life? Lucas was my dream come true.

"Don't do this to me again. If you can't speak, just nod."

I laughed and tried to swallow the tears so I could speak.

"Did you really think I could ever say no? Yes! Yes! A million times yes!"

Lucas breathed what looked like a sigh of relief and slid the ring on to my trembling finger. I threw my arms around his neck and kissed him.

"I can't believe you remembered this ring." Lucas raised his eyebrows and gave me a sideways glance.

"I actually got it that day. Remember when I went back in to get my phone?"

I hit his arm. "You little sneak. Wait, that was months ago. You've had the ring all this time?"

Lucas nodded. "I wanted to wait until your divorce was final. Once I got this ring on your finger, waiting to marry you would have been torture." Lucas brought me back to his lips, then trailed kisses down my neck.

"So, want to get married this week?" I asked. Lucas stopped kissing me and looked up at me strangely.

"This week? Where?"

"City Hall. I think we can get the marriage license the same day."

Lucas looked disappointed, and I was confused. His happiness was palpable just a moment ago.

"Babe, what's wrong? I thought you'd want to get married right away, but I understand if you want to wait." I ran my hand down his cheek, and he shook his head.

"No, I definitely don't want to wait. But I think we deserve better than City Hall, don't you think? Plus, I think my mother and sister would be pissed off at me if I did that. They'd want to be there, at least."

"Even if you're marrying *me?*" His sister wasn't my biggest fan.

"My mother loves you. And my sister will be apologizing to you the next time she sees you, I promise you that." Lucas kissed my ring finger.

"Okay, but not big. I want our wedding to be about you and me, not the party." Lucas wrapped his arms around me and pulled me closer.

"I would agree with that. I have a friend who owns a loft in the village. It's a nice place for a small party, and we could get married there, too. I'm selfish. I want to see you in a sexy dress, preferably strapless, and enjoy taking it off you at the end of the night." Lucas gave me a soft kiss and nibbled on my bottom lip.

"That sounds nice, actually. Ask him if he has any openings in the next couple of months."

Lucas wrinkled his nose at me.

"I *may* have talked to him already and set things up; we just needed a date. All you have to do is look hot and show up." I pulled back and raised my eyebrows.

"That sure I'd say yes?" I smirked at him.

Lucas shrugged and kissed my forehead.

"I had a good feeling." I laughed and kissed him again.

"You planned everything? I'm impressed; I didn't think guys liked going to weddings, much less planning them." Lucas's brow furrowed, and rested his forehead against mine.

"I've waited long enough to marry you. I wasn't leaving anything to chance. Now . . ."

Lucas moved his hands from my waist to the hem of my shirt, inching it over my head.

"We should practice for the wedding night." Lucas ran his hands down my chest, and gave open-mouth kisses across the tops of my breasts as he pulled down the straps.

"We've been practicing for a long time, Lucas. I think we'll be fi—" My voice trailed off as he sucked a nipple into his mouth. "Never know when you'll learn something new."

chapter 35

Samantha

TOMORROW WAS GOING to be a big day. Nothing about our lives would really change, except my last name. Lucas somehow managed to put everything together in a couple of months. He even took care of the menu and flowers. It was a small guest list. All I needed to do was pick out a dress and show up. I had no idea what to expect, I hadn't even seen the loft we were supposed to get married in. It was a formality more than anything, but knowing I would be Lucas's wife tomorrow thrilled me. After all my years living with a miserable frog, I was finally getting the prince I always wanted.

I wrapped my arms around Lucas's waist and nuzzled into his chest as we lay in bed together.

I rested my chin on Lucas's chest, propping my head up to look at his face. He ran his fingers through my hair as I kissed across his collarbone and up his neck. He had the sexiest Adam's apple, and I loved how he squirmed when I nibbled on it.

"Time for me to go." Lucas tried to sit up, but I pushed him back down. I didn't want Lucas to leave—at least not yet. He was supposed to stay at his apartment and meet me at the loft tomorrow. As of yet, he still didn't have a buyer. He'd asked couple of his cousins that were attending our wedding to stay there tonight instead of renting a hotel room.

"I bet I can convince you to stay a little longer . . ." I brought my lips back to his neck, searching for the spot behind his ear that usually made his entire body go limp. Lucas shrugged me away before I got there, and groaned.

"You're not making this easy. Aren't we not supposed to be together tonight anyway? The whole 'bad luck to see each other before the wedding' thing. You know I hate being away from you. I'll be sleeping in my old bed thinking of the first time you stayed over. Amazing how that seems so long ago and like yesterday at the same time, right?"

Now I *really* didn't want him to leave.

Lucas sat on the edge of the bed as he pulled his jeans on. When he stood, I sat up on my knees and inched my hand down his chest.

"You sure you want to leave me?" I pretended to lower the sheet that covered my naked body, and Lucas laughed. *So much for my seduction skills.*

"You are not playing fair tonight. Are you, Mrs. Hunter?" Lucas smirked at me. For some reason, calling me 'Mrs. Hunter' made my legs fall apart. *Tease.*

When Lucas ran his thumb over my lips, I opened my mouth to suck on it. His eyes got hooded and a sexy moan escaped him.

Sensing I might be winning, I grabbed his hand and slowly took his index and middle finger in my mouth, sucking on them like a Popsicle. His fingers almost touched the back of my throat before I pulled back, inching them out of my mouth while making circles with my tongue around his fingertips. Lucas looked like he stopped breathing, and blinking. I cocked an eyebrow at him, my silent promise to repeat the same treatment—only lower—if he decided to stay.

I let my sheet drop, and Lucas closed his eyes as he let out an audible sigh. I raked my nails down his chest and over the hard ridges along his abs. When I unbuckled his pants and wrapped my hand around his hard cock, Lucas's breathing hitched. Seeing him this affected by my touch made me feel powerful—and I loved it. As I inched my hand up and down, Lucas's jaw clenched and the expression on his face intensified.

"Get on all fours. *Now,* Samantha."

I almost squealed. Not only was I victorious, but I coaxed alpha Lucas to come out.

I scrambled on the bed to do as I was told. Lucas came up behind me and pulled me back by my hair. My heart raced as he licked along the outside of my ear.

"You don't play fair. In fact, I think you play dirty. Very, *very* dirty."

"I could keep playing dirty all night, baby." When I leaned back to rub myself against the hardness at my back, Lucas let out a sexy growl.

I *so* won.

"My sweet girl went bad. When did that happen?"

"Just take me, Lucas. *Please.*" It was hard to tell by the begging my voice how recently Lucas had already taken me. It was less than an hour ago, yet I still needed more.

Lucas pulled me up by the waist and turned me around until I faced him. He ran his knuckles down my cheek with a sly grin on his face.

"I want you to be able to walk down the aisle to me tomorrow. If I stay and do everything I want to you right now, that will be fucking impossible." I whimpered as he kissed my forehead and buckled his pants. I didn't know what the term was for the female equivalent of blue balls, but I was positive that's what I was feeling—a dull, unsatisfied ache.

I pulled the sheet back over me and scowled at my soon to be husband.

"That's not very nice." I stuck my lip out in an exaggerated pout.

"I can play dirty, too—*baby*. Get some sleep." He leaned over the bed and gave me a soft kiss.

"Stay in bed. I'll lock up. Sweet dreams, *Mrs. Hunter.*" He laughed as he backed out of the bedroom. Now he was just being cruel.

"Yeah, yeah. Whatever." I lay back down and pulled the sheet higher.

"I love you." He blew me a kiss and I giggled.

"I love you too—big tease."

I TRIED TO sleep, but couldn't. I was too wound up thinking about tomorrow and not used to sleeping alone.

"Mommy?" Bella inched the door open and tiptoed into my room. I leaned over to my night stand and turned on the light.

"Hey baby, it's late. What's wrong? You can't sleep either?" She scampered onto my bed and snuggled into my side.

"Is Lucas going to be my new daddy tomorrow?"

How should I answer that?

Marc moved to Chicago two weeks after the custody hearing, and in the past few months since he left, he hadn't contacted his daughter at all. Jeannie still called once or twice a week. I let Bella speak to her and see her for a couple of hours at a time, but we weren't ready to allow her to sleep there again.

Lucas was Bella's father in all the ways that mattered. My only hesitation in saying 'yes' was that I didn't want to confuse her.

"Lucas loves you very much, and tomorrow the three of us will officially be a family." Bella beamed from ear to ear. I hoped that meant she was satisfied by my answer.

"Lucas gave me a present before he left. Wanna see?" She bolted up to show me her new necklace. It was a white gold butterfly pendant with a diamond in the middle.

"Look, it even has my name on it!"

To Bella, always my Butterfly was engraved on the back. Tears welled up in my eyes.

"Can I wear it tomorrow?"

"Sure." I squeaked out a reply as I attempted to swallow my tears.

"Don't cry, Mommy. Lucas left you a present, too. He said to give it to you in the morning, but I'll just tell him you were crying and I needed to make you happy."

Bella jumped off the bed and sprinted out the door. She ran back in and handed me an envelope. Inside was the shark tooth necklace that had belonged to Lucas's father. Lucas always wore it for good luck, and he lent it to me once before a big presentation in school. Wrapped around the necklace was a letter.

You told me we've been married in our hearts for a while, and today is just a legal technicality. While that's true, it's still a huge deal for me. Being married to you, calling you my wife, giving you my last name, you have no idea how much that all means to me. Today you're mine, in every sense of the word.

I laugh every time you call me your Superman. You saved me as much as I saved you. I never knew what it was like to love someone so much you couldn't breathe, that thinking about trying to live without her made you go insane. I think I may've demonstrated the "crazy" pretty well a time or two. You saved me from my hollow and selfish life. When I fell in love with you, life stopped being easy. I know what it's like to live for someone else now, and I'll always live for you.

I think you remember my Dad's necklace. He would have loved you. You're beautiful with a huge heart but have a little "spunk," as he used to say. You need something borrowed and something old, and I guess this can count as both. As much as I know you love me, I know you're a little nervous about today, too. Don't be scared. We're going to have the best life together because I won't accept anything less. For the rest of the time I'm on this earth, I will always be with you. Because I can't be anywhere else.

I don't need the necklace for luck today, because I already have you.

I love you. Always you. Forever.

Instead of stopping my tears, Lucas's letter made them full-on sobs.

"I'm sorry, Mommy. I thought if you got a present you wouldn't be sad anymore." She climbed back on the bed to cuddle next to me. Her gentle hands patted my hair like I usually do when she's upset. I shook my head and kissed her cheek.

"Thank you for giving me the present, Bella. Mommy is just a little weird and cries when she's really happy. I'm mushy like that."

"Is that why Lucas calls you a mushball?"

I laughed again as I wiped the tears from my eyes.

"Yep, that's exactly why. Feel like keeping Mommy company tonight? We have a busy day tomorrow!"

Bella nodded and lay down next to me. The minute she fell back on Lucas's pillow, she was out.

It was late, but I had to text Lucas anyway.

Me: Bella gave me my present and showed me hers. I love you so much. I can't wait to marry you.

A minute later, my phone buzzed.

Lucas: You really are a bad girl tonight. You were

supposed to open that in the morning.

Lucas: But it's probably better this way, you can get all the crying out now.

He was a smug jerk, and knew me so well.

Lucas: I should confess I opened your letter, too.

I felt silly now about the gift and short note I left in Lucas's overnight bag. I had wrapped a Lego Superman keychain in a letter that said:

You're my hero and the love of my life. Thank you for making all my dreams come true.

Me: Not as amazing as your letter, but I meant every word.

Lucas: I loved it. I can't wait to start my life with you.

Me: Me too. Good night, babe.

Lucas: Good night, Baby Girl. And if it makes you feel any better, I've been frustrated as hell since I left you.

Me: A little. You brought it all on yourself.

Lucas: I know . . . I'll make it all better tomorrow night ;)

Me: Maybe I won't be in the mood.

Lucas: Yeah, right. Go to sleep, seductress.

God, how I loved that arrogant bastard.

chapter 36

Samantha

"I TOLD THE girl at the MAC counter that everything had to be waterproof knowing you. You're worse than your daughter. Sit still and close your eyes."

I shut my eyes and did my best to sit as still as possible. Daina used to be a cosmetologist, so when she offered to do my makeup for the wedding I agreed. Had I paid someone, I probably wouldn't be scolded like a child, but I knew better than to tell Daina no. When she was tense, she was a control freak with no filter, but her heart was always in the right place. If I got yelled at on my wedding day, so be it.

As it turned out, Lucas's friend didn't own a "loft." He owned a penthouse. I was getting married in a frigging West Village *penthouse*. The "small space" looked like a ballroom surrounded on all sides by windows. Rows of chairs were set up with a white runner down the middle, which apparently was the aisle I was going to walk down. I couldn't wait to ask my fiancé what his definition of "small party" was.

Daina, Bella, and I were in a dressing room getting ready. Even that looked upscale with fluffy red carpet, plush red couches, and a white vanity table. My hair flowed down my back in large curls, the sides pinned back with rhinestone barrettes. My dress was ivory satin and strapless per my future husband's request, with a silver sash around my waist. And my favorite part—it was tea length. No big puffy dress with a train that wouldn't bustle so I could barely walk or dance like I had at my first wedding. I didn't know much about the type of wedding this was going to be, especially since this place looked nothing like I expected, but I had no doubt it would beat that day by a mile.

"Okay, you're done. Go put Bella's dress on and then we'll get yours on. Go!"

"Yes, boss." I saluted her with a smirk. "Are we keeping to the itinerary, since I know nothing?"

Daina huffed and walked away. I chuckled at how she was so tense, and I was so calm. It was almost fun not knowing what was in store.

Bella's dress had been made for her—white satin with a bow in the back, very simple other than the blue butterflies at the hem. I had to hide the dress all week because she kept trying it on.

"Look, Mommy! If I twirl, the butterflies look like they're flying!" The faster she spun around, the more I was afraid she was going to fall or make herself sick.

"I know, they look pretty, but let's not get dizzy. Why don't you sit on the couch for a second?"

I put my dress over my head, and looked in the mirror. Then, it hit me. I was getting married today—to Lucas. Years ago, this seemed as likely as hitting the lottery while being struck by lightning. I still wasn't nervous, I was just anxious to get the show on the road. If I was honest with myself, I had a bad feeling in the pit of my stomach the day I married Marc—like I was settling because I couldn't do any better. Today, I was one hundred percent sure I was right where I was supposed to be, with the man I was always supposed to be with.

"Hey, can I come in?"

"Sure. Hi, Mom."

"Grandma!" Bella raced over to my mother and almost knocked her over. "See my dress. It has butterflies on it."

"You look beautiful, Bella." She took Bella's face in her hands and kissed her cheek.

"Hi, Grace! Nice to see you!" Daina said to my mother as she straightened out the hem of Bella's dress.

"You look beautiful. Happiness looks good on you,

Samantha." Her jaw trembled and her eyes reddened as she looked up at me. My mother was a smaller version of me with olive skin and bob-length black hair. She wore a silver dress with a matching short jacket on her petite frame. Even in her sixties, she was so pretty. She took my hand and smiled. It was nice to have her around again these past couple of years. Marc's nasty personality made a lot of my friends and family stay away.

"See you inside, my beautiful brave girl." I kissed her on her cheek and she nodded, turning around to leave and sit with the other guests.

"C'mon squirt. Let's see who's already here." Daina and Bella followed my mother outside so I could finish getting ready. .

"Samantha? Can I come in?" A timid looking Jessica stood in the doorway. I nodded and smiled, knowing Lucas probably sent his sister in here to apologize for telling me to back off.

"I have a delivery for you." She had a small black box with a white ribbon around it in her hand.

"Delivery? From Lucas? He already gave me a wedding gift." I held up my bouquet of lilies. I'd wrapped the shark tooth necklace around the stems.

"Well I guess you have another. You know him, always has to do everything big."

"Yes, I'm beginning to see that about your brother," I noted as I looked around the room.

Jessica wore a black spaghetti strap dress with six-inch stiletto heels. Her chestnut hair was pulled up in a loose knot with curly tendrils trickling down. She towered over me, but she couldn't face me.

"So, um, here." She held out the box and I took it from her hand. Inside were pink diamond stud earrings to match my ring. My eyes grew wide and I shook my head in disbelief.

"Your brother is nuts. These are too much." I took the earrings out of the box—they were gorgeous. I put them down on the vanity table and lifted my arms to remove the earrings I already had on.

"I didn't know Lucas gave you Dad's necklace." Jessica sat

down on the couch, still looking down.

"He let me borrow it again." I glanced at my bouquet and smiled at the memory of Lucas as just a friend. He was always so sweet and thoughtful.

"Lucas is so much like our dad was. Dad always seemed bigger than life—at least to me. He'd walk into a room and own it, no matter who was there. Everyone loved him and wanted to be his friend. He was funny and brilliant, and had the biggest heart. I saw the way Lucas looked at you that day. I knew he loved you. I was afraid you'd get back with your ex-husband, and Lucas would never get over it. I was awful to you last summer. I'm really sorry."

"It's okay. You were watching out for Lucas, I understand. Lucas is lucky to have a sister like you."

Jessica groaned and dropped her head in her hands.

"Please don't be so nice about it. It's making me feel worse." I chuckled, and was happy that Jessica and I could wipe the slate clean. I'd hate to be the cause for a rift between Lucas and his only sister.

"Go outside and tell Lucas you apologized and everything is fine. I was never really upset with you; he was bothered more than I was. He's a little overprotective of me in case you couldn't tell." I gave her a warm smile that I was surprised to see her return. "I guess I walk in soon?" Jessica nodded at me and stood up off the couch.

"Daina will let you know, I'm sure. Thanks, Samantha." As Jessica backed out the door, I realized that was as close to warm and fuzzy as she would ever get.

Not even five minutes after she left, I heard my phone buzz in my purse.

Lucas: Did she apologize?

Me: Yes, I told her to tell you everything is fine. Also, are you crazy? These earrings are too much.

Lucas: I'm crazy about you. You didn't think my dad's necklace was your only gift did you? Today is only the first day I'm going to show you what it means to be spoiled rotten. My girl gets only the best.

Me: I way under-gifted. I only got you a Lego Superman.

Lucas: I have you. That's the best gift in the world.

Even texts from Lucas made me melt.

Me: I don't want you to think I'm after your money after seeing you throwing it around today. Still only in it for the sex.

Lucas: I can understand that. The sex is pretty fucking incredible.

Me: It sure is ;) I'll see you soon. I love you.

Lucas: You bet you will. I love you, too.

Daina burst in and shut the door.

"God, the two of you are nauseating. Lucas is texting you outside with the same dopey grin on his face. You have ten minutes, doll."

"I'll sit in the front and hold your bouquet and the ring when you get up there. Bella has a basket of rose petals she'll drop before you come down the aisle. You ready?"

I laughed at my feisty best friend. My heart swelled at all she's done for me over the years, and for us. We needed someone to yell at us to "stop being an ass" a few times.

"You and I are family today." I smiled at Daina as she shook her head.

"We've always been family. Today's just more of a formality, like you said—an extravagant and flashy formality." She gave me a big hug and I whispered, "Thank you for everything."

Daina grabbed my shoulders and pushed away.

"Try to make it at least partially through the vows without ruining all my hard work. Let me make sure everything is all set before you go outside."

Daina rushed out the door. I took a deep breath and closed my eyes.

It was time to start the rest of my life.

chapter 37

Samantha

HELD BELLA'S hand as we strode over to the "room." I didn't know what else to call it. It looked like a ballroom that was divided in half by a curtain. My guess was that was where the reception would be after we took our vows. This was quite different from the traditional church weddings I was used to. Daina said when the music started, Bella was supposed to walk in before me and I would follow. By the way my little girl was clutching my hand, I knew she wouldn't make it down the aisle solo, and I didn't blame her. Now that the moment was upon us, I was a little freaked out myself.

"Mommy, I don't think I can do it. What if I drop all the flowers?" I knelt down so I could face her.

"I think that's what you're supposed to do, baby. Tell you what, can you walk in with me?" She gave me a big nod, and then I heard music. It sounded like *Here Comes the Bride,* only a jazzier version, almost like Kenny G was playing it. *Yes, this definitely wasn't a church.*

"Okay, kiddo. Ready?" I held my bouquet with one hand, and held out my other for my daughter. I took a deep breath, saying a silent prayer that my modest silver heels wouldn't make me trip, and headed down the aisle.

I marched down the aisle slowly, nodding hello to the people I knew. The room was dimly lighted and the New York City sky-line bathed in sunset made for a beautiful backdrop. Jason waved from his seat, and Lucas's mother wiped her eyes with a tissue. Then I saw him—Lucas—the man I was about to marry—in an all-black fitted tuxedo. I realized right then what the term 'drop dead gorgeous' meant, because staring at him made it hard to breathe. This man was real, and he was *mine*. Lucas gazed at me with glossy eyes, and a slow smile spread across his face as he shook his head.

"So beautiful." he mouthed to me as Bella went to sit with my mother.

Lucas reached for my hand and I quickly handed my flowers to Daina. Lucas took my face in his hands, and it felt as if we were the only ones there. I skimmed my fingertips along his jaw as a tear ran down his cheek. I wiped it away with the back of my hand. Lucas reached up to interlock our fingers before kissing my wrist.

"Now who's a mushball?" I whispered as he rested his forehead on mine and chuckled.

"If it's all right with you, I think we can get started." I glanced at the officiant, a white-haired gentleman in a black suit and tie who I'd never seen before. He looked at us with his eyebrows raised.

"Yes, please." We both answered together, making everyone laugh.

"We're here today to join Lucas and Samantha in marriage. I was given instructions to keep the ceremony short and sweet, so we can head right to the vows."

I peeked over at Lucas who shrugged with a smirk.

"Lucas repeat after me—"

"I actually have my own if that's okay." He turned to me and smiled. *His own vows, I had nothing prepared or even thought about.* The fun of not knowing anything about today had ran out. I wanted to kiss him and kill him at the same time.

"A little shy of two years ago, I asked an old friend to meet me for a drink. I remembered her as a beautiful girl, smart and sweet—but was completely unprepared for the gorgeous woman who was waiting for me. She smiled at me, and I was ruined for anyone else. I fell in love—crazy, head over heels in love—and never looked back.

It hasn't been the easiest road to get to where we are now. But I wouldn't change a thing. Thank you for giving me a second chance to love you. I know, without a doubt, we were meant to be. Today is the happiest day of my life, because I finally get to marry you. I don't think I could have waited another second."

I closed my eyes, and let the tears fall. There was no way I would have lasted through that without weeping. I had nothing prepared, but my heart was ready to burst.

"I don't have anything prepared, so I'm going to wing it. Bear with me . . . A little over a decade ago, I was captivated by the most beautiful man I'd ever seen. He was not only handsome, but also kind, and smart, and just amazing. I admired him from a distance, because I thought someone like him was out of my reach. When I saw him again years later, I realized why no one else ever measured up. Lucas, you're the love of my life, my hero, and today you're my husband. You gave me the courage to fight for what I wanted, and I never wanted anything more than you. *Always* you."

Lucas let out a deep breath, pulled me into his arms and kissed me.

"There's children here, you two." Daina yelled from where she was sitting.

"They kiss *all* the time." I heard Bella answer and laughed against Lucas's lips.

"You still have rings . . ." The judge or whoever was marrying us looked at us with a smirk.

We broke apart and my cheeks got hot. Nothing like pawing each other in front of friends and family.

"Sorry, sir. I got a little carried away." Lucas kept his eyes on mine as he slipped the ring on my finger.

"With this ring, I promise you all that I am, and all that I have, for the rest of my life."

I managed to place the ring on Lucas's finger and repeat the words without crying. I was Mrs. Lucas Hunter—finally.

"By the power vested in me by the State of New York . . ."

Lucas grabbed my waist and crashed his lips onto mine. I

laughed at his eagerness before I melted into his arms.

"I now pronounce you husband and wife. You can keep kissing the bride."

Everyone behind us clapped and cheered, but I wasn't done kissing my husband. I didn't know how long we stood there, but when it's the best moment of your life—you should never rush it.

DESPITE THE LOCATION and elaborate decorations, the reception was a small affair. There were a few small tables of close friends and family surrounding a small dance floor and DJ. Lucas, Bella, and I had our own table. Not that Bella sat with us much since she didn't stop dancing all night—she loved twirling around to watch her butterflies fly. The three of us were happy—truly and purely happy. Lucas was right; it wasn't easy getting here, but the bumpy ride made it that much sweeter.

"So, I did good?" Lucas whispered in my ear, making me jump. We sat at our table alone, watching the party going on around us. I turned my head and ran my hand down his cheek.

"Very, very good. Nice cover with saying this was a "loft" not a penthouse. Still not sure how you pulled it off all by yourself." I gave him a kiss on the cheek.

"I had a little bit of help. There's a coordinator they use for events. I just said what I wanted and they took care of the rest. I knew you'd think a penthouse was too much, but I told you, I'm planning to spoil you fucking rotten. This is only the beginning." Lucas pulled me closer until I was almost on his lap.

"Hey Luc, congratulations!" I recognized Derek, Lucas's friend from his college days. I wondered if Jason had noticed him yet, since that was *his* big college crush. Derek was still great looking; like Lucas he only got better with age.

"Thanks, man! And thanks for putting this on hold for me. I know you have a big waiting list for this place."

"Wait a minute! Derek is the friend who owns this place?"

I looked between them and Derek smiled at me and nodded his head.

"I am. You guys have a great time and let me know if you need anything."

As Derek strode away, Jason rushed up to our table.

"Congratulations, O'Rourke." Jason gave me a big hug and kiss on the cheek.

"I think it's Hunter now." Lucas gave me a wink. "Let me go mingle a little. Be right back." He kissed me on the forehead and scooted away.

"You look amazing today. Not being married to a jackass looks good on you. Talk about trading up." I laughed and hit his arm. Felt good not being married to a jackass, too. It was still a little surreal that I was married to Lucas now.

"So was that . . ."

"Derek, yes. Turns out he owns this place. And I didn't see a ring on his finger. You should go say hi."

"*Owns* the place? No shit? Maybe I will say hi. Be right back. You owe me a dance, O'Rourke. Oh sorry, *Hunter*." I laughed and shook my head.

One of my barrettes got loose and broke, and I snuck over to the dressing room to fix my hair with the extra pins I brought. Before I left the room, I looked for Bella, and found her sitting on my mom's lap, looking as if she'd lost a little steam. No one would miss me for very long.

I ran in, fixed my hair and makeup, and was about to leave when the door closed behind me. I turned to find my sexy husband with a devious grin. Lucas reached behind him to lock the door, trouble written all over his face.

"Babe, as much as I want to rip that tuxedo off you, we have a party going on in the next room. You know we can't—" Lucas's eyes raked over my body and made me forget my words. My mouth went dry as my heart pounded in my chest.

"I've been staring at my gorgeous wife in a beautiful dress, and I've held out as long as I could." He took off his jacket and threw it over one of the couches as he traipsed over to where I stood. When he reached me, he grabbed me by the waist, pulling me closer. He had a predatory gaze in his eyes as he backed me against the vanity table and cocked an eyebrow at me as he bunched up the skirt of my dress and slipped his hand underneath.

I ran my hand down his chest. Lucas in a tuxedo was temptation personified, especially when he used the word 'wife.'

"You just said you wanted to rip my clothes off. You're still my bad girl from last night." He trailed light kisses from behind my ear and down my collarbone, then changed to lingering with an open mouth when he got to the tops of my breasts. A moan escaped me as I went limp in his arms.

"Now you're the one not playing fair." My voice was husky and my head dropped back to give Lucas better access.

"You're my *wife*. All fucking mine. You have no idea what that does to me. I can't help myself, Mrs. Hunter." He put his hand inside my white lace thong and my legs opened wide. As usual, hearing him call me 'Mrs. Hunter' sent me halfway over the edge.

"Holy shit, have you been this wet all day?" He inserted two fingers and I gasped, trying my damnedest not to scream as he drove them in and out.

"My husband is really hot, especially in a tuxedo. What did you expect?"

Lucas growled and attacked my mouth with his. "Say it again," Lucas murmured against my lips as his fingers kept moving. He was out of control with need, and it was infectious. I managed to forget about the small group of family and friends in the next room, and only thought of ways to relieve the throbbing ache between my legs.

I pulled back from Lucas's lips and gave him a big smile. "I said my *husband* is really hot." I grabbed his very hard cock and stroked him through his pants.

Lucas moaned and buried his face in my neck. He lifted his head and looked at me with hooded eyes.

"That has to be one of the sexiest things to ever come out of your mouth. We have to be quick." I nodded. I was mortified five minutes ago but completely onboard now.

Lucas unbuckled his pants and moved my panties to the side. He entered me hard and quick, drawing me closer as he started to move. I pulled on Lucas's hair as his mouth covered mine. Who knew being married would be such a turn on for both of us? I hoped we had another fifty years of this to look forward to.

It was difficult not to make any noise. When we finished, we were breathing heavy and clutching onto each other so tightly I was sure we'd go back into the reception with bruises.

I glanced up at Lucas and ran my fingers through his hair.

"Did I ever tell you how much I loved being claimed?" Lucas chuckled and kissed my forehead.

"You're in luck, I plan to claim you every single chance I get—Mrs. Hunter." He went in for another kiss and I shook my head.

"No more 'Mrs. Hunter.' You and I won't leave this room for the rest of the night—and we have a party going on, remember?" Lucas narrowed his eyes and backed away to pull up his pants when we heard the door jiggle.

"Ah, the door was stuck. Jess, you can get changed in—oh my god! Seriously? You guys couldn't wait?" Daina took in the sight of my dress up to my waist and Lucas's pants around his knees and her mouth fell open so wide it almost touched the floor.

"And you can't knock on a locked door? Jesus, Daina!" Lucas yelled back. I gave him credit; it was hard to be indignant with your pants half off, but he was doing a great job.

"I'll let you two get dressed—" Daina collapsed into giggles and I heard Jessica ask her what was going on as she shut the door. I dropped my face into my hands. I had no idea how I would face them for the rest of the night.

"Hey." Lucas pulled my hands from my face and placed my arms around his neck. "Don't you dare be embarrassed! My nosey cousin will get over it." Lucas shrugged and gave me a soft peck on my lips.

Lucas finished buckling his pants and grabbed his jacket. He pulled me by the waist and gave me a passionate kiss.

"I love you. So much. Let's finish this party so we can start the rest of our lives together."

"I love you, too. Sounds good to me! Let me . . ." I motioned with my hand to the bathroom in the corner.

Lucas nodded and kissed my forehead. "Don't take too long, wife." He smacked me on the ass and sauntered out the door.

I looked at myself in the mirror. Other than the flush in my cheeks, I didn't look too disheveled. I cleaned myself up and smoothed down my dress—hoping the wrinkles weren't too noticeable. I fixed my makeup along with a couple of hair pins that were out of place and marched back outside. I tried my best to not be embarrassed about getting caught. We'd look back on today with nothing but good memories.

I went back out to our little reception and mingled with some of my friends and family. I looked over at the dance floor and found Lucas dancing with Bella. She yawned in his arms as he held her. Frank Sinatra was singing *The Way You Look Tonight* as Bella giggled at Lucas. I couldn't tell what he was saying to her.

I never got to do the 'father/daughter' dance at any event, and had always felt cheated. Looking at Lucas and Bella together healed me. She would finally have the right kind of dad—one who spoiled her, worried when she was sick, and scared the crap out of any guy who tried to take her out. It didn't matter that she didn't have his blood or his last name. She had his heart.

At the end of the song, Lucas pointed to his cheek and she gave him a kiss. He carried her back over to my mother as the beginning of John Legend's *You and I* started to play.

Lucas spotted me across the room and held out his hand. I marched over to my husband on the dance floor and he pulled me into his arms. I buried my face in his chest as we swayed to the music. When he sang *you're all mine* in my ear, I laughed and flung my arms around his neck.

I still felt at times that it was all a dream. I never knew what happiness felt like, or if it was even in the cards for me, until Lucas. He was more than just a crush, or the man of my dreams.

He was the other half of my soul, my Superman who would always rescue me—even from myself. I looked into my husband's eyes, and realized why I'd never felt whole before. He completed me in every way possible.

"I love you, Lucas." I held on even tighter, tears slipping down my face once again.

He smiled and gave me a soft kiss.

"I love you too, Sam. *Always* you."

epilogue

Lucas

Three years later

USUALLY DID a good job—with a few exceptions—of putting on a poker face when I was freaked out, but this time I couldn't fake it. I stood behind the sheet in the delivery room, holding Sam's hand and reassuring us both that everything was fine and an emergency C-section was really no big deal. But sweat poured down my face from beneath my scrubs.

Nothing about Joseph Kellan Hunter's entrance into this world had been easy. After two years of trying to get pregnant and then one month of bed rest for Sam, we couldn't wait for it to be over and have him with us. Now that the moment was here, I was scared out of my mind for both of them.

Things were momentarily quiet until a screaming baby broke the silence. Hearing the sound of my baby's strong cry was the best moment of my life, other than falling in love and marrying his mother.

Sam nudged me to go make sure he was okay. I watched as they cleaned him up—trying my best to ignore what he was covered in—weighed him, took his footprint, and spread some kind of ointment over his eyes. The nurse wrapped him up in a blanket and handed him to me. My son's eyes were wide open, and he looked at right at me—like he knew me. He relaxed in my arms and seemed to be saying, "Hi, Daddy." I saw Sam's lips, my dad's eyes, and my sister's chin. Tears streamed down my face as I tried to speak to my son for the first time.

"Hi Joey! Glad you're finally here. Wait until you see how pretty Mommy is."

Joey completely agreed. When I handed him to Sam, he melted into her arms, camped at her breast and stayed there for hours. Like father, like son.

Grace and Bella came to the hospital after Sam and Joey were settled into their own room. We set Bella up in the chair next to Sam's bed and showed her how to hold Joey. After reminding her for the tenth time to support Joey's head, I gently placed him in Bella's lap.

"He's so strong for a little guy." Bella giggled as he wrapped his little hand around her finger. He didn't fuss at all, and seemed to take an instant liking to his sister. She glanced between Joey and me, and her face fell. She'd been so excited to be a big sister, I couldn't imagine what was bothering her.

I took Joey out of Bella's arms and handed him back to Sam. Sam seemed tired and her eyes were getting heavy, but even right after having a baby, she was still the most beautiful woman I'd ever seen. It was time to go so she could get a little rest.

Sam leaned over to kiss Bella good night as she fed Joey. "Good night, baby. Be good for Daddy and Grandma, and I'll see you tomorrow." Bella nodded and lowered her gaze to the floor before joining her grandmother in the hallway. I sat at the edge of her hospital bed as I gazed at my wife and my son—life didn't get much better than this.

Sam winked at me. "Good night, Daddy." I bent down to give her a soft kiss and whispered in her ear.

"Stop trying to turn me on. You know I have to wait six weeks." She hit me in the arm, and pulled me in for another kiss.

Joey was still nursing, but he looked up to tell his old man good night.

"Bella was never like this. He dove right in and hasn't come up for air." Sam smiled as she stroked the wispy sandy brown hair on his head.

"He gets that from me. Why I'm almost late for work some days." I kissed Sam again as she laughed.

"See, big guy, we're already a team! You take care of Mommy, and I'll take care of Bella. " I kissed the soft skin on his forehead.

"Sorry about your middle name, buddy. Mommy's a sap." I turned to Sam. "Did Kellan sparkle, too?"

"No, smartass, he was a rock star."

"Hmm, another one. See, Joey. That's why Mommy's not allowed to go to concerts."

"Go." Sam pushed my shoulder. "You can bust my chops more tomorrow. Get some sleep, babe."

"Okay, okay. Good night. I love you." I gave my wife and son one last kiss and backed out of the room slowly. I was stalling. I already missed them both.

"I love you, too. Talk to Bella, make sure she's okay."

I could have spent the night with Sam and Joey, but we didn't want Bella to be without either of us for a night. She had been great throughout her mother's pregnancy, and was excited to have a little brother, but we didn't want her to think we left her for the new baby. I was especially glad we made that decision after seeing her with Joey tonight.

Home was still in Queens. I wanted to move us out of there to start over, but Sam and Bella were happy there. I didn't want to be the selfish prick who moved his family away just for his own benefit. Even though I made Sam go through listing after listing, I managed to find a great house just around the corner. I convinced Bella easily enough with the huge yard and the possibility of a swimming pool, but Sam still didn't want to leave her old house. I told her I would have the kitchen at the new house totally redone—complete with the marble top island that Rachael Ray has on her show, and that seemed to seal the deal. Maybe I was being a little petty, but when I put the key in the door, this was *my* house—not Marc's old house. To me, that was worth the time and expense.

"Hey Butterfly, can I come in?" I inched the door open in Bella's room. She was sitting up in bed watching TV, and nodded when she saw me.

Bella hadn't seen nor heard from Marc since he moved to Chicago three years ago, though she still saw her grandparents from time to time. Marc's mother had a much more accommodating attitude now, as if she realized if she pissed us off that would be the last she saw of her granddaughter. I would've loved to adopt Bella, but Marc would never sign over his rights. Not because he wanted them, but because his mother would flip at their only connection to Bella being severed.

The Father's Day after Sam and I were married, then seven-year old Bella ran home with the project that she made for me in class. It was a coffee mug with decals on it, and with all the stickers Bella decided to include—baseballs, butterflies, I could make out block letters across the middle that said *I love you, Daddy.* When she gave it to me, she said the teacher was talking about everything Daddy's do for their kids, and Bella raised her hand and said her Daddy never did any of those things—but "Lucas did." She said everyone else put *Daddy* on their mugs, so would it be okay if she called me that. I said *absolutely* and have been 'Daddy' ever since.

Sometimes, blood is bullshit. Bella was my daughter in every sense of the word.

She just turned ten and gets a little more grown up each day, but so far still lets me call her 'Butterfly.'

"Want to see the pictures we took?" I sat on the edge of her bed and dug my phone out of my pocket to show Bella the sixty-five pictures I took of the first four hours of her brother's life.

"He's really cute. He looks just like you, same color hair and eyes. Everyone will know you're his dad." She looked down and handed me back my phone.

"Everyone knows I'm your dad too. Is that what this is about?"

Bella shrugged and stared off into space. "Joey looks just like you, and he has the same last name. You're supposed to like him better than me since he's your real son." Her voice trailed off and she turned over on her side, facing away from me.

"You're my real daughter; you should know that by now. Where is this coming from, Bella?" Bella and I had always been close, from practically the first day I met her. Joey may have been my first baby, but in no way did I feel like a first time father today. Bella belonged to me just as much as her brother did. I got the feeling someone was putting things into her head.

"Grandma Jeannie said that once the baby came you probably wouldn't have much time for me anymore . . . since you're not my real dad." *And there it was.* I had forgotten what a miserable human being Marc's mother really was.

I nudged Bella's shoulder until she acknowledged me, then motioned for her to turn around. She reluctantly sat up but still glanced away. I took her face in my hands to make her look at me.

"I'm sorry I didn't get to meet you when you were a baby, but that doesn't make you any less mine. I love you. More than you can ever possibly imagine. There will never be a time that I don't have time for you. I'm your father—just as much as I'm Joey's father—and I always will be. Got it?" Bella nodded, and I hoped that meant I was getting through to her. "Just like you're my Butterfly, and you always will be."

I got a smile, followed by an eye roll. Maybe she didn't love being called 'Butterfly' anymore—not that I would ever stop.

I kissed her forehead and she wrapped her arms around my neck.

"And I better not see another eye roll," I whispered into her ear. She giggled and nodded again. "Now it's really late, so get some sleep and we'll head over in the morning." I stood up and pulled the covers over her. "I love you, Butterfly." I kissed her on her cheek, and she smiled as she settled onto her side.

"Okay. Good night, Daddy. I love you, too."

"HE LOOKS LIKE your father. Makes sense his name is Joey." My mother looked at her grandson with tears in her eyes. She'd been emotional ever since she came to the hospital and saw "Joseph Hunter" on Joey's cradle. I only had him until I was twelve, but my dad was the best. I always hoped I could be half the father he was.

Sam and Joey came home after three days in the hospital. Grace went back to New Jersey, and now my mother was staying with us for a few days until we got adjusted. At least that was the story she used. When he wasn't nursing, Joey was in his grandmother's arms.

"I think Dad would like his first grandson to have his name. I hope he looks down on us and likes what he sees." Mom was rocking Joey in the glider in his room while Sam got a little bit of sleep. I sat on the floor in front of them and kissed Joey's head. I hadn't been around babies since my sister, but he seemed to be an agreeable and easygoing guy.

"I'm sure you make him very proud. You always did. Now, why don't you join Samantha and get some sleep. There's breast milk in the freezer if I have to feed him. Go." Cuddling with my wife in bed did seem like a long-lost luxury. I nodded and stood up from the floor.

"Yes. ma'am. Good night." I kissed her cheek and turned to Joey.

"Be good for Grandma, big guy. Daddy loves you." His heavy little eyes were closing, so I kissed his forehead and tiptoed out of the room.

"Lucas? I love you, and I'm so proud of you." Mom whispered to me through more tears. I turned around and nodded, trying to hide the fact that I was about to cry. Fatherhood and being with Sam for so long had made me a mushball, too.

"I love you too, Mom. Thanks."

I crept into our bedroom and saw Sam sleeping peacefully for the first time since we brought Joey home. I slipped into bed and put my arms around her.

"Am I dreaming?" Sam's voice was scratchy. I didn't want to wake her, but I couldn't resist getting as close to her as possible.

"No rock star or vampire, just your husband." I kissed the back of her neck as she giggled, and she gingerly turned over to face me. She was still sore from the C-section.

"My husband beats any book boyfriend." She ran her fingers

through my hair and gave me a peck on the lips. "Is Joey sleeping?"

"Not yet, but my mother has no problem with staying up with him all night. Let's take advantage of her generosity and sleep for a while. Mom will feed him when he's hungry."

"I should go get him, but I'm exhausted and it feels so good to be close to you, I'll exploit your mother's kindness for a night like this." Sam snuggled into my chest as I wrapped my arms around her.

"That's my girl. We need to exploit the grandmothers every chance we get." I ran my fingers through her hair, and even though it was dark I could tell her eyelids were already fluttering closed.

"I missed you so much." Sam ran her hand down my jaw. "I'm glad it's dark in here so you can't see what I look like."

"Stop that! You're gorgeous just like your son."

"He's *all* you. I feel bad for the girls he meets. They're going to fall at his feet and won't be able to help themselves."

"I'll teach him to not have his head up his ass when he meets the woman he's supposed to marry. He may not be lucky like me and get another shot."

"I'm not gorgeous, especially not now." Sam lifted her head off my chest to face me. "Look at me, Lucas. I look scary . . . and fat. You can say it."

"I honestly didn't hear a word you just said. I was calculating in my head how many more days until six weeks."

Sam pulled me into a deep kiss, and I couldn't help pressing my body against hers. My quick calculations at that point said not fucking soon enough.

"You always know the right thing to say. I love you, babe. So much."

"I love you, too, Baby Girl. Always you. And thank you." I kissed her forehead.

"Thank you? For what?"

"For being everything I need, and giving me everything I ever wanted."

"I thought superheroes didn't need anything." Sam chuckled as I tightened my arms around her.

"Superheroes need a girl they can save, so she can save them right back."

THE END

acknowledgements

NEVER IN A million years did I ever think I would write a book. It truly takes a village, and wouldn't have been possible without the love and support of some amazing people.

First and foremost, I want to thank my very own Superman, my husband James. Many nights and weekends were spent looking at the back of my laptop screen as I wrote into the wee hours of the morning. I wore your patience very thin I'm sure. Thank you for believing in me and encouraging me when I just wanted to burn the damn thing. Not very many people meet the person they're meant to spend the rest of their life with at sixteen, and for that I will always be grateful. To my son, John—my second superhero. You're the sweetest yet toughest little five year old I know, and the best part of my day is always your hugs and kisses. You're the best thing that ever happened to me, and you always will be. You both mean the world to me and above anything else, I want to make you both proud.

To my mother, who always put me first no matter what. One of my favorite memories of writing this book will always be the way your face lit up when I told you about it. Thank you for teaching me what family is all about, and instilling a resilience and toughness in me that has gotten me through some difficult times.

To my grandparents, not a day goes by that I don't think about the both of you, and how you raised me with love and patience. You always thought that I could do anything I set my mind to, so I hope you're in heaven getting a kick out of the fact that I wrote a book. (but hopefully if you're reading this, this is *all* you read)

To my friends: Ann Marie, the toughest and bravest woman

that I know. Friends that become family are precious, and you've been family from the start. Natalie, you're always there for me, and the friend I want by my side when the going gets really tough. Your friendship means the world to me. Daina, you did triple duty as friend, beta, and character namesake. I wish more than anything else I could write you the happy ending that you deserve. I'd wrap Lucas up in a big bow and hand him right to you. You inspired the tough single mom in Samantha, and I admire you more than you know. Lisa, thank you for being the best sister anyone could ever ask for. Robyn, your excitement kept me going. Michelle, thanks for always looking out for me.

To all of my family and friends who supported and encouraged me through this long and crazy process, and got excited for me. Thank you from the bottom of my heart. I'm lucky to have so many amazing people in my life.

Stacia Newbill, you were more than a beta or CP, you were my co-pilot and the only one who knew Lucas and Samantha as well as I did. You couldn't wait to get your hands on more of them, and that kept me going the most when I wanted to give up. You're an amazing friend and one of the best and most selfless people I know. #loveyoulobster

Faith Andrews, I owe so much to you. You showed me the difference between being a writer and a storyteller, and I thank you for all the time and patience that you had for me. Who knew when I gushed like an idiot to you about how much I loved *Man of My Dreams* that I would be making a lifelong friend. I hope to someday be half the writer you are. Love you, friend.

Jennifer Mirabelli, I don't think there would be an *Always You* if it weren't for you. You told me to try writing and see what happens, and that you thought I "had something." 74,000 words all began with that one private message. You have the biggest and purest heart of anyone that I know, and I am proud to call you my friend.

Christine Mateo, one of the luckiest days of my life was meeting you on the line for the New York author signing in 2013. Thank you for taking the time to read and for your awesome ideas that made the book so much better. You are an amazing friend and I love you to pieces.

Jeannie Bell, thank you so much for taking the time to read, and for being my "morality police." You are an amazing person and I'm so grateful for all your encouragement and support.

Roxie Madar, I am so thankful that you were my beta for so many reasons. You whipped my ass into shape and helped me regain my voice after I lost it for a little while, and I owe so much to you for that. You also have become an amazing friend throughout this process, and I feel so blessed to have found you. You're courageous, strong, and funny as hell. I love you very much, my sticker queen.

Rosa Campisi, my book buddy and fellow Bronx chick. I'm so glad that books brought us together. Thank you for doing a final read through and enjoying my story.

Gia Riley, who knew all that time ago when we were just friends that loved to read that you and I would be here today? Thank you for all your support and guidance through this grueling process, and the great feedback you gave me. I'm sure it warmed your heart that I needed a country song in my New York City romance novel.

Alexis Durbin, thank you for putting so much work into *Always You*. Your attention and passion for detail meant a lot to me. You have a genuine soul and huge heart, and I thank you for all your support and friendship.

Jena Campbell, you dug *deep,* showing me how I could make things better and I am so proud of the end result thanks to you. It helped that you not only gave me great feedback, but truly loved the story and the characters. I wanted to create the best Lucas and Sam I could because of you, and I hope that I delivered.

Rebecca Yarros, thank you for taking the time to look, and even more time to explain. You helped me get on the right track, and I truly appreciated all your help.

Angela Page, you are a true friend and an amazing person. Thank you for lifting me up when I was down, and for guiding me through Indie Writer life. You are the best, I would even share

Nick Bateman with you.

B.A. Wolfe, our friendship has saved me lots of money in therapy. Thank you for always being around for advice or just to listen. You help me navigate this crazy writing world, and I couldn't be more grateful. #justiceleagueforever

BL Berry, thank you for reaching out to a new author all those months ago, and never getting tired of my constant stream of questions. You are the coolest chick I know and one of the most amazing people I've ever met!

Tabitha Willbanks, my cheerleader from the very beginning. Your support meant so much on the days it got really tough. Thank you for being such an awesome friend.

Alison G. Bailey, you're a wonderful friend and true class act. This Yankee loves you.

J.A. Derouen, your Cajun voice messages brighten my day. Thank you for encouraging me and believing in me. Aly Martinez, thank you for always being so awesome.

Mary Rose Bermundo, you are the kindest and sweetest soul I know. I love talking books with you.

To Brenda Letendre, my beautiful editor. You have truly been my rock. Thank you for your kindness and patience in helping me make *Always You* the best that it could be. You are now forever my "answer in the back of the book." Thank you for being one of the best teachers I've ever had and showing me how to be a better writer.

To the ladies of Indie Chicks Rock, I am honored to be a part of such amazing group of talented women. I love the fact that I can share my accomplishments along with my hopes and fears and get amazing support along the way. I'm humbled by the all the talent in that group, and am proud to call you my friends. #FYW

How freaking awesome is this cover? Najla Qamber somehow managed to draw out the Lucas and Sam in my head. I still get goose bumps when I stare at it. Thank you for being so amazing to work with.

To Kassi Cooper, thank you for a beautiful ebook design.

To Christine at Perfectly Publishing, thank you for fitting me in.

Thank you to Love Between the Sheets for organizing a kick ass cover reveal, release blitz, and blog tour.

Finally, a huge thank you to all the bloggers and readers who took a chance on me and read and/or promoted my book. I hope you loved it, and that you found joy and hope in *Always You*. Lucas and Samantha are the first of many characters I hope to introduce you to, and although their story is done, you may see them pop up in my next book. Your support means the world to me, and I thank you from the bottom of my heart.

about the author

Stephanie Rose was born and raised in the Bronx, New York and still lives there with her superhero-obsessed husband and son.

Stephanie has a Bachelor's degree in Business and a day job in marketing, but she always has a story in her head.

This lifelong New Yorker lives for Starbucks, book boy-friends, and 80s rock.

Spending most of her youth watching soaps, Stephanie has an obsession with angsty drama and is an avid romance reader.

She's excited to finally bring the characters she's been dreaming about to life and loves hearing from readers!

Find Stephanie Rose online on:

Facebook, Twitter, tsu and Goodreads

Made in the USA
Middletown, DE
04 March 2017